## Praise for Janet Tronstad

"An emotionally vibrant and totally satisfying read."
—*RT Book Reviews* on *Snowbound in Dry Creek*

"Janet Tronstad pens a warm, comforting story."
—*RT Book Reviews* on *Shepherds Abiding in Dry Creek*

"Ms. Tronstad creates a very enjoyable story about
learning to believe and love again."
—*RT Book Reviews* on *An Angel for Dry Creek*

## Praise for Sara Mitchell

"This tender love story holds just the right blend of
romance and sophisticated intrigue."
—*RT Book Reviews* on *Shelter of His Arms*

"A charming love story with two characters who
were made for each other."
—*RT Book Reviews* on *Legacy of Secrets*

"Mitchell is an amazing, talented author who spins
a tale of greed, love, family secrets and keeping the
faith in oneself."
—*RT Book Reviews* on *The Widow's Secret*

## JANET TRONSTAD

Janet Tronstad grew up on a small farm in central Montana. She took piano lessons as a child, but always had a particular love of bell choirs so she enjoyed learning about them for this novella. She has written many books, both contemporary and historical, in the Dry Creek series. Janet lives in Pasadena, California, where she is a full-time writer.

## SARA MITCHELL

A popular and highly acclaimed author in the Christian market, Sara's aim is to depict the struggle between the challenges of everyday life and the values to which our faith would have us aspire. The author of contemporary, historical suspense, and historical novels, her work has been published by many inspirational book publishers.

Having lived in diverse locations from Georgia to California to Great Britain, her extensive travel experience helps her create authentic settings for her books. A lifelong music lover, Sara has also written several musical dramas and has long been active in the music miniseries of the churches wherever she and her husband, a retired career air force officer, have lived. The parents of two daughters, Sara and her husband now live in Virginia.

# JANET TRONSTAD
# SARA MITCHELL

## *Mistletoe Courtship*

Steeple
Hill®

Published by Steeple Hill Books™

STEEPLE HILL BOOKS

Steeple
Hill®

Recycling programs
for this product may
not exist in your area.

ISBN-13: 978-0-373-82826-5

MISTLETOE COURTSHIP

Copyright © 2009 by Harlequin Books S.A.

The publisher acknowledges the copyright holders of the individual
works as follows:

CHRISTMAS BELLS FOR DRY CREEK
Copyright © 2009 by Janet Tronstad

THE CHRISTMAS SECRET
Copyright © 2009 by Sara Mitchell

www.SteepleHill.com

Printed in U.S.A.

# CONTENTS

# CHRISTMAS BELLS FOR DRY CREEK
## Janet Tronstad

May the bells always ring for both of you
In memory of Judy Eslick and Jim Jett

Though I speak with the tongues of men and of angels, and have not charity, I am become as sounding brass, or a tinkling cymbal.

—I *Corinthians* 13:1

Though I speak with the tongues of men and of
angels, and have not charity, I am become as
sounding brass, or a tinkling cymbal.
—1 Corinthians 13:1

# Prologue

Noise spilled into the darkness as Virginia Parker opened the saloon's back door. She braced herself as she took a few steps out into the cold while wiping her hands on her damp apron. Ordinarily, she would have searched the alley to be sure no one saw her leave at night, but she was too upset even to think of her reputation right now. It wasn't the gossips in town who were bothering her anyway. It was *him.*

Colter Hayes had interrupted her dish-washing and asked her to come out here. The saloon owner hadn't said what he wanted to talk about, but she knew it could only be one thing—he must be getting ready to fire her. When he stood there and didn't speak, she wondered if he was trying to find words to soften the blow. That's when she realized why—the man pitied her.

*Please, God, leave me with some dignity,* she prayed.

She couldn't believe someone from here would pity her. She might be living in this small Montana town now, but she would find her way back to where she belonged. She would never get used to the coyotes that slid through the streets of Miles City in the dark. Or the wide-brimmed hats the men wore low on their heads to protect themselves from the bad weather that plagued this land.

Back east in her beloved home, the days were pleasant. Servants banished any difficulties. And the music—ah, the sounds she'd heard. She had learned to play the piano looking out at the green trees surrounding the house where she'd lived for most of her twenty-four years. She'd never become the concert pianist her father wanted, but she longed to go back and play for the trees again even though he wouldn't be there to hear her.

She wondered if pity had been the reason for the brooding expression she sometimes saw on Colter's face as he watched her at the piano. She had thought it was because he had other, more tender, feelings for her. She blushed and lowered her head. Obviously, she'd been wrong about that.

"It's a little busier tonight," she finally said with a sideways glance at him.

It wasn't any more comfortable to look at him than to stare out into the icy wind thinking about him. He kept his face clean-shaven and his dark hair neatly trimmed, but that did little to offset the rough-hewn strength of him. It was rumored he had been a gunfighter and, looking at him in the shadows just now, she believed it could be true.

The man nodded. "Danny needed help washing the glasses tonight. Thanks."

"You're welcome," she answered cautiously then brushed her hand over her forehead as strands of blond hair blew across her face. The dusting of snow on the ground had grown whiter and more flakes were falling. Now that Christmas had passed she couldn't expect Colter to keep paying her to play the piano for his customers, not with business the way it was. She was helping Danny with the dishes partly to show she could do other things to earn her wage.

"It's chilly out here," Colter announced with a frown as he took off his wool coat and held it out to her.

"I'm fine—"

"You're shivering." He stepped closer and draped the coat around her shoulders. She felt the warmth of it seep into her even as she refused to let it soften her. The garment smelled of damp wool. And him. She had to admit she sometimes had stared at him, too, when he wasn't looking. He wasn't a gentleman like her father, but he was compelling nonetheless.

Thinking of her father reminded her that she would sorely miss the magnificent Broadway piano in the saloon. She had despaired of ever playing a piano that fine again after her parents had died of the flu and she had been forced to move west to live with her brother. Everyone said it had been left in the saloon when Colter bought the building and it must be so because he didn't pay it any attention. It was scandalous to see an instrument like that ignored.

"You certainly don't need to pay me for working this evening," she said. The decision to tell the men they couldn't drink anything but coffee in the afternoons when she was working had been Colter's. She was a lady, he said, and would be treated as such in his establishment. She knew he lost business because of it.

"Don't be ridiculous. I'll pay you."

When Colter had found her in the street that first day, with her bonnet dripping from the rain and desperate tears in her eyes, she'd already been turned down for a job by every respectable shopkeeper in Miles City. The Broadwater, Bubble and Company Mercantile had no work. Neither did the bank. Nor the school. Even the man with the laundry shook his head. Just last week she'd asked everyone again and they all said the same thing.

When the North Pacific Railroad came to town, there would be work for everyone. But it hadn't even made it to Glendive yet.

"I know how you must feel about businesses like mine," Colter finally said and Virginia reluctantly pulled her mind back to the conversation.

"You run an honest place." She didn't want to add that he held himself like a leader so men naturally trusted him. The white shirt he wore had been pressed at the laundry down the street and it had the sharp creases she liked. He was holding his hat and running his fingers around the brim.

She had never seen him look nervous before. His jaw was strained, too.

"You don't need to worry," Virginia finally said. She didn't want to feel sorry for him any more than she wanted him to feel sorry for her. "I'll get by. I'm truly grateful for the time I've been able to work here."

When the army patrol her brother was on had been ambushed by Indians, she didn't even have time to finish mourning his death before the officials at nearby Fort Keogh informed her she would need to move. Her job with Colter was all that enabled her to afford a room at the boardinghouse.

Virginia turned to go inside.

Colter reached out to touch her arm. "I never should have hired you in the first place. Ever since I answered the preacher's call, I've been uneasy. It's not right for you to be working in a place like this. People talk."

If people were talking, it was about him. She had been as surprised as everyone else when Colter had walked down the aisle after the Reverend Olson called for those who were repentant to come forward last Sunday.

"It's okay." She reached out meaning to pat him on the arm, but then she stopped and let her hand fall to her side. "No one seriously thinks I'm doing anything in your saloon except playing the piano. Everyone can hear the music when they walk down the street. You've paid me a fair wage. You've done all that man or God requires."

"But I—" Colter looked at her and hesitated for a moment. "The problem is you shouldn't be working anywhere. A lady like you shouldn't have to wash dishes or boil water or anything. That's why I'm going to leave enough money for you to hire someone to do the rough work around here."

Virginia blinked. "What?"

"I know I'm not saying this right," Colter took a deep breath. "I need to go away."

"I don't understand."

"I have some business to take care of—family business." He looked uncomfortable as he stared out at the night. "I'm asking you to take care of my place while I'm gone. Not to run it, of course. But to see to the boy—Danny. He's finally in school and I don't want to take him away from his learning. I'll pay you, of course."

"You're leaving?"

Colter nodded and turned back to her. His dark eyes studied her as if he was trying to decide something about her. Then a flash of something else—regret perhaps—flickered over his face and he looked away before continuing. "You'll have to close this place as a saloon, but I thought maybe you could use it to give your music lectures while I'm gone—you know talking about that Beck fellow."

"Bach," she corrected him. A few times, when the loneliness had overcome her, she had played some of the classical music she loved and told the men about the composers. She was pleased he'd remembered some of it.

Colter looked at her with a smile.

She wanted to be sure she understood. "You're planning to leave your property in my hands? For me to use?"

He nodded. "If you'd like."

"Of course, I'd like that. I could give real music lessons." Her days would be filled with joy. "I can't thank you enough."

"You don't need to thank me." He stepped closer. His eyes searched hers again for a moment and then he gently tilted her head up so she was looking at him. "All I ask is that you don't get married before I can get back."

The sight of his tawny eyes so close and warm distracted her. By the time she realized what he had said, his face was closer still. That's when he bent down farther and kissed her—quick and hard. She felt a jolt of awareness and then he pulled away.

"Why, I—" she sputtered.

"I know," he whispered. "Me, too."

She'd scarcely gathered enough wits to fully protest when he walked back through the door and into the saloon. What did he have to kiss her for? A gentleman asked before he kissed someone. It was disrespectful not to. Then it suddenly struck her. If her father were still alive, he would never let a man as brazen as Colter court her. Or kiss her either. In fact, her father would have known the man was going to be trouble long before now.

# Chapter One

*Eleven months, five days later*

The place was on fire. Virginia whipped the wet blanket over her head and beat down on the last of the embers glowing along the blackened floor of the saloon. Then she swung again.

Her pulse was racing. When Colter had left his building in her hands, he'd hardly expected her to let it burn to the ground. No matter that he was taking his sweet time in coming back to it. The air had been freezing when he left and it was just as cold outside now.

All summer she'd expected him and here it was almost Christmas again. She'd put her brass bells on the piano with some red ribbons strewn around them for color and Danny had dragged in a small pine tree that he'd set in the corner. Everything had looked so fresh this morning and now it was all coated with gray.

The smoke stung Virginia's eyes, but she wasn't crying. She was too angry. Someone had deliberately doused the floor with kerosene and set it ablaze. She'd been in the back room putting some potatoes on to boil for dinner when she'd smelled the fire. Fortunately, Danny was still in school. Someone looking in the door would have thought everyone was gone. If they had been, then the saloon would have burned down for sure.

Virginia was just hearing the cries of *"Fire"* outside. Enough smoke had escaped into the winter air that someone down the street had finally noticed it.

She hit the smoldering floor one last time. She didn't know who would do this. She should go next door and ask Lester Duncan if there had been any strangers in town. Since Colter had closed his saloon, Lester's was the most likely place for a misfit to turn up. She couldn't believe anyone who lived in Miles City would set fire to any of its buildings.

She let the blanket fall to the floor so she could arch her back to relieve the mild pain that had come as she beat down the fire. When she thought about it, she really didn't want to face Lester today either. The fire would just make him more protective of her, which would probably lead to him asking her to marry him again. Then she'd have to soothe him with some words of comfort while making it clear she planned to follow through on her application to teach in the school in Denver.

A few months ago, she wouldn't have worried about dashing any hopes he'd had. But her feelings about him had been changing since he'd started bringing over the letters his sister wrote to him. He'd read portions of the letters to her. The affection between the brother and sister made Virginia long to be part of a family again.

And then the sister had mentioned that she looked forward to hearing Lester play Bach on the violin again. When Lester read what his sister said about the beauty of his playing, Virginia began to wonder if she'd found a man who could understand her. Her father would have approved of Lester. A man who could cause such rapture on any musical instrument was a man worthy of marriage. Maybe she should say yes to his proposal.

The memory of Colter's kiss, of course, had long since turned sour. Apparently, it was all very well for her to remain single while he romanced his Patricia—if he hadn't been married to the woman all along. Just last week Virginia had gotten a cryptic telegram from the man. "Arriving soon. Leaving Helena. Coming by wagon with Patricia. Many trunks."

Virginia hadn't even heard of the woman until the telegram came and she couldn't warm up to the sound of the name. *Patricia.* The woman was probably cold and critical. And well-dressed with all those trunks. Virginia hadn't felt stylish since she'd left the east coast. She now wore her hair in a simple bun and had given up her corset. Which, she just realized, was very fortunate. A woman in a corset wouldn't have been able to beat down a fire the way she'd just done.

Virginia heard the pounding of footsteps coming closer on the street so she walked over and swung the two doors wide. "It's all right. The fire's out."

She nodded a greeting as the men stomped inside and then, one by one, stared at the black scar on the floor. They needed to see it themselves. Most of the men were old customers so they had probably been next door in Lester's saloon. She recognized Petey and Shorty.

"Smells like kerosene," one of the men she didn't know said suspiciously. He had wide black suspenders holding up his wool pants and a beat-up Stetson on his head. He had the look of a miner about him.

Virginia nodded and wiped the hair out of her eyes. She'd have to rinse her hair for a week with rosewater to get rid of the smell of it. People said her blond hair was her crowning glory and she needed all the confidence she could dredge up to welcome Colter back to town with his Patricia.

The men just stood and stared at her and then back at the floor.

"You didn't do anything?" Petey finally asked. "On account of Colter coming back with this woman—"

It took Virginia a moment to realize what he was asking her. She drew in her breath indignantly. "Set a *fire!* Of course not!"

"Now, don't go getting upset," the first man said. "Petey was only asking because he's been thinking of calling Colter out when the man gets back. We've been talking, and it ain't right him leaving you like this and taking up with some fancy woman. You had a claim on him first. We're miners—we understand if you're stirred up mad. It is claim-jumping, pure and simple. Man or gold—it doesn't make any difference."

Virginia wished the fire had burned a hole in the floor big enough for her to hide in. She should have known the telegraph operator would spread the news that Colter was coming back and that he had company. "First of all, I have no claim to Colter. He's just my employer. He's free to marry anyone he wants. Just as I am free to marry anyone." She glared at Petey. The older man knew about Lester. He didn't approve for some strange reason, but he knew they might be coming to an understanding. "No one needs to call anyone out."

She didn't add that she didn't want Petey's death on her conscience. She'd grown fond of these old men during the past year. Even if Colter wasn't a gunfighter anymore, she had no doubt who would win a contest between the two men.

"Still, it ain't right," Petey repeated stubbornly. "A man can't leave his business with a woman and expect her not to get ideas. Now that your brother's gone, it's up to us to make sure you're treated with respect."

"A woman earns her own respect," Virginia said. She was only beginning to understand that herself. She'd learned a lot this past year taking care of Danny and giving a scattering of music lessons. "Besides, I'll do fine. You know I have plans."

Even though the men were not drinking at the saloon anymore, they stopped by to talk, especially around dinnertime. She always set a couple of extra plates around the poker table. She found the table did just fine for dining if she draped a cloth over it. She'd even convinced the men to eat with the proper utensils.

"We know all about your plans," Petey said. "And we're going to be at the church for the Christmas Eve service so we can applaud you and the Wells girls, but what if it just doesn't work out?"

Petey didn't need to say any more. Virginia heard her father's voice in her head continue the litany. *What if you aren't good enough? You missed that note and your timing was off there. Do it better. It's not good enough.*

She glanced over at the piano that stood in the corner of the room. She'd waxed it until it shone and kept it covered with a cloth so nothing would damage the top wood again. She liked the way the bells looked on it, too. She had not been able to bring a piano west with her, but she had brought her mother's treasured set of ten brass ringing bells, wrapped in linen and packed in her trunk.

"We must have faith," she finally said. She'd first heard about the banker's sister, Cecilia Wells, from his daughters who were her students. They were the ones who'd mentioned that their aunt was looking for a music instructor at her academy for young ladies in Denver. If Virginia wanted, they said, their father would contact his sister about Virginia. Of course, she told him to write.

All she needed to do now was to impress Cecilia when she came to Miles City to attend the Christmas Eve service. The woman remembered bell songs from a trip she'd made to England and had said she'd be happy to consider the performance as an audition for the position at her school.

"She's sure to want to hire you when she hears you and the girls play them bells," Petey said proudly. "I've never heard anything like it. The sound puts me in mind of home."

"Everything reminds you of home."

"But what I mean to say is that even though she'll want to hire you, maybe she won't be able to," Petey continued. "Maybe she will already have promised the job to someone else before she gets here. Or maybe she won't have money to hire another teacher. Or—"

"We just need to have faith," Virginia repeated. She refused to consider defeat. The echoes of her father's criticism had stayed in her mind all these years, but she had thrown herself on God's mercy. Surely He would help her get this job. It wasn't as though she was asking to be invited on some European concert tour. She knew she wasn't good enough for that. Her father had been right to say it. But she could teach children. She knew that in her bones.

"Well, if the school lady doesn't hire you," Petey continued. "Lester says he'll let you sing over at his place. He doesn't have a piano, but we can get a rousing song or two going. And we'll promise not to drink too much while you're working either."

"Thanks," Virginia murmured. But Colter had been right about drinking and ladies. The next step to what Petey suggested would be for her to lift her skirts and dance. She shuddered at the thought. This was how young ladies were ruined.

"We can even help you clean this floor up." Petey turned to scowl at the men behind him and they eventually nodded.

She looked around the main room of the saloon. Most of it was intact. She'd gotten to the fire before it spread beyond the middle of the floor. The tables were fine even though the big mirror behind the mahogany bar would need another good cleaning. And the walls she'd just washed were now slightly gray.

"It is a mess, isn't it?" Virginia said. And then she heard the door open again so she turned to look over her shoulder.

It was probably Lester. The winter sun was starting to set so it streamed right in the open door so she couldn't see clearly. She wanted to rub her eyes. It couldn't be. But there, standing in the middle of the doorway, was the last man she wanted to see right now. Fortunately, the men standing around her put themselves to good use and, quicker than she thought possible, she was hidden behind their shoulders and broad hats.

Colter hadn't expected to see half of his old customers standing in the saloon when he came back. The place was supposed to be closed. He looked over at the bar and saw there was no lineup of liquor bottles. He looked back at the men. They were all looking guilty, except for Petey who looked like he was going to erupt with something.

That's when Colter smelled the smoke. "What's happening here?"

The last thing he needed was more problems. He had enough of a challenge with Patricia. But he could see something was wrong. Then, as he watched, someone quietly pushed their way from behind the men to stand in front of them.

"I take full responsibility," Virginia said.

Colter's heart almost stopped. With her blond head held high, Virginia was beautiful. He hadn't remembered her being quite so breathtaking.

"I'd like to know your intentions." Petey stepped out from the rest of the men and walked around until he was standing in front of Virginia.

Colter looked at the man in surprise.

"Really, Petey, he doesn't need to—" Virginia said as she tried to step around the man.

It was obvious that Petey intended to stay in front because he took a step closer.

*This could go on forever,* Colter thought, *back and forth.*

He held up a hand. He'd had enough of people dancing around their opinions. It never made anything go smoother. "Let Petey talk." He turned to the older man who had been one of his best customers. "What's the problem?"

Colter wondered if somehow Petey knew where he'd been and the trouble he was bringing back with him.

"I need to know what you intend to do about Miss Virginia here, now that you're back," Petey said with some heat to his words. "She doesn't deserve to have her heart broken."

"My heart's not—" Virginia protested.

"Tell me the man's name," Colter demanded before he remembered he'd sworn off using his guns. Being a Christian was harder than it had sounded, especially when it came to a man dealing with his enemies. He'd find something to do, though, to make the man sorry he'd dealt unjustly with Virginia. His fists would work fine for a fool man like that.

There was silence in the room.

"Well," Colter demanded as he looked the men over. They might not be as bad as the scoundrel he intended to face down, but there wasn't a man in the room good enough for Virginia, himself included.

Then Colter glanced at Petey and wondered what he was missing. The man's eyes were bulging out like he'd swallowed something with a pit in it.

"Oh, for goodness' sakes," Virginia finally said. She stepped around the older man and looked Colter straight in the eye with a snap of annoyance he found rather endearing. "They think it's you."

*"Me? What'd I do?"*

"Well, you up and got married," Petey stammered, finding his voice finally. "A woman like Virginia naturally expected—"

"I'm not married." Colter heard Petey talking, but he kept

his eyes on Virginia. She had turned pink and it was the most beautiful sight he'd ever seen. It was too bad about the two of them. He had hoped to be back months ago while the memory of that kiss would be fresh in her mind. Now, of course, everything was different.

"What about your Patricia?" Petey finally finished.

And that, Colter thought to himself, was where his life now began and ended. He turned around. "This is Patricia."

# *Chapter Two*

Virginia looked at the open door of the saloon in consternation. There was no woman standing there. A few more men from the saloon next door had drifted in and there was a boy who she didn't recognize standing beside the doorjamb. It was late afternoon and the boy was probably waiting to see Danny when school let out. She thought she knew all the boys in town, but she had missed this one.

"Patricia must have left," Virginia said as she turned back. She was relieved. She knew she'd have to meet the woman eventually, but she'd rather not do it when she had soot on her face. And her hair was coming undone. This was no time to meet anyone. Besides, she had been prepared to be polite to Colter's wife, but she wasn't sure how she was supposed to act now that she found out he hadn't even married the woman he brought back here. Virginia felt sorry for her. No wonder she was embarrassed to face everyone. At least Lester would never shame a woman this way, Virginia thought to herself in satisfaction.

"Come say hello, Patricia," Colter repeated calmly.

Virginia wondered if she should say something to Colter

about being more patient with his—she hesitated—his friend. After all, he was putting the woman in an awkward situation. She was probably just outside the door waiting for him to come out again.

"I got nothing to say," the boy Virginia had seen earlier spoke up. She no sooner noticed that than she realized his voice sounded suspiciously like a girl's.

"This is Patricia?" Virginia whispered as she realized what it all meant. Now she really did want to crawl into a hole somewhere and wait for the awkwardness to pass. She looked over at the men who'd come in earlier and they were all gawking at the child as though she was a changeling. But it was clear that the woman was a girl, which meant—Virginia had been wrong.

"You must be thirsty," she said gently as she took a step toward the child. Now that she was more focused, she could see unmistakable clues that it was a girl inside those rough clothes. The girl's nose was feminine and her dark eyelashes curled. A beaten-up old hat was pulled down over her hair. Her eyes might be defiant, but they were a lovely shade of green.

"I have some tea ready to brew in back." Virginia offered with a smile. She'd heated the water when she was peeling the potatoes.

"It's a fine thing to drink," Petey said, adding his voice to the murmurs from the other men. They'd all had her tea at one time or another. She added a little cinnamon to it. And sometimes honey. "It'll warm you right up."

"I'd rather have whiskey," the child said, taking a step forward into the saloon as if she expected to get it.

"Surely, you don't—" Virginia gave a horrified glance at Colter.

Colter had seen looks like that before. When the good church women of Helena had realized that the saloon boy they knew as Patty was really a little girl named Patricia, they'd decided that Colter wasn't a fit parent for her.

He couldn't fight them on that, but he still didn't like their judgmental nature. On one point he was firm though. God had lots of people to care about Him. Patricia only had Colter. Even the women in Helena, as indignant as they were, hadn't stepped forward to take care of the child.

Colter refused to look over at Virginia. She was no doubt planning how to scold him. He knew a saloon was no place to raise a child. But he didn't have time to worry about it, not right at this minute anyway.

"Little girls don't drink whiskey." Colter repeated the words he'd had to say a few times already.

That made the girl look up, her eyes defiant. "My mother lets me have whiskey when it's cold outside. For my bones. I have thin bones."

Colter didn't answer. He didn't need to. He saw the dawning misery spread in Patricia's eyes. Her mother, Rose, had done a lot of unfortunate things in her life, but the worst of them had been to abandon her daughter.

Rose had sent a letter to Colter saying he was the father of a ten-year-old and he'd better come to the Golden Spur and pick up the girl or she would likely starve. Rose didn't even wait for Colter to get there before she took off with some miner named Rusty Jackson who had struck it rich in one of the gulches outside of town.

"You've got to have whiskey," the girl continued, her voice clipped to show she didn't care about the other. "You own this saloon. Mama told me."

Colter walked over and put his arm on her shoulder. He supposed Rose had embellished everything to make it sound like he owned the biggest and richest saloon west of the Mississippi. Rose had been like that. She would have promised her daughter anything if it meant Patricia would do what she was told.

Colter had been one of the woman's many admirers years ago when he'd been hired to keep the peace in the Golden Spur. He'd been fast with his guns back then, having more bravado than common sense. Rose hadn't been his only mistake.

Colter supposed at some time he would need to tell all of this to Virginia, but he could see from Patricia's face that now was not the time to talk about anyone's mother.

"I might not open up the saloon again," Colter settled for saying instead. He could ignore the problem if that's what Patricia wanted. "Especially not after the fire here."

"I plan to fix the floor," Virginia said stiffly.

Colter looked up. "You don't need to do that."

"Of course I do. It was my job to take care of things. You need the building now that you have another child to care for." She nodded toward the girl.

He could see by the set of her jaw that Virginia had a rush of emotions that she was keeping inside. She looked distressed, which surprised him. Most women looked outraged with him, especially when Patricia said she wanted whiskey to drink. He looked at Virginia more closely. She appeared tired, as though she hadn't been sleeping well. And she was thinner. He didn't like to see that. She must be worried about something.

"A burnt floor won't trouble Patricia," Colter said. "Not after what she's been through."

"That's why she needs a home," Virginia persisted. "I bet she doesn't even have a pillow to sleep on."

Colter relaxed. He recognized a mothering instinct when he saw it. "She needs a family more than anything."

Virginia nodded. "You've been good to Danny since he started living with you. I'm sure you'll do fine with Patricia, too."

Her approval felt like a blessing poured over him. It made him relax inside.

"I'd do better with a wife," he said without thinking. He hadn't meant to blurt it out like that. What was wrong with him? Now of all times, he couldn't afford to forget everything he knew about women.

Virginia blinked. "What?"

The men from the saloon had started to walk to the door, but they all stopped in midstride to look back at him.

"There comes a time to get married." Now that Colter had started, he decided it was worse to back down than to go forward. It probably didn't matter how he said things anyway. He hadn't had much hope even before he left here that Virginia would agree to marry him; he'd half expected her to be someone else's wife by the time he got back. Besides, he'd been a different man when he kissed her. A man with children had to think more about marriage than a man alone.

"Do you have—" Virginia started.

By now the men were all gathered around again as though this was even more entertaining than a blaze threatening to burn down the town. He supposed it was.

Colter tried to ignore his audience. "Every man has dreams."

He looked directly into Virginia's eyes, willing her to understand what was in his heart. Maybe if he hadn't been staring at her so intently he would have noticed his daughter's reaction earlier.

Patricia had walked into the middle of the circle of men and then glanced at Colter in triumph. "He means my mother."

It took a moment for the words to make it to Colter's brain. *"What?"*

Where had Patricia gotten that idea, he wondered?

"My mama's his dream. He's pined away for her for years and years. She told me she's going to come and marry him someday." Patricia jerked her thumb at Colter. "That's why I'm with him. We're just waiting until she comes."

It must have been the letter Rose left for her, Colter thought in dismay. Trust Rose to saddle him with the explanations. He'd tracked the woman down to San Francisco just to talk to her so he knew she had no intention of marrying any man. Not even her Rusty.

No one spoke for a moment. And then Petey burst forth. "You mean you aren't marrying our Virginia here?"

Everyone's eyes turned to Virginia.

"I— No—" Virginia sputtered. "Of course, he needs to marry the girl's mother. They have a child together. Besides, I have plans. And there's Lester— I—"

Colter wished he could set everyone down and explain. But before he did, he asked, "What's this about Lester?"

"Oh, you know women," Petey said with a marked lack of enthusiasm. "If there's one bad apple in the barrel—"

"Lester is not a bad apple. Just because Lester is a sensitive musician—"

Petey snorted. "That's why I'm hoping you get that job in Denver. Maybe some time away from Lester will do you good."

"Virginia's going to get a job at some fancy school in Denver." Petey turned to Colter and informed him. "Teaching music."

"So she's not getting married?" If he'd known Virginia was going to take up with Lester, he wouldn't have left her here. Now if it was a banker or a shopkeeper, he'd wish her well. Maybe even a railroad man if any of them ever got here. But Lester? There was something he didn't trust about that man. And it had nothing to do with music.

"A woman can have a job even when she's married," Virginia replied tartly. "Besides, who I marry is my own business."

Colter's heart sank. She had that look about her that said she was rattled over some man. He should have followed his impulse and asked her to marry him before he left. She hadn't loved him, but she might have married him. And, once she did, she'd stand by her word.

When he was driving the wagon over from Helena, he'd kept thinking that things between him and Patricia would go more smoothly once there was a woman like Virginia around. He'd been captivated by her during all those days when she'd played piano for the men in his saloon. She might have been exasperated with them at times, but she always looked at them with kindness. Even if she wouldn't marry him, he'd thought on the way here, she might be able to help Patricia adjust to her new life.

Not that he could ask Virginia to do all of that now. She was so caught up with Lester that—he looked around and his eyes settled on the piano in the corner. She'd been polishing the wood, he could tell that even with all of the soot that had filtered down to the piano's surface. And she had some fancy brass bells set out like Christmas decorations.

"Even if you are getting married," Colter said in a rush, "you're the best music teacher around and I'd like you to give Patricia piano lessons. I'll pay you your usual fee, of course."

"There's no need to—" Virginia said.

"I'm not gonna—" Patricia muttered.

"Double your fee," Colter interrupted them and kept going. "Triple even. I know it might take extra lessons since she's a beginner, but she doesn't need to be able to play any of those classical songs. Just some carols—maybe before Christmas."

That seemed to leave both Virginia and Patricia speechless, although he wasn't sure whether it was the price he was offering or the speed with which he was hoping for results.

"That's not even a week away," Virginia finally said. "If

she's not already playing the piano, I don't think— I mean she's awfully young to—"

"A teacher like you can handle it," Colter said.

"Nobody wants to listen to any carols—" Patricia protested with a touch of scorn. "Babies get born in mangers all the time in that part of the world." She gave a vague wave of her hand. "It's no reason to go out and play a song about it."

That made Virginia turn to the girl. "You might want to surprise your mother," she said as she knelt down so she was eye level with Patricia. Virginia got a soft look on her face that made Colter regret he didn't have more to offer her. "Parents always like to hear their children play music."

Colter would have pointed out that Rose wasn't coming so she wouldn't hear anything, but he didn't want to interrupt the two.

"Not my mother—" Patricia shook her head. "She says that all Christmas is good for is getting people to give you things 'cause they feel sorry for you. So the best thing to do is look sad so people give you nice things. Or money. She never mentions any songs."

With that, Patricia wrinkled her face up until she did look pathetic.

Colter turned and saw Virginia's mouth tighten in disapproval.

He knew then that she was going to teach Patricia. But just to be sure, he said, "You'll need some money even if you get that job in Denver. You'll need to travel. And, once you get there, you may need to stay in a hotel for a few days."

Before Virginia could answer, there was a noise as the doors opened and Danny stepped inside.

"What's for din—" the boy began as he looked around the saloon. Then he saw Colter. "You're back."

The boy's face lit up, and, for the first time in months, Colter had hope that he might make an adequate parent. After all, neither Danny nor Patricia had anyone else to look out for them. He was better than nobody.

Then he got a second look at the boy. What had happened to him? He was cleaned up until he shone. He was wearing a shirt with a collar instead of that sacklike thing he'd been wearing when Colter left. And his hair was cut proper. His ears were probably even clean.

Colter hoped Danny didn't blame him for leaving him with a lady who insisted on that much soap.

"Welcome back, sir," Danny finally added as he took a step closer to Colter and put his hand out.

Ordinarily, Danny welcomed him back with a grunt or two, but Colter took the boy's hand and shook it. Something had changed and Colter wasn't sure it was for the better. His misgivings evaporated though when the boy left him and went to Virginia, who opened her arms and gave him a hug. Colter couldn't remember anyone ever hugging Danny. If Virginia was willing to do that, then she could scrub the whole place as much as she wanted. He'd even supply the lye for the soap.

"What's burning?" Danny said as he stepped away from Virginia.

"Oh, no," the woman muttered and started to run out of the room. "I forgot the potatoes."

Colter decided that the burnt odor of the potatoes made the smell of the kerosene-soaked floor better somehow. It proved this was still their home. He was going to need to find out who had tried to destroy his saloon, but first he'd help Virginia find something for them to eat. It had done his heart good to see the affection she had for Danny. The boy hadn't been so happy since he'd wandered into the saloon a couple of years ago. Colter hoped soon Virginia would feel the same way about

Patricia. That's what his two children needed most. If Virginia insisted in leaving, he'd have to find someone else to marry. His children needed a mother.

# *Chapter Three*

Virginia had never seen a young girl with so many trunks.
There were three dull black ones with worn brass hinges.
Patricia had opened one slightly and the bright colors peeking
out made Virginia blanch. She recognized the dresses. Well, not
the exact dresses, but the style. The shiny ones sparkled like
the dresses from the women working the saloon next door.
Virginia hoped somewhere in the trunk was a dress suitable for
a ten-year-old girl.

Patricia didn't seem worried about it though. The most immediate need was for something for her to sleep in and there
was a threadbare night shift stuffed on top of the dresses in one
of the trunks.

The night showed through the upstairs windows and it
would be time to go to bed soon. They had all eaten a dinner
of fried potatoes and canned peaches before they started to
settle Patricia into the room upstairs that had belonged to
Danny. Virginia offered to move back to the boardinghouse so
the boy could have her room, but he seemed pleased to be
invited to bunk down in the storeroom with Colter. The room
was by the back door and they were going to stand watch

tonight in case the man who started the fire came back to finish the job.

Virginia was careful not to mention any of that to Patricia. The girl had enough to worry about already.

"Maybe we can just hang up the dresses that you'll want to wear in the next few days," Virginia said. "We'll want to take our time and press them."

Patricia looked up in alarm. "I'm not going to wear them. I'm just saving them for my mother."

Virginia nodded. Of course. Now she understood why Patricia had treated the trunks with so much reverence. She had even refused to let Danny open the one with the bent latch for her.

Just then there was a commotion downstairs.

"Maybe that's my mother," Patricia said, springing up in excitement and racing for the door.

Virginia didn't get a chance to say she hadn't heard a woman's voice. Fortunately, the sounds didn't seem like trouble, so she walked over to the door and stepped out into the landing leading to the stairs. She looked down and saw it was Lester. He was wearing his black suit and holding his hat.

"There you are," Lester said as he looked up at her.

She hadn't noticed before that his hair was thinning on top of his head. The strands were kind of colorless to begin with as well. Not that it mattered. Physical attraction wasn't what drew her to the man.

She was glad she'd had a chance to clean some of the soot and grime off her just in case he cared about such things though.

"I didn't expect you," Virginia said as she smiled down at Lester.

"I was worried," he said.

Patricia went back into the bedroom when she saw who the visitor was. Briefly, Virginia's eyes scanned the saloon. Colter was sitting at a table and reading something. No one else was around. She couldn't help but notice that the top of Colter's head was covered with thick, softly curling dark hair. Not that it meant anything to her. It was just interesting to observe what a person could see from a height.

Virginia looked down at Lester and waited for a telltale skip in her heartbeat. She had always expected to have a rush of feelings when she imagined touching the man who might one day be her husband. Her heart just kept up its regular beat though. She supposed thoughts of hair and hearts belonged more to girls like Patricia than to her. She was a grown woman now and knew love was rooted in steadier things than thick hair.

Lester smiled up and she started to walk down the stairs. Truly, it was best that their relationship was a practical one based on a shared love of music; it would make it easier for Lester to understand her desire to teach. If they did marry, she hoped to convince him to move to Denver with her so she could take the teaching job if it was offered to her. Lester had talked of becoming the governor of Montana when it became a state, but until that happened, Denver would be a good place for him to meet important people. She'd told him about all the politicians her father knew, but there was no way to meet any of them in a place like Miles City. Her working for a school in Denver should help with that though.

Of course, she wouldn't be considering marriage to him if she hadn't seen from his sister's letters that he had a lifelong faith in God as well. She trusted the sister's words. Who knew a man better than his sister?

When Virginia reached the bottom of the stairs, she tilted her right cheek and offered it to Lester, who gave it a quick kiss. The sweetness of the moment was spoiled by a disbelieving grunt coming from the left of her.

Virginia looked over and caught Colter's eye. He'd glanced

up from the book he was reading. She hoped the look she gave him rivaled the one her mother had given impertinent tradesmen when they tried to peddle old fish. The greeting between her and Lester was none of *his* business.

"Sorry," Colter said, looking no such thing as he gave her a wink. "It's just that men out here don't even bother with a puny kiss like that."

Virginia sensed Lester tensing up beside her so she put her hand on his arm. She'd handle this.

"A kiss on the cheek is a time-honored way of showing a woman respect," Virginia said, looking closer. Was that a Bible he was reading?

"Back east maybe," Colter agreed. "But out here a man knows how to kiss a woman."

Lester muttered something at that, but Virginia didn't hear it.

"It doesn't hurt any man to use good manners," she continued. Lester did have the sensitive soul of a violinist even if he'd left the instrument with his sister until he could send for it. "East, west, north or south. Besides, the Bible talks about a holy kiss."

Colter looked stunned as he held up the Bible in his hand and then sighed. "I haven't got to that part yet."

Lester started to chuckle. "You haven't got to a lot of things yet."

With that, Lester turned to Virginia and tipped her head back before leaning down to kiss her fully and possessively.

Virginia tried to make him stop. She needed to breathe and—well, she just didn't like the way he was kissing her. Like he was proving a point. She pushed at him a little, but that only made him more determined. Finally, she pushed him harder.

Colter had never cared for a man abusing a woman and he grabbed Lester by the back of his collar. He'd do the same to a stray cat that had wandered into the wrong bowl of cream. Lester came away sputtering and looking mad enough to fight, but Colter wasn't worried about him.

"You all right?" he asked Virginia. Her hair was in disarray and she was gasping a little for breath. He'd seen enough women who'd been well-kissed to know that Virginia wasn't too happy with her beau.

"Of course, she's all right," Lester answered for her. "She's my fiancée."

"I've never exactly said yes," Virginia snapped at him.

That answer made Colter feel pretty good, but he could see it didn't make the lovebirds too happy.

"I'm not going to wait for you forever, you know," Lester said as he started for the door, forgetting Colter still had a hold on his shirt.

"I think you should apologize to the lady," Colter suggested.

Lester choked a little and stopped abruptly.

"I don't need to—" Lester began and almost lost his wind altogether.

Colter nodded. "A man doesn't need to do much in this life, not even breathe."

Lester's face was turning pink so Colter had pity on him and untwisted his collar a little. "Next time you have a shirt tailored, you might want to have them make the neck a little bigger."

"Aargh," Lester muttered as he pulled himself up to his full height.

"Really, you need to let him go," Virginia commanded as she stepped closer.

Colter looked at her to be sure she meant it. Then he released Lester completely. "I suppose I do need to let him talk. Anyway, I've been meaning to ask him why he wasn't over here this afternoon when everyone thought there was a fire."

"I have a business to run," Lester said as he straightened the front of his shirt. "I can't be stepping outside every time the men decide to go look at something."

"The men do get excited about things. I think they make bets," Virginia said with disapproval in her voice. "Sometimes it's a horse race. Sometimes when the stage will get in."

Colter thought a minute. "I don't suppose any of them would bet on how long it would take for a saloon to burn down."

"Oh, absolutely not," Virginia protested. "They read the telegram about you coming back and—"

Colter nodded. He knew there were rumors about his gun days. Not many of the men around would challenge him. Although, he realized, the man with the match didn't exactly leave a name. Lester was coward enough to do something like that. So he looked back at the man. "Do you have any kerosene stored in that shed in back?"

Lester's face darkened at that. "Anybody could have gotten some from there. I'll bet that's what happened."

Colter grunted. "Well, I guess we're not going to figure it out tonight."

Now that Lester was free to leave, the man didn't seem too eager to go. Which made the man a fool as well as a coward in Colter's eyes.

"Is there something you want to tell me?" Colter finally asked. After what had happened today, he'd only lit a few of the lamps around so the shadows were deep in parts of the saloon.

"A man has a right to say good-night to his fiancée in private," Lester said.

Colter shrugged. "He does if he's saying it in his own establishment."

What was it about Lester that reminded him of a rooster? Maybe it was the way his neck stretched when he got indignant.

"It's still snowing out there," Lester protested. "I can't ask Virginia to walk outside just to say good-night."

Colter nodded. "I suppose not."

"You can say good-night here," Virginia said as she reached out her hand to Lester.

Colter had to respect the woman for not letting the man kiss her after his earlier performance.

Lester still didn't look any too happy, but he finally shook Virginia's hand before saying good-night and shuffling out the door.

When the other man had left the building, Colter turned to Virginia. He figured she would want to thank him for coming to her rescue, but he didn't want her to fuss over it. He would do as much for any woman who was in trouble.

"What did you think you were doing?" Virginia turned to him and demanded.

Her voice wasn't as grateful as Colter had been expecting and it turned him cautious. "I—ah—"

"I had it perfectly under control," Virginia continued without letting him answer. "If you'd waited, I would have explained to him how a gentleman should behave and—"

"I don't think he was set to listen," Colter added mildly.

"I would have explained how he should behave," Virginia kept on going. "And then we would have been of one mind on how to be when we're together. We'd have had an understanding."

Colter was flabbergasted. "I interrupted all that?"

"Yes, you did," Virginia declared and then she sat down in a chair and burst into tears.

Colter was silent for a bit. "I could go get him and bring him back."

"I don't want him back," Virginia said, as she lifted her tear-streaked face and then hiccuped. "But he plays the vi-oo-lin."

She hiccuped again.

"Breathe easy now," Colter said as he moved close and patted her on the back.

Then he stepped over to the bar and brought back a cup of cold coffee. "Here, take a swallow of this."

Virginia took the cup and drained it. They were both quiet for a minute, but she didn't have another hiccup. Colter had never listened so intently to another person's breathing though, and he began to have some sympathy for poor Lester. In the light of the lamp, Virginia's skin glowed and her hair shone and—

"That holy kiss you were talking about," Colter finally said, his throat thick enough he was afraid Virginia would know his thoughts by the way his voice sounded. "Is it something like this?"

God was going to have to forgive him, Colter thought as he leaned down and touched his lips to Virginia's. He was a doomed man.

"That's not right," Virginia whispered against his lips.

Colter moved his head back.

She cleared her throat and continued, "A holy kiss is for church." Her face was flushed pink, but she was smiling a little.

"It's almost Sunday," Colter said as he straightened up and smoothed Virginia's hair back. "I don't recall any kissing in church before I left here. 'Course I didn't get a chance to go more than a few times before I left."

He had wished he had time to talk a little more with the pastor before he was called away to get Patricia. He'd been reading the Bible alone to try to make sense of things, but he had some questions.

"I've been taking Danny with me."

"I appreciate that," Colter said and then realized something. "I haven't paid you yet for taking care of everything. And the bank's closed now."

"Monday's fine," Virginia said as she stood up, too.

Before he knew it, she had said good-night and walked back up the stairs.

Colter supposed it was for the best. Virginia deserved a newly minted penny, not an old beat-up coin like him. So far, he was doing all right by Danny and Patricia, but they had even fewer expectations of life than he did. Someone like Virginia was different though. She'd grown up with china dolls and tea parties—and those pianos she talked about. She should marry a man who could give her those things again. She hadn't talked much about her life back east, but he'd noticed she had a way of doing things that showed she'd known some fine things in life. She was very precise in her movements.

She'd certainly never had much to do with ex-gunfighters who were trying to be fathers. That much Colter could guarantee. He was better at trail grub than normal meals. He'd been meaning to get Danny a regular shirt, but he'd never quite made it to the mercantile to do it. Frankly, he wasn't even sure how he was supposed to make a home for the two children he was taking on. He'd been raising Danny in this saloon here, but it wasn't suitable for Patricia. Besides, he didn't have a taste for that kind of life anymore himself.

Maybe in church tomorrow he'd talk to Jake Hargrove, his old friend who lived over by Dry Creek. Jake had gone from a trapping life to raising his nieces and it hadn't seemed to hurt him any. Of course, he'd convinced Elizabeth to marry him shortly after his nieces came to live with him so he was probably making out just fine. A wife would make all of the difference.

## Chapter Four

Virginia woke up and almost screamed. Thin streaks of morning sun were coming in the window and a purple bird was staring down at her. She blinked to clear her vision and noticed the bird had odd feathers. And a little girl's nose was sticking out of its beak, quivering with excitement.

"Well, who do we have here?" Virginia leaned up on an elbow so she could be eye to eye with her visitor. "I wonder if anyone wants fried chicken for breakfast."

That made the nose and the beak shake even more with barely stifled giggles.

"This looks like a nice plump bird," Virginia continued, pretending to consider the idea. "I bet it tastes good."

With that, Patricia put down the feathered mask that must have come from her mother's trunks and giggled freely.

"Are you finished trying to terrify me?" Virginia asked as she stretched.

"You weren't scared. You were hungry. My mother would have screamed."

"I'm sure she'd have swooned from fright," Virginia agreed.

Patricia was silent for a minute. "Sometimes she liked to play if she wasn't busy."

Virginia nodded. And sometimes purple birds came to visit at dawn. No matter how much Patricia loved this mother of hers, Virginia didn't think much of the woman. She reached out to sweep a stray feather out of Patricia's hair.

Then she pushed the covers off and swung her legs around to the floor. "If you get dressed, I'll show you how to make a sock doll this afternoon."

The girl shrugged. "Okay."

Patricia was leaving the room when Virginia remembered. "And put on your best clothes. It's Sunday today and we're going to church."

Patricia turned around. "My mother doesn't take me to church."

*Now why aren't I surprised?* Virginia thought.

"Well, it's time you went then," was all she said.

Virginia knew it wasn't really her decision to take the children to church. Colter was their parent. He should make that decision. But since she was going to church regardless of who else did, she decided she would wear her best gray wool dress with the brass buttons trailing down the front and the small bustle in the back. And, of course, her black hat and gloves.

Even when she was giving lessons to the Wells girls, she dressed like a lady. She was afraid to relax her standards for fear she wouldn't fit into her world anymore when she was able to return. Being caught without a corset yesterday was lazy on her part. A lady had to put the proper effort into dressing. Her father, she couldn't help thinking, would be appalled if he could see her now. He had expected more from her.

Virginia heard Patricia's footsteps going down the stairs while she put the last pins in her hair. If she knew Danny, the boy was already up and dressed for going to church.

When Virginia got to the stairs, she looked down and wondered what had happened. By the smell of things, pancake batter was burning somewhere and a gray barking dog was chasing an animal—it must be a cat—around the tables. Colter had just opened the doorway coming in from the back room. He was holding a wooden spoon in his hand and ignoring the smoke starting to billow out behind him. He must have heard the children. Danny was sitting in one of the chairs laughing as a wild-haired Patricia threatened to throw a small spittoon at him. If it was the spittoon from the bar, at least it was clean.

Virginia walked down the stairs and over to the piano. She didn't have much experience with chaos, but she did know sound. She reached for one of her deepest bells and rang it sharply. The pure sweet note floated over the saloon. Then Colter shut the door to the back room, closing the cat and dog in there. Patricia sat and gazed up at the bell with a look of rapture on her face. Even Danny had stopped laughing.

There was blessed silence in the room.

*Now how did she do that?* Colter asked himself as he walked over and set his spoon down on a table. When he'd gotten up this morning, he'd figured he'd make some pancakes for breakfast just like he used to do every Sunday morning for him and Danny. Two more people to feed didn't worry him.

But then Patricia had come down and opened the front door to get her morning breath of fresh air, something she claimed her mother always advised. A gust of wind made her hair blow this way and that. Then, Danny started to laugh at her hair and the cat ran inside, trying to escape that dog following her. Before Colter knew it, everything was out of control.

With one bell ring, though, Virginia had brought it all back to normal.

He hadn't realized until this very minute that he was a fool to think he was ready to be a father to two children. When it had just been him and Danny they had done all right. But how would he manage with Patricia as well? He didn't know anything about girls.

"How'd you do that?" Patricia was demanding of Virginia. Colter needed to sit down. He'd faced ambushes with less panic than he was feeling right now. How did ordinary men manage to raise children like these? A person couldn't just put them in a corral like spring colts. Or let them scatter like chickens. Could he?

Fortunately, Virginia rang the bell again and Patricia walked slowly over to the piano.

Life was full of surprises, Virginia thought to herself. Who would think that a slip of a girl more familiar with a spittoon than a musical instrument would be blessed with such an exceptional ear for music. By the look on her face, she figured the girl had also heard the slow slide of the bell tone. Most ears didn't pick that up. "The note's a D. It can also do this."

By hitting the bell slightly differently, Virginia made a lighter sound.

"It's beautiful," Patricia said as she stopped in front of the bells and reached out to touch one of them reverently.

"My mother's father had them engraved." Virginia smiled as she stepped closer to the girl. The etched cross was surrounded by curls on the front of the brass bell. "He was a change ringer with a cathedral guild in England. Very proud he was of it, too."

Virginia handed a bell to Patricia and the girl ran her finger around the rim of it.

Virginia guessed that, even if they hadn't started lessons, the girl was now a student so she should tell her more. "My grandfather's job was to mark the hours of the day and other important times and places. The different series of rings were called changes. He was most grateful for these small bells because he could use them to practice at home in front of the fire instead of in the church's cold bell tower. He left them to my mother when he died and she left them to me."

"I wouldn't have minded the cold," Patricia said.

Virginia smiled. "If you turn the bell over you'll see a mark. That means they were made by the Whitechapel Bell Foundry in England."

Virginia loved to teach about music. She picked up a couple of more bells and rang out part of a scale.

"Does the church here have bells?" Patricia asked. "I didn't know churches had bells."

"We have an organ, too. We're not planning to ring the bells until Christmas Eve. And we're not doing any changes, we're playing 'Silent Night.' But the organ plays every Sunday."

"Then I'm going," the girl said simply.

Virginia nodded. She knew what the love of music could mean to someone. It was too bad that Patricia couldn't go back east and discover the richness of the music there. Virginia sighed. She wished her father could have met the girl. It might have made up for some of his disappointment with her if she could have brought him a student with a natural talent for music that might even have rivaled his.

Colter felt his heart ease as he watched Virginia talking to Patricia. Maybe he wasn't as alone as he had thought. Virginia sounded as though she was willing to help Patricia. The girl needed affection almost more than she needed musical training, but he wouldn't tell either one of them that yet.

The only reason he knew how barren the girl's childhood had been was because he'd gone to Rose before he'd brought Patricia back here. That woman was drunk when he talked to her or she probably wouldn't have admitted she hadn't been sure he'd go to the Golden Spur, especially when the girl wasn't even his daughter. Rose had laughed like crazy at that, saying he should have asked the girl her birthday. He'd remembered Rose as being irresponsible, but he hadn't known she could be cruel until then.

On the ride back to Helena, he had decided he wouldn't mention birthdays. Or tell Patricia what her mother had said about him leaving her if he wanted. Colter figured God had tapped his shoulder to help the girl and that was that. He'd already learned with Danny that feeling like a father didn't always have much to do with the facts of the matter.

Colter shook his head as though to clear it. Patricia was safe with him now and, in time, her mother would become a distant memory. A little smoke was still in the air so he excused himself and went into the back room. The door to the outside had been pushed open by the escaping cat and dog so most of the smoke had left as well. He decided he'd just make oats for everyone for breakfast. If they were all going to church, he wouldn't have enough time to make pancakes now anyway.

He put the water on to boil and went back into the main room.

"Braids," Patricia was demanding. "I want braids."

"I think brushing your hair will be enough." Virginia was proceeding to do just that.

"But it tangles," Patricia protested. "Unless I wear my hat."

"No hats," Virginia said.

"Why not? He's wearing his." Patricia eyed Danny.

Colter noted that the boy did have his hat on. That was unlike him. He was probably making sure no one took a comb to him though. Or a spittoon.

"Oh, but you have such pretty hair. We don't want to cover it up." Virginia said to Patricia as she untangled everything.

Colter wondered when Virginia would notice they had bigger problems than Patricia's hair. He hadn't truly seen how ragged her clothes were until she sat next to Virginia. As near as he could tell, Patricia was wearing a cut-down man's shirt cinched in with a piece of cowboy rope. Her trousers were made of coarse wool and were starting to fray at the seams.

"You'll have to sit by me in church," Colter told Patricia. People wouldn't notice her clothes so much if she was sitting by him. At least they would be less noticeable than if she sat by Virginia.

How did that woman manage to always look so good anyway?

"I think there's a community dinner after church services today," Virginia remarked as she started to guide the brush through the girl's hair. "Elizabeth Hargrove is making her doughnuts, too. She passes those out between Sunday school and church."

"My mother made doughnuts once," Patricia said with longing in her voice. "She said doughnuts are the way to a man's heart."

"Yes, well—" Virginia hesitated and looked up at him. "If it's all right with Colter, we'll invite the Hargroves here some afternoon and make doughnuts with Elizabeth and Spotted Fawn. I don't know if they'll make their way to any man's heart, but they sure are good."

Patricia started to frown. "Spotted Fawn? Is that an Indian name?"

Colter wondered if he should have said something to Patricia earlier. He'd grown so accustomed to the Hargrove girls now that he often didn't remember they were part-Sioux.

"She'll be in church?" Patricia asked.

"We hope so," Colter said.

Patricia frowned as she looked up at him and then back at

Virginia. "My mother won't let me sit down with no Indians. They can't even get whiskey at her saloon. They're no good. Everyone says they're a regular bite upon the face of the earth."

"The word's *blight* and it's not true," Virginia said with some heat.

Patricia still looked undecided.

"Spotted Fawn is a lovely girl. And you'll treat her politely." Virginia looked over at Colter. "That is, if your father agrees."

"Of course I agree," Colter said, wondering what was going through Virginia's mind. "You don't need to ask me if I agree with every little thing."

"They're your children," Virginia said.

"Well, yes, but—" he stammered to a halt. He could hardly admit he was adrift in that particular job and wasn't sure he could be trusted to decide all of those questions.

"I don't know if we can fix any of my dresses to fit you, but we can try." Virginia bent down to say to Patricia.

"I have my own dress." Patricia stood up. "I'll show you."

Colter watched as his daughter ran toward the stairs. "I should have bought her a dress before I left Helena."

Virginia got a worried look on her face. "Her mother must have given her the dress then."

Colter shook his head. "Everyone at the saloon there thought she was a boy. I doubt she has a dress."

Virginia was aghast. If she was ever so fortunate as to have a daughter, she wouldn't deny the girl her birthright. "Tomorrow morning I'm going to take her to the mercantile and let her pick out a dress. Any dress she wants. If they have any that will fit I mean—"

Virginia stopped. The realization sank into her bones that she was only a temporary guest in this girl's life. Or Danny's life. She'd already made the mistake of getting too attached to both of them. And, before she knew it, Patricia's mother was going to come here and expect to marry Colter.

She looked up at the man in annoyance. "You need your hair cut, too. It wouldn't hurt to set a good example for your children."

"I've been making breakfast," he defended himself and then stopped to groan. "Ach, the oats are probably burnt, too."

With that, he rushed back to the cookstove in the other room.

The air inside the saloon was gray again and Danny had removed his hat and was trying to swat a fly with it. But Virginia felt as if her heart was pounding a little too fast. Nothing unusual was even going on. Except for the fact that this morning she'd been part of a family.

She went over to the table where a stack of bowls and some spoons were lying and began to arrange them for the four of them.

Music had been so central in her family's life that she had seldom sat down just to talk with her parents and brother. She'd spent hours practicing in hopes she would wake up one day with the miraculous talent her father kept saying she must have inside her since he had such a gift. She had been consumed with the search for that talent, only to be disappointed time and time again.

She could not remember a single day in her childhood when there had been the kind of chaos she had experienced this morning. She wouldn't have thought she would enjoy it. But something about Colter trying to take care of his two wards melted her heart. She felt a longing to be a mother.

She sighed. That led her back to Lester. Maybe he would be back to normal by today. She needed to be patient; she supposed any man needed some training to be a good husband. It wouldn't hurt for them to sit together after church and talk a little more about their future. She'd welcome a chance to tell him about the concerts that they could attend in Denver. Maybe they'd even attend the opera if there was a performance in the town.

She smiled. Patricia's mask would make a worthy prop in an opera. Maybe the girl could come visit them when they were settled in Denver. And Danny, too, of course. She thought for a moment and then frowned. Somehow she couldn't picture Colter with them, sitting in her parlor and drinking tea with Lester and her. No, she couldn't see him doing that at all. She supposed that meant the children would need to be older before they could come. She frowned. She didn't like that thought at all.

# Chapter Five

V irginia would not have guessed that Patricia was shy. Maybe she hadn't been when she was dressed as a boy, but now, in her girl clothes, she was as demure as a flower sitting beside Virginia. The snow still blew outside and the wood-plank floor inside was covered with wet splotches from the heat of the cast-iron stove melting the ice from the men's boots. Next year, the town planned to build a proper church, but until then they were using the schoolhouse for religious services, which meant they sat squeezed together on benches made for children.

Virginia was glad Patricia at least had good button-up shoes. They had chosen to sit on a front bench so they could see the organist play. The tips of the girl's shoes peeked out from beneath her clothes in a perfectly polite way. Colter had given them a quick polish before they had all left the saloon. Unfortunately, there wasn't room for Colter and Danny to join them on the bench so they were several benches behind them.

"This is Patricia," Virginia said for the tenth time as people filed past. Reverend Olson had said the final prayer and church was over. "She's moved down from Helena and she'll be in school when it starts up again after Christmas."

Everyone smiled and said hello while the girl beamed. Virginia had decided not to mention that Patricia was Colter's daughter. She would let him give that explanation; she only hoped he mentioned that he was planning to marry the girl's mother when he told people. Marriages around here were often irregular, but everyone seemed more comfortable when children were set in proper families.

Fortunately, they had been able to dress Patricia so she looked like the other children. The girl did have thin bones and none of Virginia's dresses would fit her, not even when they were tucked and hemmed. The dress Patricia thought of as hers was much too large, being cut down from one of her mother's saloon dresses and being too flashy by far for any respectable woman, let alone a school girl.

Virginia had a white apron, though, that wrapped around the girl's waist several times before they tied it and, with one of Danny's new white shirts and a few pale blue ribbons, she had emerged from her upstairs bedroom looking almost like the other girls. When she pulled Virginia's gray shawl around her shoulders, no one could tell that what she was wearing had been pieced together.

The people started going outside and Virginia saw Lester walk over to her.

"I don't know why you have to introduce her," Lester muttered as he sat down on Virginia's left side. "She's *his* daughter."

Virginia turned just in time to see the scowl Lester sent toward Colter's back.

"Would you like to go up and see the instrument closer?" Virginia bent to ask Patricia.

The girl nodded.

"Go ahead then."

Virginia waited for Patricia to walk away before she turned

to Lester. "It's no trouble to introduce her to people around here."

Virginia had decided during the sermon to work on improving Lester's manners, but she hadn't wanted to say anything in front of Patricia. Children, she believed, should look up to the adults in their lives.

Virginia noticed Lester hadn't even turned to look at her. Instead, he was continuing to stare at the other man's back.

Colter must have sensed someone looking at him, because he turned and started walking right toward them. Virginia couldn't help but think that he was coming to her rescue once again. Maybe it was the way he walked, balanced and sure on his feet as though he wouldn't back down from any trouble— not even the trouble he clearly could see on the horizon if his frown was any indication. As he got closer, she noticed his scowl disappear and his eyes start to sweep her with warmth. Then it became more than warmth. Really, a man shouldn't look at a woman like that in a church, she thought to herself as her face heated up. Or anywhere else either.

"Who does he think he is?" Lester hissed in Virginia's ears. "You're practically my fiancée."

"He's only smiling," Virginia said quietly to Lester. She was sure Colter didn't know the way his eyes were shining anyway. If she meant to train Lester, the lessons might as well begin now. "A gentleman doesn't cause a disturbance in church anyway. A soft answer turns away wrath."

"I'm not going to just let—" Lester started, but by then Colter was standing right in front of them.

Virginia didn't think it was advantageous to remain seated while Colter stood over them, so she rose to her feet as well. My, she realized as her stomach flipped, his eyes did speak to a woman, whether she wanted to hear him or not. Maybe if she could demonstrate, Lester would see the value of being polite in public places regardless of what other people were doing though.

"Wonderful sermon, wasn't it?" Virginia said to Colter as she gave him just the right kind of social smile. Not too cold, but not warm either. Just very correct.

Lester stood to his feet, too.

Colter ignored the other man and kept his eyes on Virginia. "When the reverend was preaching about all that squabbling over who was supposed to be first, it made me think back. I've seen gunfights started over less."

"I don't think they had guns back in the Bible days." Virginia thought the conversation was going fairly well so she added, "Which is most fortunate, don't you agree?"

"People just killed each other with rocks," Lester interrupted to say, his voice deeper than usual.

The fact that her would-be fiancé sounded menacing when he delivered his observation was only accidental, Virginia told herself. Some men just needed to develop the art of social conversation.

Colter grunted as though to prove her point.

"People aren't so easy to kill with rocks," Colter added. By now he'd taken his eyes off Virginia completely and they were boring into Lester.

Virginia was getting ready to say that this was the very reason that public conversation was to be kept neutral, when she noticed that Lester's neck was getting pink.

"Well, the reverend clearly said Christians were to be the peacemakers," she tried to remind them both of the point of today's sermon. "All people need to do is—"

"You got a gun on you?" Lester interrupted to ask as he kept glowering at Colter. "I figure you've got one hidden some place."

"My goodness, there's no need to speak of guns!" Virginia was appalled. Her explanation must be lacking something.

"Of course, there's no need to talk of guns," Colter agreed smoothly as he pointedly ignored Lester again. "We're in church, getting ready to have dinner with our friends and neighbors." Colter smiled down at Virginia. "I'll go find us all a place to eat. They're putting some tables up by the window on the side."

"Virginia will be sitting with me for dinner," Lester said from his position to her left. He'd said the first to Colter, but then he turned to Virginia. "You can't ignore me forever. I'm going to apologize, you know. For last night."

Virginia smiled at him proudly. He seemed to be learning.

"You're more than welcome to join us," she countered Lester's invitation. There was no reason to have divisions in church. "Isn't he, Colter?"

Virginia appreciated that Lester had brushed his suit and shined his shoes, too. How could she refuse to forgive him when he'd gone to so much work? All men and women probably had disagreements before they married.

"I plan to sit with you *alone*," Lester responded. His face was flushed and he ran his finger around the collar of his white shirt.

Virginia was torn, but she knew what she needed to do. After all, the children and Colter were only temporary family in her life. She hoped Lester would become permanent. He needed a little more work, but she remembered her mother saying how much trouble she'd gone through to teach her father his manners. And her father was flawlessly polite even when something displeased him.

"Virginia?" Colter asked.

She smiled up at him. "Lester and I do have a lot to talk about. You'll be fine with the children, I'm sure."

Colter's heart sank with her words. Of course, he'd be fine with the children. The fact that it was the children and not him on her mind told him he was in trouble though. He never used to have a problem charming women. And then it struck him—he'd never even tried to impress a churchgoing woman before. He'd liked more ankle and flash. Women like Rose had been the ones he wanted to be around.

This agreement he'd made with God was turning him inside out and shaking him upside down at the same time. He'd come to peace with the fact that being a Christian had changed his gun-carrying ways. But women? He hadn't particularly expected it to make any difference in regards to women. At least not in ways that affected his heart. And he'd long since realized that it was his heart leading him toward this particular woman.

"You and Lester have a good dinner," Colter said, although he almost choked on the words. One thing he did know was that God intended for him to respect a woman's wishes. "As you said, the children and I will be fine."

With that, Colter turned and walked away. He would find Danny and Patricia and get them both settled at a table with him.

Virginia watched Colter walk away. "Maybe I should just help him find the children."

"I never get to spend time with you," Lester complained softly at her side. "Let him take care of his bas—"

Virginia gasped and shot him a look of horror. They were standing in the middle of the schoolhouse, but fortunately no one else had heard. She sat back down on the bench.

"His children," Lester continued as he sat down with her and then added defiantly, "I don't care what anyone calls the girl. I just know she's not your concern."

Virginia looked around to see that no one was walking close enough to them to hear their words.

"Of course, she's my concern," Virginia said quietly. "She's only a little girl who needs some help adjusting to her new home. What's wrong with you lately anyway?"

Lester had been so pleasant those evenings when he'd sat and read her the letters he'd received from his sister. Maybe that was it. "You haven't had bad news from home, have you?"

If anyone knew how devastating that could be, it was her.

Lester shook his head. And then he gave a weak smile. "Can't a man just want to sit and talk with his fiancée?"

"We're not engaged. Not yet," Virginia corrected him. She studied his face though. "Is it your violin? Maybe you should ask your sister to send it out here. I know how it is to want to play music and not have an instrument to express all you're feeling."

"Oh, I couldn't ask her to do that," Lester said.

Was it her imagination or did his face turn a little white? In any event, he didn't look at all welcoming of the idea. Maybe he didn't understand.

"It's not that difficult to send things by steamer," she explained. "You don't need to fear for the safety of your violin either. Just get your sister to pack it well. You probably have some sheet music, too, that you'd like sent with it. And that wool vest your sister mentioned in one of her letters. I'm sure she would be more than happy to send you a few things to make your life more comfortable out here."

Lester felt the same way she did about the harshness of these small Western towns. A few comforts from home would be most appreciated.

Virginia tried to remember where his sister lived. She couldn't recall him saying. She knew the other woman was a lady though because she used the most beautiful lavender paper to write her letters. Lester was very protective of the letters themselves or she would have asked to read one just so she could feel the paper.

"She can't send anything," Lester said with a gulp. "She's sick."

Virginia chided herself as he abruptly stood up and walked away. No wonder the man had been acting peculiar these past few days. He was devoted to his sister and must be terribly worried. And, instead of being a comfort to him, all she had done was add to his troubles by criticizing him.

Well, it wasn't too late to show she was a supportive almost-fiancée. She would not only sit with him while they ate, she would encourage him with every breath she took.

Colter was sitting beside Reverend Olson and chewing on a piece of fried chicken. Elizabeth Hargrove had asked Patricia to eat with them so she could get acquainted with Spotted Fawn, and the girls were starting to say a few words to each other. Danny had eaten and was outside, no doubt throwing snowballs at some of the other boys.

"We have such bounty," the reverend said as he lifted up a piece of corn bread.

"Yeah," Colter said and tried to smile. His stomach felt sour though, as he kept his eyes focused on Virginia fawning over that worthless fiancé of hers. She had been like that through the entire meal. She had practically cut his meat for him. He would never understand what women saw in men like him.

"I don't suppose God has changed His mind about shooting people?" Colter asked.

The reverend saw where Colter's eyes were going and he started to chuckle.

"Women are strange creatures," he finally said. "But you have to be careful. Sometimes they take to the man who's wounded and not the one who did the shooting."

Colter grinned. "I guess they do at that."

The reverend finished his corn bread.

"Do you know of anyone around here who has a violin?" Colter asked him then.

"Can't say offhand that I do. Maybe Wells has one—his wife is real fond of music. And, his sister, too, with her school and all."

"I'll ask him. Thanks."

He decided there was more than one way to compete with Lester. Virginia seemed impressed with the fact that Lester could play the violin. Colter had never seen anyone play the instrument, but he knew his hands were nimble enough to learn anything that required quickness. He'd practiced many techniques to train his fingers to move with sensitivity because a gunman needed nimble fingers. He'd seen Lester fumble around outside just trying to get a leather knot tied so his horse would stay where it was supposed to be. If Lester could play the violin with his clumsy fingers, Colter decided he could, too. All he needed was a violin and a few pointers from someone.

Just then, there was a rush of boys through the door into the schoolhouse and it looked as if Danny was in their lead.

"We found it," Danny announced in triumph. "The empty can for the kerosene."

"Ah." Colter noticed that got the attention of everyone in the place.

"I forgot about the fire," the reverend said in the silence that followed. "I meant to pray about it this morning in the service. We can't have that kind of mischief in our town."

There were murmurs of agreement from some of the men present.

"It could be an old can," Lester said from where he sat on the far side of the room.

"It's got no rust from the snow," Danny said.

Colter figured there wasn't much to be proved from an empty container, but he liked Danny's enthusiasm for finding out what happened. So he stood up. "Let's go take a look."

Halfway to the door, Colter decided he wasn't ready to leave Virginia there with Lester. There was no telling what would happen.

"Maybe Virginia can identify it," he said loud enough for the crowd of men to halt and look over at her.

"She was the only one there when it happened," old Petey spoke out from where he stood on the side of the church. After he spoke his piece, he grinned back at Colter.

Colter nodded. He owed the man.

"So, is she coming?" another of the old men took up the cry.

By that time, Virginia had stood up. She didn't look reluctant to leave, not if the eagerness with which she wrapped her shawl around her shoulders was any indication.

"I don't know what you can tell them," Lester said. He was speaking to Virginia, but his voice carried throughout the room.

"It's the fire," she said to him as she walked toward the door. "We can't be too careful about fire."

And, with that, Virginia paused briefly as she came up even with Colter and the two of them walked out of the church, leading the band of men and boys.

Colter felt victorious.

The day was warmer than anyone had expected, and he stopped along with Virginia at the foot of the church steps. Snow covered the ground, but the winter sun was shining down. A path had been trampled from the church steps down the main street in town.

"I don't want you to get snow in your shoes," Colter said as he knelt down to make sure her shoes were securely buttoned. "Who knows where those boys are taking us."

Colter figured he couldn't be blamed if he lingered a bit. Virginia's high-topped shoes fitted a trim ankle. And the ruffle of her underskirts teased against his hands as he tugged on the fasteners to be sure they held strong. The fine wool of her dress rubbed lightly against his cheek and he forgot all about the kerosene can. He practically forgot his name.

"Hey," Danny shouted from someplace ahead. "Where is everybody?"

Virginia reached down and put her hand on his shoulder. "We need to catch up."

He guessed she was right, so he stood and brushed the snow off his knees. He figured if he knew who wanted to burn his saloon to the ground he would sleep easier tonight.

# Chapter Six

As the sun went down that evening, Colter lit all the lanterns in his saloon. Then he opened the front door and waited for his friends to arrive. What a day he'd had.

The dark red kerosene can had turned out to be one the mercantile had left outside last spring. It had apparently gotten dragged around by a dog or a coyote and lodged up against a clump of sage in back of the livery stable. Boys and men alike examined the can, trying to decide if it had been used in the fire until Colter eventually stepped forward and sniffed at the can's spout. The kerosene smell was so faint he voiced his opinion that it hadn't held anything recently.

By then the men and boys were having a fine time stomping through the snow, looking for clues about the fire and throwing a few snowballs. Finally, the owner of the mercantile declared that, in honor of the boys finding his missing can, he would offer up chocolate enough to make cocoa for any children around if someone had milk to go with it.

Jake Hargrove offered to ride back to his farm and bring in a bucket of milk. By then Colter was feeling affectionate toward the town he'd missed those long months he'd been gone, and he invited everyone over to his saloon. They'd make up the hot chocolate for the children, he said, and there'd be plenty of hot coffee and tea for the adults. He even had some hard biscuits in a couple of tins he'd brought back with him from Helena. He remembered after he made the invitation that his place had been a saloon and some people might not be comfortable going there, but no one hesitated, not even the women carrying babies.

The graciousness of it all made Colter feel glad to be home. He had wandered all over this country in his younger days, and now that he'd seen the last of his twenties he was fortunate to have friends and neighbors like these. The truth was he had come home in more ways than one during this past year. God had become an anchor for him. And the children—he hadn't asked for either one of them, but they had become his and he planned to raise them as best he could.

When everybody had something warm to drink, they convinced Virginia to play the piano. She started out with some Irish ballads about ill-fated lovers and swollen rivers. Half of the men sang along as she played "Danny Boy." The women shed a tear or two when the song changed and Virginia herself sang "The Orphan's Prayer."

The light of the lanterns flickered on the intent faces of everyone as they listened to Virginia sing of the child who had been ignored and left to die. More than one person looked over to the corner where Patricia was sitting with the other children, so Colter figured her story had been passed around. He tensed up at first, but then he saw the glances were all kind. He wondered if the emotion he heard in Virginia's voice was because she, too, recognized the song as being repeated in Patricia's young life.

There was respectful silence when Virginia finished the orphan song, and then a man yelled out from where he stood at the bar, "Play us the mountain one. The she'll-be-a-coming-around one."

Virginia's fingers started again with a changed tempo and the men began to clap and stomp. Colter felt deep contentment as he sat there and listened. He'd been the last to sit down and he was alone at a table in the back until Petey came and sat down next to him.

"She sure is something," Petey whispered as he nodded his head toward Virginia. "And not just with her piano. She's been real nice to me and the boys this winter. Had us over for soup on many a cold night."

Virginia paused at the end of her song to catch her breath and everyone applauded. As the sound died down, Colter turned to the older man. "Soup, huh?"

Petey grinned at him and continued in a low voice. "She can't cook worth much, but she always asks after us like she cares about whether we have holes in our socks and things like that. It does my heart more good than the soup. I'll tell you that much. I never have had the courage to tell her I don't even have socks. I just wrap an old piece of something around my feet when it's cold."

"Ah," Colter said with a nod. He wasn't the only one halfway in love with Virginia Parker.

"I've been asking around," Petey continued. "It seems Lester wasn't in that back room over at his saloon when we smelled the smoke coming from over here. I was holding a pretty good poker hand so I didn't notice, but Shorty was working at the bar then and he went back to check about something. The door to Lester's office was open, but he wasn't in it. He's usually there that time of the day."

"I see." Colter had watched as people came inside the saloon earlier and Lester hadn't been among the crowd. Colter thought the other man hadn't come because they were rivals, but maybe there was more to it. Now he felt cautious as well.

"I know it doesn't prove anything," Petey continued. "But

that morning Shorty had just said he thought he saw Virginia walking down to the mercantile, too. Lester was there to hear it. I don't see him wanting to hurt Virginia. He seems real set on marrying her, but—"

His voice trailed off.

Colter nodded. He had the same questions.

"I think we need to keep an eye on things is all," Petey finally finished.

"You won't get any argument from me on that," Colter said. "In fact, if you want a job helping fix this floor here, let me know."

"It might be nice to be close," the older man agreed.

"And if you see Lester doing anything else peculiar, let me know," Colter said.

Petey nodded.

The music continued for another hour or so and then the children started to get tired and parents were bundling up their families for the ride home in the cold. Even though the snow hadn't melted much today, there was no wind and everyone would do fine if they had a blanket to wrap around themselves in the backs of their wagons.

Virginia went around wishing everyone a good night. Colter wasn't sure everyone here tonight had even realized how talented she was until now. People were all complimenting her. He thought she would be exhausted, but, when the children had both gone off to bed and he was the only one left, she went back to the piano. That's when she started to play the Bach music.

Colter had taken some of the used cups into the kitchen so he didn't clearly hear the first chords she played. He'd put some hot water on to heat and offered to do the dishes in Danny's stead tonight. The boy was tired.

The music coming from the other room pulled Colter back

from the kitchen. Empty cups were still stacked at tables around the room, but he sat down anyway at the table in the shadows. He didn't want to interrupt Virginia. She was playing a song that had haunted him during the months he'd been gone. Many a night, he'd tried to figure out why he was drawn to the thin loneliness he heard in the echoes of that song. Virginia had played it twice when she was working in the saloon. Both times she'd looked sad, as though she was remembering things she'd do best forgetting. When he'd been gone, he'd regretted not asking her about it before he left.

How could a song say so much, he wondered, and not use any words?

Sorrow wasn't comfortable for Colter, but he let Virginia take him there with her. She played the song with her whole body as she stretched out to reach keys far from the center of the piano. He had no illusions that Virginia was playing for him or even was aware he was there; he knew she was playing for herself. He was just blessed to be carried along with her.

Time passed and Colter continued to listen as Virginia played through many classical tunes. A few of them she'd played before in his saloon, but most of them were new to him. Finally, the music stopped and Virginia looked up from the piano.

"Oh," she said when she saw him sitting there.

"That was beautiful."

"I didn't know anyone was still here," Virginia apologized and then smiled. "I try not to play quite so many classical pieces when someone is listening."

"Never stop yourself for me. You play—" He did not know how to explain the depth of it all. "Very well. You obviously love what you're playing and it's very special."

For the first time, Colter wished he was a man with a smooth tongue. A man like that could put the feelings inside him into words telling her what her music inspired in him. He felt a jolt—maybe that's what Lester could do. Maybe that's what she saw in the other man.

Virginia pushed back the piano stool and stood up. "Thank you for saying so, but I'm sure you're tired, too."

"There's still a little hot chocolate left." Colter had held back a couple of cups of milk in hopes she'd drink some with him after everyone had gone. She hadn't had a chance to enjoy any since she started playing the piano.

"That would be nice," Virginia said as she walked toward the kitchen. "Just tell me where it is and I'll get it."

"I can put the milk on to heat," Colter said as he stood as well and picked up the small lantern from his table.

They walked to the back room together and Colter set the lantern on the top of the cupboard where he'd stored the chocolate. Warm shadows made the plain workroom feel like home. He poured milk into a cast-iron pan and set it on the stove. The coals from the previous fire were strong enough to heat it although it would be slow.

"Oh, the dishes," Virginia said as she looked at the large cast-iron kettle on the back of the stove that was steaming with water ready for washing.

"I figured you'd want it hot," Colter said, as he picked up a towel and reached over to move the kettle to the side of the stove to stop its boiling. "But we'll do the dishes in the morning. Tonight is too—" Again he was at a loss for words. "I'd rather have you tell me about your music tonight. I can tell you love it from the way you play."

Virginia smiled. "I forget sometimes that I had to grow to love it. My father was the musician in our family. His teachers always praised his skill. When he was sixteen, he was invited to tour Europe with some older musicians and everyone said his future was bright. Then there was a fire in a friend's house where he was sleeping. He survived, but his hands were burned badly. He went to the best doctors, but when his hands healed there were deep scars. He could still play, but it was no longer the same. He'd lost some of his movement. Another student replaced him in the concert tour and there was no more talk of Europe."

There was silence for a moment and then Colter realized something. "I'm so sorry. It must have been terrifying for you—with the fire here," he said. "Just remembering what happened with your father."

"I did not even think of it." Virginia looked up at him ruefully. "I was too upset about someone burning down your building when I was supposed to be protecting it."

Colter felt the vise's grip around his heart tighten. "I'd never want you to risk getting hurt to save any building of mine. Promise me you won't do anything like that. Just get yourself and the children outside and call for help."

He'd rather lose everything he owned than to have her try to fight another fire by herself. How terrible it would be if she burned her hands. Or worse. She could have died if that kerosene fire had had more time to burn before she noticed it. What if she had been asleep upstairs?

"Maybe you should get a room at the boardinghouse," Colter said. "I'm sitting guard, but a fire— I'd pay for the room, of course."

"I have money. Besides, I couldn't leave without the children. And it's too late tonight to get a room at the boardinghouse anyway."

"We'll look into it tomorrow then. For you and the children, too."

"We don't even know if the person who set the fire is still in town," Virginia said. "Besides, my father—he wouldn't want me to be a coward. He was quite strong on that point."

Colter noticed that Virginia had started rubbing her hands when she talked about her father. Maybe she was just beginning to realize the damage the fire yesterday could have done as well.

"It must have been frustrating for your father not to have the use of his hands," he probed further.

"Yes, it was hard. He missed so much," Virginia agreed.

By now all the joy had drained out of Virginia's face. The pleasure she'd had in playing her music had gone still.

"Maybe it was hard for you, too," he guessed.

Virginia looked up at him as if she was surprised at his question. "Yes, but it was different. He'd lost the place that was to be his. It was only hard for me because I couldn't give him what he wanted. I knew he wanted that place to be mine. He'd trained me for that since I was a small girl. But I was never good enough. I used to think I was when I played in a room alone looking out at the trees, but when someone else was there—my fingers just didn't work right."

Colter nodded. "I've seen the same thing with men who want to be gunfighters. When a man's alone with a tin can, it seems easy. But it takes some getting used to pulling a trigger when someone else is around."

He could see by the shocked expression on her face that he'd picked a bad example.

"All I mean to say," he said quickly, "is that you might just have needed some time to get used to the people listening. I've given up guns, just so you know. I did that even before I bought the saloon here. And then when I walked forward in church—well, I'm not planning to go back to living by my guns."

"I'm glad," Virginia said simply.

By then the milk was steaming in the pan and Colter reached over with the towel he'd been holding to pull the pan to the side of the stove. Then he stepped over to the cupboard and brought down two clean cups. He poured the milk into the cups and Virginia put the chocolate in it.

"It must have been hard for you to lose your father," Colter said a few minutes later as they sat down at the table in the main part of the saloon. He'd left the one lantern in the kitchen and there was only one other in the room so the shadows were deep.

"I would have died in his place," Virginia said. "Or at least taken his scars onto my hands if it would have been possible. But there was no way—"

Colter nodded. "I wish I had known my parents. To feel that way about them."

Virginia didn't answer so Colter took a long sip of cocoa.

"Playing snowballs with the boys this afternoon must have reminded you of things you did with your family?"

"Oh, no," Virginia said abruptly. "We never did anything like that."

That surprised Colter, but he didn't let it show. "Well, I suppose each family does different things."

"I wanted to learn to ice skate, but my father was afraid I'd fall and hurt my hands."

"But surely—"

"That's why I'm just learning to cook. I wasn't supposed to be near a stove either."

Colter had to restrain himself from standing up and going over to take Virginia in his arms. What kind of a childhood had it been if she had to worry all the time? Even he had been allowed to grow like a wild weed.

Virginia bit her lips. She'd never told anyone that much about her childhood and she was regretting it already. She didn't want to make her father sound unfair. He had his reasons for protecting her. He envisioned great things for her. It wasn't his fault that she wasn't good enough to step into the life he wanted her to have.

"I was allowed to plant a tree outside my window," Virginia finally said. She wouldn't admit that it was actually the gardener who had handled the shovel. The tree had been hers in the way that mattered.

"That must have been fun," Colter said.

She eyed him carefully to see if he was mocking her, but he wasn't. His eyes gazed at her with kindness though, and a hint of pity.

"I've always loved trees, too," Colter said. "I plan to plant a whole bunch of them when I find a place out by Dry Creek. Cottontail grass grows strong there so there's water for trees."

"Is that where you plan to move?" Virginia was happy to leave behind the subject of her miserable childhood. After all, many people had far worse childhoods. She'd had everything she needed. Food. Clothes. Music lessons.

Colter nodded. "I've got my eye on some land out by the Hargroves. Jake says there's talk of cattle coming to the area. Longhorns coming up from Texas. They'll do good in the sage-brush land out there."

"It'll be nice for the children to have a home." Virginia felt a wistfulness rise up in her. "You'll plant the trees by the house, won't you?"

Colter nodded. "Just as soon as I get a house built."

"Ah," Virginia said. She shouldn't have gotten so caught up in the dream. "There's not much around there to build houses out of."

The steamer from Fort Benton brought in cut timber and the boards were freighted down to Miles City in wagons. But it was expensive. If Colter built a house out by the Hargroves it would likely be built of sod. Even that wouldn't happen until the snows melted.

"I'm sure the children will appreciate any house you build them," Virginia said. And then she drained the last of her cocoa from the cup.

"I can afford to build a house," he said sharply.

"You won't be getting any income from the saloon for a while," Virginia pointed out. "And you'll have other expenses. The children will need shoes before long. And probably a new winter coat for each of them. Not to mention food."

"We can't keep living at the saloon though," Colter said. "Not if I'm out at Dry Creek getting things ready to buy a herd of longhorns."

"At least wait until spring," Virginia said. "They get snow drifts six or seven feet tall out there. I was out to visit Elizabeth Hargrove one day and couldn't get back to town for two days. The Hargroves don't suffer because they've spent months filling in every gap in the walls. And they are a family—"

Virginia stopped. She had no right to be concerned about any of this.

"And the children and I aren't?" Colter asked, obviously misunderstanding her stumble. She couldn't explain her feelings about his family though. She hardly knew what it meant herself.

Virginia looked down. "It's just I don't think Patricia has really decided to stay. In fact, I think she wants to leave and go looking for her mother."

"That'd be a disaster," Colter muttered.

"I don't want her to go either," Virginia said. "But I think I understand why she wants to. Her mother is all she has."

"She has me now."

Virginia looked at the determination in Colter's face. His jaw was set, his eyes flashing. He'd protect Patricia with his life.

"Yes, she has you," she agreed.

Virginia hadn't intended for the forlorn sound to be in her

voice. She looked up at Colter, her eyes stricken, and saw him gazing back at her with kindness on his face. And something more that she wasn't sure about.

"She has you, too," Colter said gently. "If you want, you can be part of our family—me and the children."

Virginia swallowed. She didn't know what to say to that. She had her plans. Her dreams. And what about Lester? It was all going to make her cry, and she didn't want to do that in front of Colter. So she stood up.

"I find I'm a little tired, after all," she said.

And with that, she stood up and walked over to the stairs leading up to the second floor. The tears started to fall after she had taken a step or two up, but she kept her head high. She knew Colter couldn't see her tears and would have no idea she was crying unless she dipped her head.

She reached her room and closed the door before her tears blinded her. She realized it wasn't thoughts of Lester that brought the tears. He might be her destiny someday, but he wasn't the one who broke her heart.

It was Colter. What was she to do? The one thing she had learned from her father was that it was crippling to try to live a life for which she didn't have the natural talents. She had not been able to play the piano as well as her father wanted, but with Colter her inadequacies would be even more glaring.

Just watching Elizabeth Hargrove in the past had made her aware of how much a woman needed to know to make a comfortable home for her family in this land. Virginia didn't know how to can vegetables, or grow vegetables. In fact, she realized with a final sob as she threw herself on her bed, she didn't even know how to cook vegetables. They always ended up burnt or mushy. And often both. She could brew a good cup of tea and make a passable kettle of soup, but— Oh, dear, she just realized…Colter loved fried chicken. She'd seen how many pieces he'd eaten at the church dinner. She'd be hopeless at cooking chicken.

She wasn't sure even God could cure her deficiencies. Her gaze was drawn upward anyway. She didn't know who else to turn to with the churning inside her. It was as though hope was shining somewhere, but it was out of reach for her. *Please, Lord,* she prayed, *make your grace shine upon me.*

The thought came to her that maybe her desire to move back east was only hiding the real longing of her heart—to have a home where she was loved and accepted.

# *Chapter Seven*

Colter woke to the sound of a dog barking. The sky was still dark outside, but the sun was struggling to come up. He couldn't find any enthusiasm to greet a new day. His back hurt and the rest of him felt worse.

He had slept in a hardback chair so he'd be ready to stop anyone from entering the saloon. He'd bolted the back door so no one could get inside that way without making enough noise to wake him. He hadn't counted on the stray dog going between the front and back doors all night whimpering as if he knew someone was inside.

Finally, Colter put the rest of the milk in a dish with some scraps from dinner and opened the door. The dog came up to him, its gray fur matted in places and a rib or two showing. Dogs generally protected the places where they ate and Colter reasoned the animal would earn the food by barking if anyone came close. He might have even said something like that when he bent down to let the dog smell his hand. He stayed to rub the animal's ears.

Now that dawn was showing up, Colter figured he might as well stretch his legs and see what the day held. The air was chilly and he could see thin layers of ice along the dirt street where the snow had melted yesterday. He set his feet down softly so his boots wouldn't make any noise as he walked around the side of the saloon. He heard a low growl from the dog before the animal passed him by and raced around to the back of the saloon. Colter flattened himself against the side of the saloon and got ready to fight.

It was the cat. Colter was glad it was still dark enough that no one could see him make his legendary fast draw on a scrawny yellow cat. Although when he saw how the cat managed to outrun that dog, Colter concluded he wouldn't want to underestimate the furry ball of fur as an adversary.

Since the morning was growing lighter, Colter decided he might as well check around the saloon for footprints. The only tracks in the snow between his saloon and Lester's were from the dog and cat. He wondered if Lester ever put food out for them in back of his saloon.

Naw, Colter shook his head. The other man had never struck him as the generous type. Or really any kind of a good type. Which was why it was such a mystery to him that the man had won over Virginia.

The thought was enough to sour a man's morning. Virginia couldn't have left him any faster last night if the place had been on fire. It was downright discouraging when even a hint of a proposal drove her away from him that quickly.

He stood for a bit, looking down the alley to be sure no dark shape was hiding in the shadows. He'd spent a night or two stretched out in an alleyway himself years ago and it wasn't the worst place he'd laid his head.

Colter turned to go back to the front door when he saw the dog coming back down the street toward him again. The poor fellow looked as discouraged as Colter felt with his mouth open and his tail hanging low. Colter figured he might as well wait and greet the dog before he went back inside. Maybe it would cheer them both up.

Neither one of them had an easy life. He'd bet that dog had been the runt of the litter. Colter hadn't been small, but he'd always been the one to get the least at his uncle's table. Not that he blamed his uncle. As the man had said many times, he'd been under no obligation to take Colter in when his parents had died. His uncle counted every bite of food Colter ate and made sure he paid for it through his work.

"Hi ya, fella," Colter said as he crouched down to scratch the animal's ears.

The chill of the morning felt good on Colter's face as he stood up. The sun was growing brighter and he could see clearly down the street now. The quiet of night was over. Colter opened the door to the saloon. He'd expected the dog to slip in and it did.

"Lookin' for something more to eat, are you?" Colter said as he followed the dog inside. "You just had a bite. Let me get my own breakfast first."

He'd noticed there was a side of bacon in the storeroom. Virginia looked like the kind of woman who would keep fresh eggs in the cupboard, too. First, he needed to get the water heating for a shave. And put the coffeepot on. He'd even go ahead and make those flapjacks that he hadn't made yesterday.

Back on his uncle's farm, flapjacks would have brightened his whole day. He guessed he wasn't so easy to please anymore. It was hard to admit that he had nothing in his life now to satisfy the longings that had overtaken him in the past year.

When he'd walked forward in church last winter, he had figured it was good to make his peace with God since he was planning a better life for Danny. The church folks had been kind to the boy and Colter wanted to be sure he kept his place in their affections. Colter thought it wouldn't do him any harm, but truthfully, he wouldn't have bothered if not for Danny.

But somehow things had gotten tangled. He'd started reading the Bible the reverend had given him. No one had warned him God would crack his heart wide-open. And now he just didn't know what to do about people. Danny. Patricia. And then Virginia. She was the one who troubled him most right now. He didn't want to press her about marrying him, not if it made her unhappy. She had looked stricken as she'd walked up those stairs last night.

Before he'd left for Helena, he had felt a stirring toward her. But last night when he saw the scars in her life, he knew he'd devote his life to protecting her if she'd let him.

Ah, that was the problem, he thought as he bent down to scratch the dog's ears. A man didn't always have control over how close another person let him get to them.

He heard the sound of footsteps overhead. That must be Virginia getting up.

"Danny," Colter gave a call toward the storeroom. They might as well all face the day together.

When she awoke, Virginia got out of bed and determined not to spend any more time wishing things were different. The distress of the night had passed. In the morning light, everything seemed clearer. The truth of the matter was that she had lived most of her life without the things she most wanted. Her concert-pianist dream had eluded her. She'd lost her home amidst the trees. Her father had never said he was proud of her or that he loved her. Her mother had been a gray shadow urging her to work harder. But what was the point in feeling sorry for herself? Virginia suspected it was about the same for everyone. It seemed that most people learned to be content without being happy.

There was no reason to expect her desire for a family would come easily. She was about ready to give up on trying to love

Lester. She couldn't marry him. But she didn't think she would make Colter happy either. When he knew how inept she was at the usual things women knew, he would regret marrying her even if he ever made her an offer. No, her best plan was to hope to receive an offer for the job at the school in Denver. Sometimes having half of a dream come true was better than nothing.

As she washed her face, she remembered the feathered bird that had been waiting for her yesterday and she decided it was only fair to give Patricia a morning surprise, too. Years ago, she had purchased a shiny gold pin in the shape of a bird. It was little more than a trinket really, but any girl would enjoy it. So she tiptoed into Patricia's room and pinned the golden bird to a scarf and then draped the scarf over the back of a chair facing the girl's bed.

Following that, she tiptoed out and returned to her room to wait.

She dressed quickly in her old cotton day dress, the one she used when she needed to haul water or scrub the floor downstairs. Then she added a clean apron. A life of work held satisfaction and she would be busy today. First, she needed to take a better look at the scarred floor and see if scrubbing and mopping would make it any better.

Just then there was a squeal from Patricia's room and Virginia went out into the hall.

"Thank you, thank you," Patricia said as she threw herself into Virginia's arms. "It's a present. I've never had a present before."

Virginia nodded as she bent down and kissed the top of the girl's head. "Just for you. Your own little bird."

For a sweet moment, Patricia leaned into her with a hug. Then the girl moved back and looked up in excitement.

"I can't wait to show it to my mother," Patricia said, her eyes shining. Her longing to see her mother was written plainly on the girl's face.

Virginia ignored the pang of jealousy she felt. What would it be like to be loved like that by a child? "It's time to get dressed. We have a busy day."

Patricia nodded. "We need to go to the stage office. My mother promised that she'd send me a letter. It should be here by now."

And with that the girl danced her way back into her room.

Virginia shook her head when the girl shut the door to her bedroom. She, too, had known the tug of loving a difficult parent. It was a peculiar thing—sometimes the less love the parent had to give the more love the child offered them in return.

Well, Virginia thought as she started down the stairs, all she could do right now was to pray Colter had the wisdom to help the girl when she realized her mother was never coming. He'd shared with her some of the conversation he'd had with the girl's mother and Virginia was appalled.

There was nothing she could do about it now though. In the meantime, she could stack up the rest of the dirty cups from last night and take them into the workroom. She could smell coffee brewing so she assumed Colter, and maybe even Danny were up already.

"Good morning," Virginia called out as she took several cups in her hands and headed toward the workroom door. "I'm bringing dishes."

She leaned against the door and pushed. It was unlatched so it swung in easily. "I have—" She stopped and looked. "What'd you do?"

There was a big splotch of coffee on the wood floor and Colter was holding a towel over his hand. He was obviously in pain and that stray dog from yesterday was looking at him with mournful eyes.

Colter winced. "I'm just clumsy."

"You scalded yourself," Virginia said as she set the cups down on the nearest surface and started looking in the cupboard. "I know we have something in here to make it better."

When Danny had scraped his arms while climbing a tree last summer, Virginia had bought an ointment at the mercantile.

"I'll be fine," Colter muttered.

"Here it is," Virginia said as she spied the green tin. She pulled it out and started to take off the lid. Then she turned to Colter. "You'll need to open your hand so I can put this on it."

Virginia wasn't prepared for how blistered his hand was. The skin was an angry red. She dipped her finger into the ointment and reached out to put it on his hand when the dog gave a short bark that settled into a deep growl.

"It's fine, old boy," Colter said as he reached down to put his good hand on the dog's head.

"Looks as if you have a dog."

Colter shrugged. "I guess he needs a home, too."

The pain started to ease and Colter looked down. Virginia was concentrating on his hand just like she did on every task. Her movements were precise and controlled. He'd had a gunshot wound or two in his life that had been treated with less compassion.

"It must be because you play the piano," he finally said. "That you have such gentle fingers."

Virginia looked up at him with a small frown on her forehead. "Your hand will be all right, won't it? I wouldn't want any scarring," she added.

"I'll be fine." Colter gazed right back into her eyes. They were the color of fall grass, where the browns and sun-striped greens melted together on the flatlands. The colors suited her eyes, letting her hide what she was feeling. Even now, despite the concern filling them, he had a feeling secrets lurked behind her eyes. "Whatever that ointment is, it feels good."

Virginia nodded and started walking around the kitchen. "I'll need a strip of cloth to wrap around your hand. It'll keep the ointment on and the dirt out."

She found an old piece of cotton cloth in a drawer in the cupboard. Colter figured it had been part of a shirt at one time, but it was clean enough to be useful.

"Now, you be sure and keep your hand free," Virginia said as she wrapped the cloth around his hand. "Don't use it for anything if you can help it."

"Well, I'm going to need to get to work around here," Colter said. Besides, his hand did feel a lot better now that it had the ointment on it. "I have supplies that came in down at the mercantile a couple of days ago and I need to get them in the storeroom."

"The other men can help you," Virginia said. "I'll ask Lester to spread the word that we could use some help over here."

Colter snorted. "Lester? I think we'd do better to ask Petey."

"I can do that," Virginia said. "Later. The men won't be at Lester's yet anyway. Noon is when they show up."

"I suppose the supplies can wait that long."

"If you're going over to the mercantile, you might want to get a length of cotton cloth for a dress for Patricia. She can wear her boy clothes, but she'll need a dress for church." Virginia stopped. Then she took a deep breath and continued. "I wish I could do the sewing on it, but I'm afraid I'm not very experienced at that. I apologize. I'm sure Elizabeth would help if we asked her, though. I wish Patricia had something better for school, too."

"What are you apologizing for? I'm the one who neglected to buy her a dress before leaving Helena. Besides, don't they have some ready-made dresses at the mercantile?"

"Not many. Most of their dresses are for women. Usually mothers make the dresses for their daughters." Virginia hesitated. "I think every woman around can sew well enough to make a girl's dress, except for me."

Colter knew Virginia was trying to tell him something important. Her whole body was tense as though she was expecting some reaction from him. "I don't see what it matters if other women know how to sew," he said.

Virginia glared at him. "Of course, it matters. How's a mother supposed to clothe her children if she doesn't sew?"

"Didn't we buy a shirt at the mercantile for Danny?"

"That's not the point," Virginia said after a pause.

"What is the point?"

"I can't sew!"

Virginia looked like she was on the verge of tears, but the dog must have heard the cat outside because he'd raced to the door, a low growl in his throat.

"Stand away from the window," Colter ordered Virginia. It might not be the cat and no one else would be at his back door before dawn unless they were up to mischief.

He gripped the butt of his gun at the same time Virginia whispered, "Your hand."

Colter looked over to see she'd moved closer to the cupboards and wasn't visible from the window. Then he walked to the door and gently opened it.

The dog shot outside before Colter could even see the cat. He heard a furious meow though so he figured that as the end of it. He turned to go back inside when he glanced over and saw that the dog had run right past the cat and headed over to the back of Lester's saloon. There in the snow was a red kerosene can. The dog gave a triumphant bark when he stood guard over the can at Lester's back door.

"Good dog," Colter said as he started over to the other man's saloon. He wanted to know what the man had to say for himself now.

# Chapter Eight

Colter headed back to his place within minutes, his gun holstered and the skin on the palm of his hand tight and painful from straining against the cloth Virginia had wrapped around it. The dog followed at his heels, looking as defeated as Colter felt.

"What happened?" Virginia asked when he stepped into the workroom. He saw that the spill on the floor had been wiped up and another pot of coffee was on the cookstove.

"Lester says the kerosene can isn't his," Colter admitted.

"Of course, it's not his—I mean, not if you're thinking it's the kerosene can from the fire. What possible reason would he have to harm me?"

"From what you told me, he probably didn't know you were in the saloon at the time." Colter walked over to a stool by the cupboard and sat down. "I smelled the can's spout and the odor was strong. That can was full not too long ago and now it's empty. Who else would have used so much kerosene in the past day or two?"

"Yes, but still—"

"I know," Colter acknowledged. "Not even Lester would be

fool enough to drag that can out there and leave prints in the snow going to and from his own back door. That's what I can't figure out."

"Someone just wanted you to think it was Lester," Virginia suggested.

Colter nodded. "Could be."

Then he looked at her. It pained him to see her defend the other man. Loose strands of blond hair fell from the bun she had on top of her head. And her skin put him in mind of pearls, all white and pink. "We need to ask at the boardinghouse and see about a room for you."

"First, let me look at your hand," she said. "You probably worked that bandage loose with all of your moving around."

Colter figured it must be the Bible reading he'd been doing of late. He'd turned poetic. That had to be it, because all he could think of was that the ointment she used smelled like spring grass. He figured he'd remember her standing in the morning sun like this with her brow furrowed with worry as long as he lived. He'd heard an old man once talk about how he could remember the exact color of the dress his wife had been wearing when he first met her. This morning would be that memory for him. He was trying to think of the words to tell Virginia all of this, when Danny walked into the workroom.

At first the boy was sleepy and then he was wide-awake. "We've got a dog!"

"It's the same one that was here yesterday morning chasing that cat," Colter told him. He didn't want him to think he'd gone out in search of a dog, as if they needed a dog or anything.

That fact didn't seem to dim Danny's enthusiasm. He knelt down and wrapped his arms around the gray dog. The old mutt lifted his eyes to Colter, although whether for rescue or forgiveness he couldn't tell. Colter figured it was the latter when the dog moved in closer to the boy and settled in like he was planning to stay.

"You'll have to feed him." Colter decided he might as well give up any claim to the dog gracefully. "That way he'll know who his master is."

Danny nodded. "He likes roast beef."

"You've already been feeding him?"

"He was hungry."

"We'll talk about what to feed the dog after we have breakfast," Colter said. "So why don't you bring out that slab of bacon that's hanging in the storeroom. We're all hungry by now."

"I'll get Patricia," Virginia said as she stepped toward the door leading to the main room. When she got to the door, she glanced back. "But wait to cut the bacon until I can do it. You shouldn't be using knives with your hand the way it is, anyway."

Colter nodded as she slipped out of the room. He liked having someone worry over him.

She just needed a moment to think, Virginia told herself as she stopped on the other side of the door. The big black circle in the middle of the floor reminded her that this whole building could have burned down and her with it. As Colter had been talking, she remembered that Petey and some of the other men had taken to sleeping behind the bar in Lester's saloon. They boasted that he couldn't see them and he had no idea they were enjoying the warmth of his establishment long after he'd gone to bed. She wondered if one of the men had found the kerosene can. Maybe they even knew who had started the fire.

She didn't get a chance to walk over to the stairs before Patricia came out of her bedroom.

"Look," the girl demanded as she stood on the top landing,

pointing at the bird pin on the collar of the shirt she was wearing—Danny's old shirt.

"You have to come closer so I can see," Virginia said and the girl obligingly started down the stairs.

"It's a singing bird," Patricia said as she reached the bottom. "I didn't see it right off, but see its beak? It's singing. It loves music just like me."

"Why, yes, it does," Virginia agreed in satisfaction. This must be how it would feel to teach in that school down in Denver. To awaken young people to an appreciation of music would make a worthwhile life for her. "Don't forget we have a lesson this afternoon."

"On the bells?"

"You need to start on the piano, that's what Colter—I mean, your father requested."

Virginia noted the surprise on the girl's face. She had probably not heard anyone call Colter her father until now. Besides, as far as Patricia was concerned, he was just someone temporary in her life until her mother came for her.

"But couldn't I just do something with the bells?" Patricia asked.

"The Wells girls are coming over to practice them later this afternoon. Maybe you can ring one of the bells with us."

The deepest bell didn't have to be rung very often and Patricia would probably enjoy that one because it had the most sliding echo to it.

The girl beamed.

"But first we need to cook breakfast," Virginia said as she led the way to the workroom.

Virginia told herself that she might not be as good a cook as Colter, but at least she had the use of both of her hands.

She looked around as she entered the other room. Danny had set the bacon on the counter and Colter had pulled the butcher knife down from the shelf. He was obviously considering how to go about slicing off some of it.

"I can do that." Virginia walked over to the cupboard.

"Thanks. I should be able to do it, but—" Colter apologized.

"There's no shame in being wounded," Virginia said as she took up the knife and started slicing the meat.

Patricia, meanwhile, was standing in the middle of the room, studying Colter. "Are you Danny's father, too?"

Virginia turned around and noticed Danny stop patting his new dog. The boy looked up with a flash of longing on his face and then bowed his head down again.

"I just do the dishes," Danny mumbled.

"You do more than just the dishes," Virginia said indignantly as she set down the knife and put her hands on her hips. Then she realized she'd said that wrong. Danny was still looking down and she could see his misery from here. "I mean who you are is more than just someone who does the dishes."

There was a moment's silence and then Colter cleared his throat.

"I should have said it earlier," he said. He looked a little awkward and that melted Virginia's heart. "But I'd be honored to call you my son."

Virginia blinked back a tear.

Danny lifted his head and nodded shyly. "I'll work hard."

"It's not about the working," Colter said firmly. "You're my son, no matter what."

Patricia furrowed up her face where she stood. "He doesn't have to be my brother, does he?"

"Well, now," Colter said, his voice low and easy, "I'd say that's up to the two of you. I figure you might like to be kin though. I never had a brother or a sister and there were many times I wished I had someone on my side who claimed me as family."

Neither Patricia or Danny said anything, but at least they weren't scowling at each other.

"I had a brother," Virginia offered as she slid the bacon slices into a cast-iron skillet. "And I'd be happy if I could sit down and talk with him today. I never appreciated him as much as I should have when he was alive."

Virginia took the skillet over to the hot cookstove and set it down. "Now for some eggs."

Colter went out to the other room to put the plates on one of the tables for breakfast. Virginia had told him where to find the cloth she used to cover the table and he brought that out from behind the bar. He got it a little crooked because he just had the use of the one hand, but he knew it didn't matter. She'd also suggested napkins and he pulled four of those out as well. If it had been growing season outside, he'd be half a mind to go pick a rose or two from the bushes that the last owner had planted behind the saloon.

Colter liked setting the places for four people. His family.

Before he knew it, Virginia was bringing a platter of fried eggs and bacon through the door. The two children followed her, one carrying a plate of biscuits and the other a crock of butter.

"Elizabeth Hargrove made the biscuits," Virginia said as she set the eggs and bacon on the table. "And the butter, too."

"Everything smells good," Colter said.

They were all seated, faces scrubbed and hands clean, when Colter asked if everyone would bow their head so he could pray. "Our Father, thank You for these provisions and the hands who have prepared them. Protect us today. In Jesus' name. Amen."

Colter didn't think he could grow more contented. He felt like a true father when he could put food on the table and lead his children in a prayer of thanks for it.

* * *

Virginia dabbed at her mouth with a napkin. Her words had been going around in her mind since she'd spoken them earlier this morning. If one of the men next door did know something about the kerosene can, she needed to find out what it was. After all, she had been responsible for Colter's building when the fire was set.

"I can go get Petey when we're finished," Virginia said as she picked up her last piece of biscuit. "He said he'd help with the floor."

Colter nodded. "I'm happy to pay any of the men next door to come over and work—as long as they're sober anyways."

"Of course, they're sober," Virginia rebuked him. "It's not even nine o'clock."

Colter raised an eyebrow at her statement, but he didn't contradict her. It reminded her that she knew better though. She hadn't even considered that the man who had dragged the kerosene can out in back of Lester's saloon might not have been sober when he did it. She knew she wouldn't rest easy until she solved the mystery of the fire. She had told Colter that she was sure Lester would never do anything like that, but little things were coming to mind. Times when he wasn't the man she thought he was. She knew he was worried about his sister so she didn't want to judge his recent behavior severely, but what if he were the kind of man who could attempt burning down his competitor's establishment?

The good thing about asking Petey and his friends to come over and work on the floor was that she could pose her questions subtly without raising anyone's suspicions.

"I'll go next door and ask them for you," Colter offered as he stood up from the table. "I'd worry about you going into a saloon alone."

"What do you mean? I worked in a saloon and I was fine."

"Yeah, but that was my saloon and I was here all the time."

Virginia would have protested, but she suddenly realized that the men would be more likely to come if Colter asked them. She didn't really care how the men got to be here, she just wanted a chance to talk with them, especially Petey.

"After I get back, we can all head down to the store," Colter said. "It'll take a while for the men to get themselves in shape to work."

"And the mail," Patricia spoke up. She had been quietly finishing her eggs. "I want to check to see if I have a letter from my mother."

Virginia saw Colter's lips tighten, but he didn't say what he was thinking.

"That's not a problem," he said instead. "We can check on the way to the store. The stage office handles the mail."

"My mother." Patricia turned to Danny. "She promised to write to me."

Danny just nodded. Virginia thought perhaps he was so awestruck at acquiring a father and a dog today that he wasn't too concerned about not having a mother.

The smells were what Virginia liked best about the mercantile and she took a deep breath as she stepped across the doorway. Patricia and Danny had gone in ahead of her and Colter was following. The shelves at the back of the store held spices and teas from distant places. On the left side of the counter in front of the shelves was a tobacco cutter. Bolts of calico and unbleached muslin were arranged on a table on the right-hand side of the room. Another shelf to the side of the counter contained face powders and hand mirrors.

The children headed straight for the jars of hard candy. There were red and green ribbons of spun sugar for Christmas. Virginia had already made mittens for Danny, but she didn't have Christmas gifts for Patricia and Colter yet. And Christmas Eve was just two days away.

"Annabelle Bliss," Colter called out as they stepped farther into the store.

The woman was past middle age and had some slight graying in her hair. She wore a freshly ironed white blouse and a gray wool skirt. Virginia had always found Annabelle to be extremely fair-minded—maybe it came from weighing goods so often. Something was always sitting on top of Annabelle's swinging scale. Even the crackers were sold by weight here.

"It's about time you got back in town," Annabelle said as she stepped around the counter to shake Colter's hand. "I know Virginia has been waiting for you for a long time now."

Virginia felt herself panic. She didn't want Colter to think she'd hung around like a schoolgirl waiting for him to return home.

"Well, fortunately, I'm back now." He didn't seem taken aback by Annabelle's remark. "We were hoping that you might have a ready-made dress for my daughter here, Patricia."

Virginia watched the girl look up and beam. Even Christmas candies couldn't compete.

Annabelle cocked her head and studied Patricia, then she turned back to Colter. "Almost all of our ready-made dresses are for women. Even the smallest dress would be too big to cut down that much. You'd be better just to buy material and start fresh."

"It's just that school is going to start again soon," Virginia said. "We were hoping—"

"I understand," the store clerk said. "You might talk to Elizabeth Hargrove. She bought a length of yellow calico here a week ago for a dress for Spotted Fawn. The two girls look almost the same size. She might let you buy the dress from her. If I know Elizabeth she probably has it almost sewn by now."

"We're also interested in shirts for boys," Colter added. "To fit my son here."

Virginia noticed that those words distracted Danny from the jars of candies as well. The boy was too far away to hear though as Colter quietly asked Annabelle to wrap up a pound of the candies and put it aside for him to pick up later.

"What else do I need?" Colter leaned down and asked. "For the Christmas stockings."

"Add a pound of those walnuts, too," Virginia whispered back. "And maybe some hair ribbons for Patricia and a pocketknife for Danny."

Colter nodded for Annabelle to include those things as well.

As it turned out, there was a blue shirt that fitted Danny and Colter was able to order two more to come in with the next shipment. By then, Patricia was anxious to go to the stagecoach office and see if there had been any mail for her.

The stage office had its own smells, too, Virginia thought as they stepped inside the wood-frame structure. Wet leather seemed to predominate, but she could also smell faint traces of horses and sweat. There was a long counter with a clerk seated behind it and on top of that were various letters. Virginia had never actually received a letter here; Colter had said he would always telegraph anything to her so she hadn't even checked. She hadn't realized that the letters sat out in batches so people could look for any mail that was to go to them.

That's when Virginia noticed a familiar lavender envelope. She didn't even need to read the address to know who it was going to. Lester was getting a message from his beloved sister. Even if he had been difficult lately, Virginia did want him to have reassurance that his sister was all right. At least, she prayed that's what the letter said.

Unfortunately, there was no letter for Patricia even though she looked though the stack twice.

"It's still coming," Patricia said defiantly. "You'll see."

"There have been some bad blizzards this time of year," the clerk behind the counter said. "Some roads are blocked, but I'm sure it'll get here in a couple of days if you're expecting it."

They thanked the clerk and Colter led them out of the stage office and down the street to home.

The air still smelled of bacon when they got home and the first thing Danny did was to go call his dog from the back of the saloon. Colter went after him. Virginia took off her hat and took it upstairs to her bedroom.

When she came back down, Patricia was sitting alone at one of the tables. Her dark hair was hanging down and hiding her face. Virginia wondered if it wasn't also hiding her tears.

"I'm sorry you didn't get your letter," Virginia said softly as she went over and put her hand on the girl's back. She could feel a quiver as the girl swallowed back a sob.

"It must be the snow," Patricia said as she wiped a hand across her face.

Virginia didn't know what to say to that. "It's hard to know what to think when a parent disappoints you."

Patricia kept her head down.

"With me and my father," Virginia said, sitting down and making another attempt, "I never did make him happy."

That made Patricia lift her head. Her cheeks were blotchy and she still had a lone tear trailing down her cheek. But she was listening intently. "What did you do?"

"I just kept trying harder and harder to please him," Virginia said. "He wanted me to be a special kind of pianist and I made too many mistakes."

"He shouldn't count mistakes," Patricia protested, her eyes snapping. "That's not fair."

"No, it's not." Virginia was quiet for a minute. "He was nothing like your father though."

Colter seemed to accept the girl no matter what she could or couldn't do. Virginia envied Patricia because she was facing a life of encouragement rather than scolding.

"I like my father," Patricia said quietly. "But I still want my mother to write to me."

Virginia nodded. She hadn't really expected to be able to spare Patricia the rejection she was bound to feel at some point.

Just then Petey knocked on the front door to the saloon. Virginia called out for him to enter.

"The others will be over when they're able," the older man said as he shifted the mop he carried on his shoulder. "I don't know what we need to use to clean up that burn, but I figure we'll have to mop it up at some point."

"I expect so," Virginia said as she stood up.

She decided she didn't want to wait for the other men to get here before she talked to Petey so now was her chance. She looked and saw that Patricia was walking toward the stairs.

She stepped over and quietly asked the older man, "You know about the kerosene can? The one with tracks from Lester's place?"

He nodded.

She didn't know how to do this except to be straightforward. "Do you think someone over there wanted us to think it was Lester who had set the fire?"

"Well, now, I reckon there are several men who'd like you to think that—"

"But why would they want to cause trouble like that? It just makes everyone upset."

Petey was quiet for a minute. "I know there's no reasoning it out as to why someone loves someone else. I've seen women grieve something fierce for men who are locked up in prison and not likely to live free again. And I've seen men who were desperate in love with women who didn't want them. But it's a misery. I don't want to see you take up with someone like Lester. He'll break your heart."

"He doesn't have my heart—" Virginia stopped. "But I still don't want everyone to be unfair to him. His sister clearly thinks he's a man with deep—"

"Lester?" Petey said incredulously. "He doesn't have a sister. At least not one who'd claim him."

"Sure he does. He's read me parts of the most wonderful letters from her."

"Letters, huh? Shorty mentioned something about letters he'd seen over there. Purple things."

"That's them," Virginia said.

"Humm, we'll see."

"I wanted to know if anyone knows about that kerosene can."

Petey got a belligerent look on his face. "Shorty found it in Lester's back room. That's why he rolled it out of there this morning. He wanted Colter to know."

"But no one really knows?" Virginia asked. "It's all just suspicion."

"Well, now that depends on how you figure it. I trust Shorty."

Virginia wanted to say that she trusted Lester. And she did, sort of. It's just that she was no longer sure. Could a man hide his real nature from his sister who had known him his whole life though? Unless the woman wasn't his sister. Still, some things she knew. "Lester would never set a fire when I was in the building."

"That's just it. Shorty had just remarked that you must be walking down to the store. He saw the back of a gray dress out the window and thought it belonged to you, but I noticed in church that Mrs. Baker has a dress that exact same color, too."

Virginia only had time to clear her throat, before the other men burst into the room all carrying brooms or hoes or some utensil. At the same time, Colter came back inside, too.

"Well, you're ready to work," Colter said with satisfaction as he saw everyone.

"You can count on us," Shorty said.

The older men looked steadfast and honest. *How does a woman know the truth of the matter, though?* Virginia asked herself. Her father would criticize her for being in a muddle like this, but she would give anything if she could ask for his opinion. She felt a surge of sympathy for Patricia. Sometimes even a very imperfect parent could be deeply missed.

# Chapter Nine

Christmas was new to him, Colter thought as he sat at the table farthest from the piano. Oh, he'd passed the day of December twenty-fifth before, but usually the only joy to it was a friendly game of poker with whoever happened to be around and, if he was fortunate, a sip of brandy from their not-yet-empty bottle.

And, now, all of the music of Christmas was ringing around him. The two Wells girls were lined up next to the piano and Virginia was demonstrating how to hold the clapper inside the bell to mute a note. She wanted the bells to fade out when they played "Silent Night."

"Just go soft at the end," Virginia said as she demonstrated it with a bell.

Patricia was standing on the other side of the piano and ringing one of the bells, too. Colter couldn't have been prouder if he was up there doing it himself. Even from back here, he could see the shine on those brass bells. The Christmas Eve service was tomorrow night and Colter wanted to watch the faces of the townspeople as they heard the music.

He'd never seen bells that rang out songs, but then he hadn't seen many Christmas celebrations. When he was a boy at his uncle's, he remembered once or twice having a dinner of roast beef and hard potatoes on the day. There were never any presents or decorations though. Or even any kind words passing from one to another.

This Christmas, though, it was going to be different. He was going to celebrate with everything he had in him. He finally understood the miracle that had happened on that night long ago in the manger. He saw just a glimpse of the hope it brought to everyone, including him.

This year his family was going to honor that by celebrating.

"Lift the bells higher on that note," Virginia said from the piano as she showed with her hand where it needed to be.

He liked that Virginia and Danny had already put some red ribbons around and brought in the little pine tree. Tonight they were all planning to make popcorn strings and hang some shiny pennies on the tree before heading over to the boarding-house to sleep.

He'd arranged a room for Virginia and the children. He hoped they wouldn't have to stay there for long, but he didn't know. In the meantime, Christmas was coming.

On Christmas Eve, after the service at church, they would light the candles Virginia had saved back for the tree and read the story from the Bible that talked of the blessed baby.

Only after that would they open their presents. He knew Virginia had gifts for the children and he had some, too. For Patricia, he'd bought a hat that was halfway between the boys' hats that she liked and the girls' hats that she needed to wear. Danny had been a little more difficult until Colter saw the picture frame sitting on the shelf in the mercantile. He'd bought the frame and planned to give it with the promise that the two of them would go to a photographer after Christmas and get a photo taken together.

With the two children taken care of, Colter had sat down to

think about Virginia's present. He hoped to find some inspiration by watching her play the bells with the girls. He noticed the way Virginia bent her head down, listening to each of the girls, as though they were the only ones in the room. And when she stopped to rest her hands on Patricia's shoulders, he could hear the murmured words of praise even where he sat. His new daughter glowed after Virginia talked to her.

"Let's do it again," Virginia said from the front to the girls. "You're doing an excellent job."

He knew Virginia was convinced Patricia had a special ear for music, but Colter figured some of that was simply Virginia. She knew how to open the world of sounds to the girl. He had caught Patricia yesterday in the workroom, beating a rhythm on the metal tub hanging on the wall. She was listening to hear the sounds as she beat it in different ways. He knew she was adjusting to her life here because she hadn't asked for a drink of whiskey since that first day they got here. And she wore that bird pin from Virginia everywhere she went.

Colter looked down at the paper on the table. None of that gave him any ideas on what to give Virginia for a present though. He knew she liked his piano and he'd wrap that up and give it to her, but it didn't seem personal enough. He wanted a gift that told her she'd become close to his heart.

The music lesson ended and the girls put their bells down on the piano cloth. Colter put his pencil down and started to clap. Which made the girls giggle—and Virginia blush.

Just then Danny banged open the door from the workroom, holding something wrapped in his jacket. His dog trailed in behind him, making sharp quick barks.

"What's the matter?" Colter said as he stood up. He figured Danny wouldn't have given up his jacket on a cold day like today if something wasn't wrong. And he'd never heard the dog as frantic. Virginia was walking across the room to help, too.

Danny laid his bundle down on the nearest table. "The cat's hurt."

The folds of the jacket fell away and Colter could see the yellow cat had been in a vicious fight. He looked up. "Get the dog away."

Virginia gasped as she walked up. "Is the poor thing alive?"

"Barely." Colter reached down and started examining the cat. Then he looked back at Danny. "The dog."

"The dog didn't do this," Danny protested. "It was another cat. The dog saved our cat's life."

Colter figured now wasn't the time to debate the point about who the cat belonged to. It was a stray. "You're sure? Because this dog has been chasing this cat around for the past few days at least."

"They just like to chase," Danny protested. "They're really friends."

Colter had found a deep scratch along the cat's side and a bite along its leg. He turned to Virginia. "Do we have any more of those strips of muslin?"

"I'll get them," she said as she walked to the workroom.

"And bring that salve, too. The one you used on my burn."

By now Patricia had walked up to the table and the Wells girls had left to go home.

"Is she going to live?" Danny asked.

"I expect so," Colter said as he reached out to put his hand on the boy's shoulder. "You did the right thing to bring her here."

"I could go kick that other cat for you," Patricia offered as she stood beside Danny.

"No kicking," Colter said with a smile to the girl. "But I appreciate you offering to help your brother."

"Well, it won't do any good to talk to the cat," Patricia muttered. "I know that much."

Virginia came back into the room with strips of muslin draped over her shoulder and a tin of the ointment in her hands.

"Here," she said as she laid it all out on the table in front of Colter.

Ten minutes later, Virginia was standing at the cookstove heating up some milk for the poor cat. She thought of Danny's words about the dog and the cat really being friends and it appeared to be true. Colter had wrapped the bandaged cat up in a piece of wool blanket and laid her in a warm corner of the workroom. The dog had lain down next to her looking as if he was going to stand guard for the day.

"My days back home were never like this," Virginia muttered to Colter as he put another stick of wood in the stove.

She sensed him stiffen up at her words, but then he took a deep breath. "You're still planning to go back east then?"

She nodded as she poured the warm milk into a bowl she had sitting close. "The only reason I'm going to Denver is to make enough money to go home again. I have friends there who would help me get started teaching there."

"How much?" he asked. "What would it cost to go home?"

"Fifty-six dollars for the steamer down to Kansas City. Then eighty-four for the train to Connecticut."

"One hundred and forty dollars then?" he asked.

She nodded. "When I came out, my brother bought my ticket. Otherwise I don't know what I would have done."

"Sometimes home can disappoint you," Colter said as he picked up the bowl of milk and walked over to set it down by the cat.

It wasn't until Colter left the room that Virginia realized she hadn't included Lester in her plans. Even if she were more enthusiastic about him, she probably would not have counted him. She was used to thinking of herself as being alone when she thought of going back east. Oh, she'd had family back there—her father, her mother and her brother—but she had spent most of her time with the piano. Sometimes she felt she knew the hearts of the composers better than those of the people living around her. Until now she had always considered herself fortunate to have the music. Now, she wondered.

She had been consumed with becoming a pianist worthy of her father. She had never thought how much that quest had cost her. She'd never even had a pet. She glanced over at the cat and dog. She had friends, but not one who felt strongly enough about her to dive into a fight and rescue her if she needed it. Her friends would help her get students and a place to live. But that would be all.

Suddenly, the thought of being in a home like the one where she'd been raised made her feel lonely. She looked a little closer at the cat. Maybe when she went back she would get a kitten.

Colter went back to the piece of paper he'd left lying on the table. He didn't need to spend any more effort thinking about what to give Virginia for Christmas. There was one thing she wanted more than anything—a way to go home.

By the time she came out into the main part of the saloon, he had reined in his feelings.

"The floor is looking good," he said when she glanced over at it. "I think we have one day left with the scrapers and we'll have all the dead wood gone. Then we can replace it with new lumber in the spring."

"The men are doing a good job," Virginia said.

"Yeah."

Virginia just stood there and it suddenly occurred to him that she wanted to tell him something. For a wild sweet moment, he wondered if she was going to say she didn't want to go east after all. That she wanted to stay right here.

"I was wondering," she started. "About Christmas. I've never cooked a holiday meal, but I was hoping. That is—the men who came to help with the floor… I know most of them. They don't have any Christmas dinner planned and I was thinking maybe we could invite them here."

"All of them?" Colter did a quick calculation. "That must be twenty men."

Virginia nodded. "I'm not a good cook. But I was thinking if we did something easy."

"Of course," Colter said. He didn't know why he hadn't thought of this. "It's not the food, it's the company anyway."

"And they love canned peaches," Virginia said.

"I can make a pretty good biscuit," he said.

"I can make soup."

Colter stood there and smiled. A woman who was willing to cook for her friends might just be persuaded to stay with them. He couldn't help checking though.

"Do you have a lot of friends back east?"

Virginia shrugged. "Some of my schoolmates are close enough friends to recommend me as a piano teacher. I was already giving lessons before I left and several of them offered to help me get set up again when I come back."

"Well, that's good."

She nodded. But Colter consoled himself that she looked uncertain. If she were going to be happy there, he would let her go and wish her well. If there was any weakness in her resolve to move back though, he intended to find it.

"What kind of soup?" he asked.

"If I can find a chicken, I can make soup with that," she said and then looked at him anxiously.

"Jake Hargrove told me they have some chickens for sale. I could ride out and get a couple."

Virginia nodded. "You could pick up that dress for Patricia, too. We wanted her to have it for the Christmas Eve service when she plays her bell."

"So she is playing with you for the church service?"

Virginia nodded. "She loves the bells."

"She loves her teacher," Colter said softly.

Virginia blushed slightly at that. "I only show her how to play the notes."

It was quiet for a moment. They just stood there companionably. And then Colter felt his skin break out in a sweat. That was his first clue that he was going to climb up on the cliff and jump off.

"Come with me," he said. "I can rent a buggy from the livery and we can take a ride out to the Hargroves. It's not a spring day, but it's not freezing. No storms anyway. I have a buffalo robe in the storeroom we can use to keep warm. You'll want to pick out the chicken yourself."

*Come with me, come with me,* his heart sang.

"But what about the children?" Virginia looked bewildered.

"I'll ask Petey to come over here. We'll be back before supper anyway."

Virginia didn't answer. For a long minute Colter just stood there worrying that the sweat on his face would become obvious. A fair number of grown men would pay to see him sweat, he thought to himself. They'd be surprised, but they'd pay.

"Why, I think that would be lovely," Virginia finally said.

"Good. That's good." Colter decided he'd best not give her time to change her mind. "I'll go get the buggy and be right back. I want to show you the place I plan to build my house, too."

Colter muttered to himself the whole way to the livery. Had he made it too obvious by telling her he wanted to show her where his house would be? He wasn't sure if she would be flattered or alarmed if she knew how much he wanted her to come with him.

By the time he got back to the saloon with the buggy, he'd

convinced himself that he needed to wear a suit. He had most of the pieces for a suit, but not a tie, so he went next door to ask Petey to watch the children and lend him a tie. Fortunately, Petey had worn his tie today as a salute to the coming holiday so he could just hand it over when Colter asked.

Petey wished him well and advised him to be a gentleman.

"She sets a great deal of store by manners," the older man said. "See you mind yours."

Colter was careful to take Virginia's arm and escort her to the buggy before lifting her up so she could sit. Once she was settled, he tucked the buffalo robe around her knees. Then he patted her hand and asked if she'd like a peppermint.

"I didn't even know they had such a nice buggy at the livery," Virginia gushed and turned to Colter as he climbed up into the buggy, too.

The smell of peppermint floated over to him and he breathed deeply.

"We can be fairly civilized out here," Colter exaggerated. It might be more accurate to say they'd be civilized when the railroad came to town. At least, that was what he'd heard. But now was not the time for a man to be timid.

The road to the Hargroves' place was sprinkled with old snow. For most of the winter, the sides of the road had been piled high with drifted snow. But today the sky was blue.

"I haven't been out of town for months," Virginia said.

"Any time you want to go, just let me know," Colter replied. "I'm planning to buy a buggy like this now that I have Patricia to take around."

"She'd rather ride a horse."

"Maybe, but I want to see her turn out to be a fine lady— like you."

"What?" Virginia looked up at him and squeaked. "She'd hate that."

"Well, I do figure that being a bachelor father, I'm bound to make some mistakes with the children. There are things that women just seem to understand easier."

He gave a heavy sigh after those words and let Virginia sit in silence for a bit. He hated to use guilt, but he hoped it would work.

"Just don't force Danny to play the piano." She finally couldn't stand it. "I already gave him quite a few lessons and he hated it."

"Patricia though—"

"Patricia should have the best lessons you can buy," Virginia said. "On any instrument. She's a natural with it."

Colter congratulated himself. The conversation had flowed in the direction he wanted it to. Maybe Petey didn't need to worry so much.

"I could use your advice. When I build my house out here on the Dry Creek, should I plan to keep the piano in the parlor or in its own room?"

"Oh, don't put it off by itself. The person playing the piano misses out on too much that way. Patricia needs to have others around."

Colter asked her more questions and, before much time had passed at all, they were making the turn to go into the Hargrove place. Jake had added corrals around his place since Colter had been here last. And there were a row of chokecherry bushes growing along the lane leading to the wood-frame house Jake had built after he married Elizabeth. There were snowdrifts melting along the south side of the house and a couple of sheets hanging on the clothesline to the north.

They didn't even need to knock at the door. Elizabeth had heard them and came outside before he'd finished pulling the buggy to a stop.

"Well, what a wonderful surprise," Elizabeth shouted out

as she wiped her hands on her apron and smoothed back her dark hair.

Colter studied Elizabeth. She was wearing a brown cotton dress and her dark hair was swept back into a bun. Her cheeks were pink, and he could see her breath in the cold air. She looked so happy he could only believe she was. She'd come from the east just like Virginia had. Granted, Elizabeth had been more of a servant than a lady, but she had found happiness on the banks of the Dry Creek. If she could do that, couldn't Virginia, too?

## Chapter Ten

Virginia had never envied her friend as much as when she was in her kitchen. And it wasn't the string of dried onions that hung from a hook by the far cupboard or the jars of spices and herbs that lay so colorfully on the small shelf. It was that Elizabeth knew how to use the onion and the spices. She could probably make a wonderful meal out of dried grass for her family if she had to.

The kitchen smelled like cinnamon. A plank table stood below a small glass window that was frosted over. The heat from the cookstove made the room comfortable. Colter was with Jake and Spotted Fawn out in the shed catching chickens.

"You came just at the right time," Elizabeth was saying. "I was going to go and get a chicken ready for our dinner tomorrow, too. I should have thought about Petey and his friends. You'll need—what? Six chickens?"

"Goodness, no. I think one old hen will be enough." Virginia closed her eyes and added, "I plan to make soup."

"Oh." Elizabeth stopped pulling jars off the shelf by the cookstove. She turned to look at Virginia. "Soup?"

Virginia had been afraid of this. "It's all wrong, isn't it? I don't know what I was thinking. I was talking to Colter and before I knew it I had said we should invite Petey and his friends to dinner. Of course, you know all I can make is soup and—"

"You make a lovely pot of tea, too," Elizabeth interrupted to proclaim loyally.

"I know this Christmas is special for Colter and I wanted to give him—" Virginia spread her hands in despair. "I wanted him to remember this Christmas forever."

"He can remember soup."

"He's going to be wishing it was fried chicken with every spoonful he eats," Virginia said as she went over and sat down in a chair by the table. "He's even going to have to make the biscuits."

"There's nothing wrong with a man cooking. Jake does it sometimes."

"And you're kind, too," Virginia said, half wailing the words. "You're the one he should marry."

Elizabeth started to laugh at that. "I don't think Jake's ready to give me up quite yet."

"Well, you know what I mean."

"I sure do," Elizabeth said as she came over to the table and sat down. "And I'm all for it. I always thought you two should marry. I was going to say something, but Jake said I should mind my own business."

"Oh, no. You don't understand. We're not getting married. I just want him to remember me."

"But why aren't you getting married? I've seen the way you two look at each other."

Virginia blinked back a tear. "I can't make soap either. Children need soap."

Elizabeth reached over and put her hand over the one Virginia had resting on the table. "You can manage soap. The big question is—do you love the man?"

"I don't know. We're just so different."

"It's this place, isn't it? I know when you first came, everything was so new and you missed your home. But how is it now?"

"I've gotten used to a lot of things. And I do know that if I go back, I won't be here to celebrate when the railroad finally makes it to town and when the church gets their own building."

"Then stay. Find out if what you feel for Colter will grow."

Virginia took a shuddering breath. "It's not that simple. I worked all my life to please my father and all I did was disappoint him. What if it's the same with Colter? I keep thinking I should take the job in Denver if I get the position. I just— It would certainly be safer. I could save enough to move back east. And I love music."

Elizabeth stood up. "Virginia Parker, I know you love music, but I never thought you'd scare easy. Don't give up so fast. I say it's time you learn to make fried chicken."

"Colter loves your fried chicken," Virginia said as foolish hope rose in her heart. "I think he ate three pieces at the church dinner."

Elizabeth laughed again. "Then, when we're done with you, you're going to make it even better than I do."

Elizabeth walked over to the cupboard and pulled out a piece of paper and a pencil. "Just do everything the way I write it down. When you've made it a couple of times, you can change things to your taste. I'm giving you some spices, too. Pepper, salt, ginger, cinnamon."

By the time they heard the men walking back to the house, Elizabeth had managed to write instructions for frying chicken, making gravy and mashed potatoes, as well as cooking gingered carrots. Virginia confessed she was not to be trusted with vegetables, but Elizabeth assured her she had written every step down so simply a child could do it.

"We'll still let Colter make the biscuits," Elizabeth said as she stood up from the table. "Just so he doesn't come to expect all this every day."

Virginia thought nothing would be more wonderful than to be so competent he would expect meals like that. But she knew Elizabeth had cooked and waited on people for years before she married Jake. The other woman didn't know what it was like to have men rush to do the cooking because hers was so bad.

"I'm sending some pickles back with you, too," Elizabeth said as she handed her several small cloth bags with spices. "It's not Christmas without my dill pickles."

Virginia put the spices in the pocket of her dress.

When the men came in, their hands cold and their boots muddy, Elizabeth insisted Colter take Virginia over to see where he was planning to build his house. She and Jake would bring the chickens to town with them on Christmas Eve.

Virginia folded up the sheet of instructions Elizabeth had given her and put it in her pocket next to the spices. Then Elizabeth put the yellow dress for Patricia in her hands and handed the jar of pickles to Colter.

"I can't thank you enough," Virginia said.

Elizabeth grinned. "Spotted Fawn is happy to give it to her. She remembers how it was not to have the same kind of clothes as the other children."

Virginia nodded. "We'll see you soon."

Colter felt nervous as he drove the buggy farther down the road. He'd only shown a few people besides Jake and Elizabeth where he hoped to build his house. A person had to be able to see what the place would look like when it had trees around it in order to truly appreciate the site.

"You're still warm enough?" he asked Virginia as he turned the horses off the main road and headed up the nearby rise.

Virginia turned to him. "I'm stronger than I look. I don't need to be coddled."

So much for Petey's advice on being polite, Colter thought. If he kept this up, she would think he was a snake-oil peddler.

"Of course you don't need to be coddled."

They topped the rise and Colter pulled the buggy to a stop. The area was covered with light snow, but it would be green in the spring. The soil was good.

"We have to go a little way for water," he started to explain, "but I've always liked to be a little higher than what is around me." He knew Petey would despair of him. "I suppose it goes back to my gunfighting days."

Virginia nodded. "I can see that."

Colter had known many women and their response to his mention of being a gunfighter had either met with fascination or repulsion. Virginia showed neither. She just looked at him straight across, like she could accept it, even if she didn't like it.

"Not that anyone who lived in my house would have to worry much about men coming to gun me down." This was the reason he'd mentioned it. He'd wondered if she was worried about this and it was holding her back. "I entered a couple of shooting contests and lost. It took the shine right off my reputation."

"That was a clever thing to do."

He gave her a quick glance. "Not many people understand that."

"What way will you have the house facing?" Virginia asked as she turned to look around.

"Northeast." Now that the buggy was at a complete stop, he was free to watch her reaction. She had a smile on her face, which he figured must be good.

She nodded. "If you're going to put in a kitchen, take a good look at Elizabeth's first. I've never seen one so well-organized."

"Jake plans to help me with the house."

"Good."

The sun was shifting as they sat there in silence.

"I figure two stories with the top for bedrooms."

Virginia nodded. "The children will like that."

Colter let her look around in silence for a bit. Then he figured that if she looked too long at the area she might find some reason to not approve of it. Besides, it was best to leave now so they'd get back to town before dark. He knew Petey would stay with the children as long as they were gone, but he would still worry until they were back.

Virginia saw that lanterns were beginning to be lit in the windows of Dry Creek as Colter drove her back to the saloon.

"I don't mind walking from the livery," Virginia said. "If you want to just go there with the buggy."

"There would be no end to the scolding I would get from Petey if I didn't bring you back to the saloon. Besides, it's as easy to go to the livery afterward."

"It's just…" She hesitated. "I wanted to stop by Lester's for a minute."

"Oh."

"I need to talk to him," she added.

Colter looked over at her face. She looked miserable.

"I appreciate you coming with me. I don't think Lester should mind if you go out driving with a friend."

"He has sensitive feelings."

Colter grunted at that. A buzzard could look mighty sad; that didn't mean his feelings were honest. It was just a ploy to fool his dying prey. Colter pulled the buggy to a stop in front of the livery though. If the lady wanted to walk, she could. He swung himself down from the seat and walked around to offer Virginia his hand.

"Thank you," she said as he took her hand.

Colter could feel the tremble in her fingers. "It'll be fine."

She looked up at him with worried blue eyes. "I just have to talk to him. It won't take long."

He nodded. The way the men gossiped in Lester's saloon the man would have probably heard about their drive. "If he gives you any trouble, let me know. I'll talk to him."

"I don't think…" Virginia looked alarmed.

"Not to argue," Colter explained. "Just to let him know we went to the Hargroves' to order chickens."

He helped Virginia step down from the buggy. "I can walk with you. I don't like you being on the streets at dark."

"It's still light enough," Virginia said as she pulled her shawl around her shoulders more securely. "I'll be home before you know it."

Colter nodded. Nobody could stop him from keeping watch over her as she walked down the street. For the moment, she called his saloon home. That meant she was his to protect even if she planned to give her heart to another.

He stood there until he saw her enter into Lester's establishment.

By then the livery owner had come out to get the buggy.

"How'd it work for you?" he asked. "Have a nice ride?"

"I can't fault the buggy," Colter said as he paid the man.

With that, Colter started walking down the street, too. In his past life, he'd follow Virginia into Lester's place and either start a fight or get roaring drunk. In the morning, he'd wake up sore and sick. Now he was learning a new way. He'd go back to his place and see how that old cat was doing. And make some supper for his children. God would have to help him accept Virginia's decision if she agreed to marry another man.

# Chapter Eleven

Virginia stepped inside Lester's saloon and squinted. It was almost too dark to see. She could make out a couple of men standing at the bar though, and she could tell it was Shorty serving them drinks.

"What's happened here?" she asked. "There's no light."

"Virginia!" Shorty said as he set down the bottle he held and walked around the bar, heading toward her. "What are you doing here?"

"I just wanted to talk to Lester. Is he in back?"

"He's trying to find another can of kerosene," Shorty said. "I keep telling him there was only the one and it—well, it's empty."

"The lanterns are dry?"

Shorty nodded and lowered his voice. "I don't think he knew it was the last can when he— Well, Petey said you don't believe it was him that did it, but—"

Shorty looked behind his shoulder into the dim room. "I think I hear him coming out."

"I'll just sit over here," Virginia said as she pointed to a table. No one was sitting at any of the tables so it would be quiet.

"Petey said you were asking about some letters." Shorty's voice went even lower. "There was a miner who came by here last fall. His sister has been sending him mail in care of Lester's place since then. I haven't read them, but I noticed some of the letters are opened."

Virginia nodded. She supposed if Lester would set fire to a building, it wouldn't be much of a stretch for him to lie about some letters. But she was still disappointed. It had all been such a pretty picture, thinking of him and his sister and that wonderful violin. "Did she write the letters on lavender paper?"

Shorty nodded as he stepped away.

Lester was walking toward them. "Virginia! What a pleasant surprise!"

"We need to talk," Virginia said as she walked over and sat at the table. Lester might not be the gentleman she had thought he was, but she would treat him like one as she kindly explained why she could never marry him. She refused to let the emotions she had for Colter keep growing when there was another man who seemed to feel she belonged to him instead.

Lester might be willing to deceive someone else, but she wasn't. She would have her talk with him and then go next door and try to find something for the children for supper. *This,* she thought to herself, *is how civilized people handled their lives. Orderly and with concern for others.*

Colter had one of Virginia's aprons tied around his waist. He had just sliced some onion and put it in the cast-iron skillet. He'd added some wood to the fire a few minutes ago and when the blaze got higher he would put some bacon in with the onion. He'd sliced some potatoes and had them ready to add after the bacon.

The cat by the cupboard meowed. Colter had checked her bandages when he first got in and they were in place. Petey had left a note on the table saying he and the children would be back soon. Patricia wanted to check on the mail from the last stage of the day.

Colter told himself he had put the apron on so he could wrap it around his hands when he moved the skillet. He didn't want to injure the skin on the hand he had scalded. But, the truth was, the apron reminded him of Virginia.

He was getting ready to put the bacon in the pan when someone knocked loudly on the back door.

"Come," Shorty said when Colter opened up. "Hurry."

Just then, a woman screamed. It sounded like it came from Lester's place.

"Let's go," Colter said as he reached back and grabbed the gun holster he'd left hanging from a peg on the wall. It was dark outside, but both men moved swiftly to the open back door of Lester's saloon.

Shorty stood back so Colter could enter first. The hall to the main room was dark, but there was one lantern lit by the bar. A couple of the regulars were staring at something in the corner of the room. The fact that they weren't moving made Colter worried enough to draw his gun.

He slid around the corner and his heart stopped. Lester was standing there with a knife in one hand and an arm wrapped around Virginia's neck.

"Let her go," Colter said as he stepped farther into the room. *Please, Lord,* he prayed.

Lester laughed. "And let you shoot me? No, she stays with me."

"You're frightening her." Colter kept his voice even. Desperate men were easily spooked.

"Well, that's her own fault," Lester said in disgust. "Coming here and accusing me of setting that fire. Saying she was going to tell you all about it. That you would handle it. I know what that means. And I'm no match for your gun."

"I meant he'd talk to the marshal in Billings," Virginia said. Colter was glad her voice still had a little starch in it.

"And then she played me for a complete fool by saying you'd given up your guns."

Colter knew there was enough light for the other man to see what was pointing right at him. "Let her go, Lester. That's the only way for you now."

The other man didn't move.

"You've heard of me." Colter knew the longer he talked the less chance there was of violence. At least, as long as he kept his voice steady. "All the stories are true."

"I heard you'd been beat in some shooting contest over by the Rockies," Lester said. "Heard you weren't as fast as you used to be."

"Let Virginia step outside and you won't have to worry about how fast I am."

"It's not my fault anyway. I thought everyone was gone. I wasn't going to hurt anyone. I just didn't want to lose all my business when you got back."

"You did this over *money?*"

"You could have burned up that piano," Virginia scolded the man. Colter noticed the color in her face was a little better. Her hair was falling down, but her eyes were fierce. She'd managed to move a few inches away from Lester and was using her hand to reach into the pocket of her dress.

*Don't do it, Virginia.* He didn't know what she had planned, but anything was too dangerous.

"I did it for us." Lester turned to Virginia, his voice pleading for understanding. "If business stayed good, I thought I could sell the place when the railroad came in. It was for our future. With those friends of your father, I could have made something of myself in politics."

Colter didn't like Lester talking to Virginia. "If it's money you want, we can talk."

"Huh?"

Colter nodded. He'd gotten the man's attention back. Now all he had to do was get Virginia away from him before she used whatever it was she'd grabbed from her pocket. He could see her fist had closed over something even if it was still hidden. He wondered if she had one of those little guns women carried. He hoped not. So many things could go wrong with them.

He spoke clear so Lester would hear. "I have three hundred dollars over at my place. How much would it take for you to let Virginia go?"

"Three hundred?"

Colter nodded. "Let Virginia go and we can go count it."

Lester snorted.

Colter saw Virginia take a deep breath and he knew the talking was over.

He steadied his gun as he saw her hand move. Lester must have felt her turn and he looked down just in time to have seen Virginia throw something. Then Lester sneezed. Virginia slipped away from him and dropped to the floor.

"Hands up." Colter stepped closer.

He saw Virginia crawl under one of the tables.

"Drop the knife," Colter added, in case the other man didn't believe it was over.

Lester sneezed again and the knife fell to the floor.

"Anybody have some rope to tie him up?" Colter asked without taking his eyes off Lester. He heard footsteps so he knew the men that had been standing at the bar were getting what they needed.

"What's going to happen?" Virginia said as she pulled herself up off the floor. She'd managed to put several tables between her and Lester.

Colter took a deep breath. He'd grown up thinking men settled their own differences with a gun. Those days were over for him though. "We'll hold him in the back room at the stage office until the marshal can get here. There's no windows and a good lock on the door."

"We'll get him there," Shorty promised and a few of the other men nodded as they came back with rope. "I just saw Petey outside and he says— Well, he'll tell you. He's next door at your place."

Colter walked over to Virginia as the men started tying up Lester.

"Are you all right?" He brushed back the hair from her face. That's when he felt the grains on her skin. He looked closer. "Pepper?"

She nodded. "And some ginger. I think I still have the packets of salt and cinnamon."

"Well, if that doesn't beat all." Colter smiled as he brushed the spices off her face. "I'm sorry. I guess this territory is still a little rough."

"There's greed everywhere."

Once Colter finished getting rid of the spices, he didn't have any reason to keep on touching her except that—he pulled her into his arms. "I was so afraid something would happen to you."

"I know," she said and he felt her head move against his chest as she nodded.

Then there was a man clearing his throat.

Shorty spoke up. "Petey said it was kind of urgent—I know we've had our own problem going. But Patricia—"

Colter nodded. Virginia had already turned to the door.

*Dear Lord, what now?* Virginia prayed as she walked over to Colter's place. At least kerosene lamps were lit in the place, which meant someone was home. She supposed Patricia was upset because there hadn't been a letter from her mother. She heard Colter's footsteps coming behind her and it was a great comfort to know they were both there to help with the tears.

Before Virginia opened the door to the saloon, she heard the dog barking excitedly.

"What's wrong?" she asked as she stepped inside. She didn't need anyone to answer to know that something was happening. One of Patricia's trunks was halfway down the stairs, with its lid locked tight and Danny standing over it with a scowl on his face.

"Patricia's moving out," Danny said.

By then Colter was in the room, too.

"She can't be that upset." Virginia turned to Colter. His face looked as worried as she felt. "Can she?"

Virginia looked up and saw Patricia come out of her bedroom. She was dressed in the clothes she'd worn when she arrived. She had a big smile on her face. "I got my letter."

"From your *mother?*" Virginia asked in astonishment.

Patricia nodded as she bounced down the stairs. "I need to get everything packed and down to the stage. She's not at the Golden Spur anymore, but she's not with that man either. It will be just her and me again. Like it's supposed to be."

"It can't be," Virginia said as she turned to Colter.

"I won't let her go," Colter vowed as he walked over and crouched down by Patricia. "Now, tell me everything."

Patricia started to talk, sounding more excited than Virginia could ever remember hearing her. Not even when she was playing the bells. It seemed that her mother had indeed written a letter, telling Patricia that she had parted company with Rusty the miner.

"He completely ran out of gold," Patricia told Colter. "So my mother isn't going to stay with him anymore. But she sent me her address. So I can bring her trunks to her. She's already paid the money to the stagecoach place in San Francisco."

That's when Patricia turned to Virginia. The girl's face was beaming and she ran over to Virginia with her arms wide. "I'm going to live in San Francisco. I'm sure my mother will take me to the opera."

Virginia opened her arms and held the girl close. Then she looked over at Colter. He seemed as stunned as she was. Virginia bowed her head and kissed the top of Patricia's head.

Then Patricia drew back and looked up. "The stage leaves tomorrow so I won't get to play the bells."

"I'll miss you," Virginia said as she drew the girl into another hug.

Meanwhile, Colter had stood up again.

"I'll get supper ready," he said and then walked into the workroom.

Virginia wondered how anyone could think of food even if the children needed to eat.

Colter braced himself against the cupboard. He'd never felt so powerless. He hadn't thought Rose would ever send for Patricia. Not after the things she'd said. But Rose was the girl's mother. He knew he didn't have any legal rights to keep the girl here. He wasn't prepared to let her go either though.

How could he be losing all the people he loved? The next thing he knew Danny would remember a grandfather that he wanted to live with. Colter knew he had pieced his family together from various places. That's just the way it had happened. But it never occurred to him it could be taken apart so easily.

The cat meowed and Colter remembered supper. He'd pulled the skillet to the back of the cookstove so the onions were not burned. He added the cut-up bacon to the onions and put it back on the front of the stove.

Petey came in the door. "I've been up in her room trying to get the second trunk ready to go."

"She really got a letter?" Colter asked as he reached back for Virginia's apron.

Petey nodded. "The clerk at the office said something about prepayment made from San Francisco. He had some official form that he'd gotten on the same stage that Patricia's letter had come."

Colter nodded. He must not know anything about families. It wasn't surprising given his childhood, but he was still astonished. "Did it say what stage she's to go on?"

"Tomorrow morning."

"I'll miss her."

The other man came over and put his hand on Colter's shoulder. "You know, I'm going to miss her, too. And from what she's told me of that mother of hers, I'm spitting mad that the woman has the nerve to ask her daughter to come live with her again. After leaving her there in that saloon all by herself. Doesn't she know what kind of things can happen to a little girl in a situation like that?"

Colter nodded. "She knows."

The cruel fact was that love could be very selfish. It might be true that, in her own way, Patricia's mother loved her. But it wasn't a love that ever considered what was best for the other person. Colter knew how easy it must be to fall into the trap of loving like that. All he wanted to do was to take Patricia and Virginia and lock them in their rooms upstairs and never let them go.

The door opened again and Danny and the dog came inside.

"They're just crying out there," the boy said in disgust.

Colter turned to the boy and gave him a fierce hug. "Tell me you're not leaving me, too."

"Me?" Danny looked alarmed as he squirmed his way out of the hug. "Where would I go?"

"Nowhere if I have my say." Colter turned around to tend

# HOW TO VALIDATE YOUR
# EDITOR'S FREE GIFTS!
# "THANK YOU"

1 Peel off the FREE GIFTS SEAL from front cover. Place it in the space provided at right. This automatically entitles you to receive two free books and two exciting surprise gifts.

2 Send back this card and you'll get 2 Love Inspired® Historical books. These books are worth over $10, but are yours absolutely FREE!

3 There's no catch. You're under no obligation to buy anything. We charge nothing — ZERO — for your first shipment. And you don't have to make any minimum number of purchases — not even one!

4 We call this line Love Inspired Historical because every other month you'll receive books that are filled with inspirational historical romance. This series is filled with engaging stories of romance, adventure and faith set in historical periods from biblical times to World War II. You'll like the convenience of getting them delivered to your home well before they are in stores. And you'll love our discount prices, too!

5 We hope that after receiving your free books you'll want to remain a subscriber. But the choice is yours — to continue or cancel, anytime at all! So why not take us up on our invitation, with no risk of any kind. You'll be glad you did!

6 And remember... just for validating your Editor's Free Gifts Offer, we'll send you 2 books and 2 gifts, *ABSOLUTELY FREE!*

## YOURS FREE!

*We'll send you two fabulous surprise gifts (worth about $10) absolutely FREE, simply for accepting our no-risk offer!*

Steeple
Hill®

® and ™ are trademarks owned and used
by the trademark owner and/or its licensee.

# The Editor's "Thank You" Free Gifts Include:

- ● Two inspirational historical romance books
- ● Two exciting surprise gifts

## YES!

PLACE
FREE GIFTS
SEAL
HERE

I have placed my Editor's "thank you" Free Gifts seal in the space provided above. Please send me the 2 FREE books and 2 FREE gifts for which I qualify. I understand that I am under no obligation to purchase anything further, as explained on the opposite page.

We want to make sure we offer you the best service suited to your needs. Please answer the following question:
About how many NEW paperback fiction books have you purchased in the past 3 months?
❏ 0-2 ❏ 3-6 ❏ 7 or more

### 102 IDL EZNZ                    302 IDL EZQP

|  |  |
|---|---|
| FIRST NAME | LAST NAME |

ADDRESS

|  |  |
|---|---|
| APT.# | CITY |

|  |  |
|---|---|
| STATE/PROV. | ZIP/POSTAL CODE |

FOR SHIPPING CONFIRMATION

EMAIL

# The Reader Service — Here's How It Works:

Accepting your 2 free books and 2 free mystery gifts places you under no obligation to buy anything. You may keep the books and gifts and return the shipping statement marked "cancel." If you do not cancel, about a month later we will send you 4 additional books and bill you just $4.24 each in the U.S. or $4.74 each in Canada. That is a savings of at 20% off the cover price. It's quite a bargain! Shipping and handling is just 50¢ per book.* You may cancel at any time, but if you choose to continue, every other month we'll send you 4 more books, which you may either purchase at the discount price or return to us and cancel your subscription.

*Terms and prices subject to change without notice. Prices do not include applicable taxes. Sales tax applicable in N.Y. Canadian residents will be charged applicable provincial taxes and GST. Offer not valid in Quebec. All orders subject to approval. Credit or debit balances in a customer's account(s) may be offset by any other outstanding balance owed by or to the customer. Please allow 4 to 6 weeks for delivery. Offer available while quantities last.

the skillet. It was time to add the potatoes. "Go ahead and put some plates on the table in the other room."

"I hope they're done crying," Danny said as he walked over to the cupboard.

"They were both crying?" Colter asked.

"Yeah. Girls," the boy said in disgust as he pulled down some plates.

Colter looked over at Petey. "Is that good?"

The older man shrugged. "I don't know for sure. But at least she must be sad at the thought of leaving everyone here."

"She'll miss the dog," Danny said as he balanced the plates and opened the door.

Colter heard the sizzle coming from the stove. If he had his way, she'd also miss the cooking.

## Chapter Twelve

When Virginia woke the next morning, it took her a few minutes to remember why she held a handkerchief in her hand. She'd gone to sleep with tears in her eyes. Everyone had been gloomy last night as they ate supper together, except for Patricia, who had been feverish with excitement.

Before they went to sleep, Virginia had given every gentle reason she could think of to make the girl change her mind about taking the stagecoach to San Francisco. Colter had assured everyone that if Patricia was set on going, he would go with her and make sure she made it to her mother's place.

His declaration had made Virginia cry even more.

She did not want to send Patricia off with memories of tears though so she dressed and went downstairs to make breakfast for everyone. The morning light was just coming into the main room as she made her way down the stairs. The trunk that had been sitting on the stairs last night wasn't there any longer. Neither was the one that had been dragged to the door.

The smell of coffee was coming from the kitchen and before she walked across the room, Colter opened that door and came inside. He looked as exhausted as she felt.

"I thought I'd help get breakfast," she said.

He nodded. "I have batter made for pancakes. I just haven't—"

He sent her a look so bleak her heart broke.

"She'll be fine," Virginia whispered as she walked toward him. "She's bright. And tough."

Virginia opened her arms and he stepped into them.

"The stagecoach had someone come and take the trunks," Colter said as he wrapped his arms around her, too. "Patricia was up. I don't think she slept at all last night."

"Is she in her room?"

"I think so."

Virginia's heart slowed. She'd never grieved like this before, with someone to hold her who knew the same anguish. She could feel the strength in Colter's arms as he held her, but it was the tenderness in his heart that comforted her the most. They stood wrapped together for a few minutes and then Virginia stepped back.

"I wanted to play some music for her before she leaves," Virginia said as she looked over at the piano.

"Oh." She stopped then looked up at Colter. "I have a bell missing."

Virginia walked over to make sure she was right. She looked all around, but there were only nine bells instead of ten. "The one that's missing is the one Patricia was going to play in the Christmas Eve service tonight."

"Well, I think we need to go upstairs and talk to her," Colter said.

"Maybe she took it upstairs so she could practice."

When Virginia and Colter knocked on the girl's door, there was no answer. They looked at each other and Virginia slowly opened the door.

"Patricia," she called softly but she already suspected what she would find. "She's not here."

Colter followed her into the bedroom. Everything was gone. Patricia's old hat. Even the rope she'd worn cinched around her middle for a belt. The closet was empty except for the yellow dress Elizabeth had made.

"She's probably down at the stage office," Colter said as he turned to go.

Virginia followed him down the stairs. She was surprised that Patricia would try to leave without saying goodbye. Unless she was ashamed for stealing the bell. Virginia knew the girl would never enjoy the bell either since she'd stolen it. Which was such a shame with her ear for music.

"Wait a minute," Virginia said as she went back upstairs.

When she came back down, she was carrying ten small pieces of linen and some cord to tie them together. She went to the piano and quickly wrapped the remaining bells in the linen. Then she tied them together with the cord.

"You're not going to…" Colter asked when she walked back to him.

Virginia nodded. Music had separated her from those she loved when she was a child. She didn't want it to come between her and Patricia now. "Let's go."

The morning air was cold and gray clouds promised snow later today. There were a few people on the street, but it did not take long to arrive at the stage office. Virginia looked in the window and she saw Patricia sitting on a bench inside with a small bag nearby.

"She looks so forlorn," Virginia said as she glanced up at Colter.

"Yes, she does," he agreed as he opened the door.

A rush of warm air greeted them as they stepped inside.

Patricia looked over and, when she saw them, shifted farther away on the bench.

Virginia put her hand on Colter's arm. "I'll talk to her. She's feeling guilty."

He nodded.

"We're just coming to see you," Virginia said softly as she walked slowly toward Patricia. "We missed you and your father is making a wonderful breakfast. Besides, I wanted to bring you these."

By now Virginia was standing in front of the girl and she held out the bundle of bells. "One bell is lonely by itself. It needs others to make music. If you want them, they're yours."

Patricia looked up wide-eyed. "But you need them for the songs tonight. For the church service. For that lady with the school."

For the first time that morning, Virginia remembered Cecilia Wells was coming tonight to make a decision about whether or not Virginia could be a music teacher at the school. If she didn't have the bells, she wouldn't appear like a worthy teacher at all. But her heart told her it wasn't only bells that got lonely. She looked down at Patricia's scared face and hoped the girl would remember she was loved when she played those bells.

"I still want you to have them," Virginia said as she sat down on the bench next to the girl.

"But—" Patricia began and then she burst into tears.

Virginia put the bells down on the bench and opened her arms to the girl. "Come here."

"I was talking to the clerk," Colter said as he came over and joined them on the bench. Patricia stopped sobbing in Virginia's arms long enough to look up at Colter.

"He's made a mistake. That's all," Patricia said as she pulled away from Virginia. "My mother sent money for me to go, too. Not just her trunks. He just made a mistake."

Patricia sat with her arms crossed on the bench.

"Oh, dear," Virginia said as she glanced up at Colter.

"Well, you will always have a home with me," Colter said as he opened his arms to the girl, too. "There's no need for you to go anywhere."

The girl started to weep again, this time even harder. Her face was pressed against Colter's shirt, but her voice was clear. "My mother didn't send for me."

Then Patricia looked up at Virginia. "I was going to bring the bell back. I know they're yours."

Virginia shook her head. "In the future, we'll share them."

"But we'll use them tonight for church, won't we?" Patricia asked as she wiped her eyes.

Virginia nodded. "We'll need to practice some later today."

Colter went to the church an hour before the Christmas Eve service was set to begin. He brought a load of firewood over because he had volunteered to heat the room up so everyone would be comfortable as they remembered the day Jesus was born. As long as he was heating the church, he decided he might as well provide some green boughs and a few red ribbons to make everything look festive.

When he was done, he sat on one of the benches to pray. It was about this time last year that he had walked up to the pulpit in this very building, pledging to become a Christian. He figured it wouldn't hurt to begin this next year with prayer either. His family was just beginning to find themselves. Patricia had spent the rest of the day without mentioning her mother. Danny had welcomed Patricia back with a pat on the back and an offer to let her name the cat since he had already named the dog. Virginia—well, she was the one who might be leaving.

Tonight the woman from the school would hear the bells

ringing out those Christmas carols. Colter had heard the practicing that had taken place this afternoon. The girls could play
those songs flawlessly. He had no doubt Virginia would be
offered the job. All he could do was pray that God blessed her
and gave her the desires of her heart. He'd never felt so helpless.

A few hours later, Virginia and Patricia carried the bells over
to the church and arranged them on a table before anyone else
was there. When they opened the door, warm air welcomed
them. Virginia knew that was because of Colter's thoughtful-
ness and she appreciated it. The girls would not be able to ring
the bells right if their hands were all freezing.

"May I?" Patricia asked. Virginia nodded and the girl picked
up one of the bells and rang it. The sound of the note filled the
schoolhouse and the girl grinned.

Reverend Olson and his wife were the next to arrive, but then
families started to arrive in clusters. The Hargroves were there.
The Bakers. Annabelle and Higgins. Mr. Wells and his daughters. And, with them, a woman dressed in black silk who had
to be his sister.

Virginia saw Mr. Wells nod for her to come over and she
went to greet them.

"This is my sister, Cecilia," Mr. Wells said. "With the school
in Denver. We've been telling her all about you."

"I've heard some wonderful things," Cecilia said as she
offered to shake Virginia's hand.

"I'm so glad you could come," Virginia said as she accepted
the woman's hand. "This is a special service for us tonight."

By the time the Wells family was seated, everybody was
ready for the Christmas Eve service to begin. Higgins began by
reading the story of the baby's birth from Luke. Then Reverend
Olson and his wife sang a duet. Spotted Fawn recited a Christmas poem that she had written. And then it was time for the bells.

Virginia barely had to prompt the girls. They knew their songs so well and the intense sweet smiles on their faces probably moved the listeners as much as the clear tones of their bells. Whichever it was, the building was completely silent as the bells rang out. Virginia wondered if there wasn't some of the wonder with them tonight that had been present thousands of years ago. She could almost hear the sigh from the listeners when the deep tone of the last bell finished ringing.

The girls walked back to their places on the benches and no one made a sound.

At last, the reverend stood. "After that beautiful reminder of the spirit of Christmas, let us pray."

Everyone stood and bowed their heads. "Bless us on this beautiful Christmas Eve. May You give peace and joy to us all and be with us on our journeys home."

When the prayer was done, people rushed over to tell the girls how much they enjoyed the bells. And to tell Spotted Fawn that they thought she should have her poem published in one of those magazines from back east.

Cecilia Wells came over to Virginia as she started wrapping the bells up in the pieces of linen.

"Those bells of yours are magnificent," the woman said. "And my brother tells me you've only given lessons on the bells for a couple of months. It's truly remarkable what you've managed to teach. I just want you to know that the job is yours if you want it. I'll be in Miles City for a few days, so think of any questions you want to ask about the school. I'll invite you over for tea before I leave and we can talk more."

"Thank you," Virginia said with a nod of her head.

She had never thought it would be that easy. Surely the woman should ask her questions about her character and her references and—Virginia stopped. She wasn't ready to make a decision yet. She looked over at Colter. How was she ever going to decide?

"Can we do that again?" Patricia asked as she came over. Her eyes were bright and her smile radiant.

"Not right now," Virginia said with an answering smile. "Maybe for New Year's Day."

Elizabeth and Jake came up to tell them how much they enjoyed the bells.

"And you're worried about frying chicken?" Elizabeth whispered in her ear as she gave her a hug. "When you can make music like that? You don't even need to cook to put a smile on everyone's face."

"It was a pleasure to hear those bells," Jake said as he offered Virginia his hand.

By then most of the people were leaving and Colter came up to ask if he could walk them home.

Virginia nodded yes and put her shawl around her shoulders.

The moon was shining high in the sky when they left the schoolhouse. The clouds from earlier had moved on so they could see the stars, too.

"Chilly?" Colter bent down and asked her when they stepped onto the street. He didn't wait for an answer, but put his arm around her. She liked feeling his warmth so close beside her. Patricia and Danny raced on ahead. The night was peaceful and Colter didn't seem in any hurry to get home. Neither was she.

"Quite a day, wasn't it?" Colter said as they walked along.

Virginia nodded. Maybe that's why she wasn't as excited as she'd expected to be about learning she had the position at the school in Denver. When she remembered the panic she'd felt when Patricia was going to leave, her heart still raced. But now that those she loved were safe, she would have to consider the school position. But not until after Christmas. Tomorrow she didn't want any distractions. She planned to make a feast that everyone would long remember, whether she was here or not.

# Chapter Thirteen

The carrots were sticking to the bottom of the skillet. Virginia had her best apron on and she'd banished everyone else from the kitchen. This was part of her Christmas gift to those she loved. She'd coated the pieces of chicken with flour and spices, just like Elizabeth's instructions said. She had the potatoes boiling on the back of the cookstove. Colter had mixed up the biscuit dough, but she was determined to bake them.

"I need more spoons," Patricia said as she put her head inside the door. She was wearing the hat Colter had given her last night along with the locket Virginia had given her. She was dazzling as she set out dishes for twenty-four people on the gaming tables in the main room. Virginia didn't have enough tablecloths so she had suggested Patricia use a couple of old sheets from upstairs.

"Come in then," Virginia said.

Colter had suggested the two of them exchange gifts tonight, but they had given their gifts to the children. Virginia enjoyed seeing Patricia display her treasures proudly.

"You have to keep everything secret that you see when you come in here though," Virginia added.

Colter still thought she was making soup. Danny probably did, too. Although the boy was so taken with his picture frame and new mittens, he probably didn't care what he ate.

When Patricia came in the workroom, the cat slipped in behind her.

Virginia went back to reading her directions.

She was ready to start frying the chicken. She put some drumsticks in the skillet because Elizabeth said she always did these first to test the heat. Virginia smelled the chicken start to cook. She looked up at Patricia. "Keep Colter away from the door. If he smells this he'll know for sure what we're having. Better yet, send him outside for something."

"What?" Patricia looked blank.

"Oh, one of those things men do," Virginia said. "He could go get something for dinner. Maybe more wood."

Patricia opened the door to go back into the other room and that was when it happened. The dog raced through the opening and the cat arched her back and hissed. That signaled the dog to begin the chase. The cat jumped up on the counter and knocked the plate of seasoned flour on top of the dog. Which made the dog growl at the cat so it ran over and took up a position on top of the pans holding the unbaked biscuits.

"Scat," Virginia said to both of the animals as she waved her apron at them, trying to get them cornered. Unfortunately, she was the one who caught the handle of the skillet and knocked it off balance. None of the drumsticks fell on the floor but they landed on top of the cookstove and started to burn until smoke started to rise up.

Virginia didn't know what to do first so she went to the cause of the problem. She picked the cat up by its fur and took it to the back door. She opened the door, getting ready to throw the cat on the porch, when the dog ran out first and Colter came around the corner carrying a load of firewood.

"I heard you need more wood," he said as he looked around. "What happened to the dog? It's all white."

"That dog is destroying our Christmas dinner," Virginia said, her voice full of outrage.

"I see." Colter stood there looking sympathetic.

If he hadn't looked so calm, Virginia might have been able to keep it in. "No, you don't see at all. I have to be able to make Christmas dinner."

"I'm happy to help."

"But you shouldn't have to do that," she said as she stepped back inside and closed the door. She could get really frustrated at the way Colter acted when she couldn't do something. He didn't criticize. He didn't blame. He didn't— It hit her so hard she had to lean against the door. He didn't act the way her father did even though she kept expecting it. She did not have to worry about disappointing him with every action she took.

Realizing this gave her added determination. A man like that deserved his Christmas dinner. She went over to the counter and smoothed out the piece of paper that had her instructions. The problem was that everything was off course.

She opened the door to the main room and saw the man she needed.

"Psst! Petey," she hissed. Fortunately, the man was close enough to hear her and he came without causing anyone else to look up and see who was calling him.

Petey slipped into the kitchen.

"You can cook, can't you?" Virginia demanded. "I need help with dinner."

"Well, why didn't you say so?" the man said in delight. "I can make a pot of soup that will make your tongue dance."

"We're not doing soup," Virginia said. "It's fried chicken."

* * *

Colter checked his watch again. He had expected Virginia to be out of the kitchen an hour ago. How long did it take to put together a pot of soup? Granted, it would have to be a large pot of soup to give everyone a bowl, but it shouldn't take this long.

Patricia was the last one he knew of who had spoken to Virginia, so he called the girl over.

"Do you know what's taking so long in there?" He nodded toward the workroom.

"I don't know a thing," Patricia said emphatically as she backed away.

Just then, the doors opened. Virginia came out bearing a platter of golden fried chicken. Petey followed with a couple of bowls of something that looked like potatoes and carrots.

"Merry Christmas," Virginia announced. "From Petey and me."

The older man ducked his head in a slight bow and Virginia went to the head table and set down the platter. Then she went over to Colter and looked him in the eye.

"I don't know a thing about frying chicken," she said. "I'm trying to learn, but what you see here is because of Petey."

"Well, I'm grateful to whoever made it."

"And," Virginia continued, "I don't know how to make soap. Or sew up a dress. Or make bread. I'm willing to learn, but you may as well expect me to be hopeless until I do. I've never churned butter or raised chickens or milked a cow."

Virginia was halfway through her list of what she couldn't do when Colter realized what it meant. At least, what he hoped it meant. "You're going to marry me?"

Colter hadn't meant to say it that way. His words had no grace or beauty to them and Virginia set great store by both those things. But before he could take the words back and put new ones out there, she was answering him.

"It seems so," she said. "If the offer is still open."

"Of course, it's still open," Colter said as he swung Virginia into his arms and lifted her up before bringing her down and kissing her.

Virginia was breathless. Her heart was pounding in her. Her feet were still not touching the floor. And she thought a herd of buffalo had found its way into the building and was stampeding until she realized it was the men stomping their feet on the floor and throwing their hats in the air.

It took a few minutes for everyone to be calm enough to eat, but Virginia wasn't about to let this dinner grow cold. It was their first Christmas together and she knew both she and Colter would remember it forever.

"Everyone may take their places," she said. Which, of course, was the wrong thing to say because suddenly no one knew where they were supposed to sit.

"The bride needs to sit by the groom," Patricia announced as she pulled two chairs out from the table.

Virginia wasn't sure she could eat, but she felt a definite need to sit. Then Patricia seated Colter on the chair next to Virginia.

"We should visit Denver—or San Francisco," he muttered to her as he reached over and held her hand. "I promise I'll be a good husband. That's it—we'll honeymoon in Paris. I know how you like other places."

The noise faded as Virginia met Colter's eyes.

"We don't need to go anywhere else," Virginia said softly. When had his face grown so dear to her? She smiled at the anxiety she saw. "You and the children. That's all my heart needs."

"I love you, Virginia Parker," Colter said as he leaned over to kiss her.

"And I you," she said just before his lips met hers.

* * * * *

Dear Reader,

By now you probably know I love a Christmas story. Whether it's snow or bells or lights, the sight of Christmas decorations makes me feel festive. Part of the reason is that I take great joy in celebrating a day that brings people around the world (and through time) together to remember one central fact—that God came to earth to show us He loves us.

I hope this book reminds you of that love. During this season, with all the decorations and the sounds of carols, take time to reflect on the reason we even have a day such as this to celebrate together. May you also hear Christmas bells at some point and remember they have been used for generations to remind people of God's church and His love.

If you are feeling lonely during this time of year, find a church to attend where you can share the story of Christmas with others who hold it dear. I pray you have a joy-filled holiday.

And, if you get a chance, I would love to hear from you. You can e-mail me at my Web site at www.janettronstad.com. Or send me a note in care of the editors at Steeple Hill Books, 233 Broadway, Suite 1001, New York, NY 10279.

Sincerely yours,

Janet Tronstad

# QUESTIONS FOR DISCUSSION

1. Virginia Parker felt abandoned in Miles City in the beginning of the book. She had lost the home she had with her parents back east and then she'd lost the humble army quarters she'd shared with her brother when he died. Can you think of a time in your life when you've felt you had no place to go? Did you blame God? Others? How did you feel?

2. When Colter Hayes found Virginia wandering the streets of Miles City, he felt sorry for her and hired her to play piano in his saloon. Later, he wondered if he should have just given her money instead. What do you think? When you see someone in need, do you debate about giving them money versus helping them in other ways?

3. Virginia Parker tried to educate the men in the saloon about classical music. Have you ever tried to "make a silk purse out of a sow's ear"? What happened? There is a fine line between improving someone and accepting them as they are. How should we decide what to do in such a situation?

4. Virginia loved her father and worked for years for his approval. How did this impact her life? How did this influence her relationship with Colter? With Patricia?

5. When Patricia steals one of her precious bells, Virginia decides to give her the whole set. What prompted her to do this? What would you give up to keep a child's love?

6. Christmas made Virginia more sentimental than usual. Do you feel your emotions change around the holidays, for better or for worse? The Christmas bells were a tradition for her. What are some of your traditions?

# THE CHRISTMAS SECRET

## Sara Mitchell

to a different drummer and keep tripping over their feet. May you learn to hear the divine rhythm of God's Voice, and keep time with Him.

Come to me, all you who are weary and burdened,
and I will give you rest.

—*Matthew* 11:28

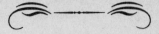

# Chapter One

❧

*Canterbury, Virginia*
*December 1895*

An eye-watering sun beamed from a sky the color of her favorite blue hydrangeas—a deceptive bit of nature hoodwinking housebound humans, whose calendars proclaimed the month December. Shivering, Clara Penrose buried her face in her muffler because the sturdy thermometer she had mounted beside the cottage's door read thirty-six degrees Fahrenheit. The air smelled metallic, with a bite that stung her nostrils as she made her way along the uneven flagstone path toward the garden shed.

For Clara, winter remained a difficult season, despite the determined jollity of Christians preparing throughout the entire month of December for the annual Christmas celebration. This particular Christmas, however, promised to be more than difficult. She tried with little success to convince her racing heart that it was doomed to disappointment, that a woman her age should have outgrown girlish dreams.

Her heart refused to listen to reason.

Congressman—no, now he was *Dr.* Harcourt—was moving to Canterbury. And…if the gossip was true…his wife was dead, and he had never remarried. Nobody knew what he'd done with his life over the past three years, including Clara's brother Albert, who had known Dr. Harcourt when the gentleman was a congressman. Albert might be an annoyingly officious lawyer, and three years earlier he might have bullied Clara into attending that Christmas fete…but if she'd resisted, she never would have met the most fascinating man ever to cross her path.

*He won't remember you, Clara,* the relentless voice in her head repeated. There had been a crush of guests at Senator Comstock's Annual Christmas Gala, over four hundred of them. Dr. Harcourt had still been a congressman, and couldn't take a step without someone demanding his attention. As for his wife… Clara grimaced. An undeniably stunning beauty, Mrs. Harcourt certainly knew how to draw heads, as well as lop them off: she scarcely acknowledged Clara with a single dismissive glance. The skinny old maid in her four-year-old evening gown was about as memorable as a grain of sand. Her only conversation with Congressman Ethan Harcourt had meant nothing to him, nor had she nurtured—until now—any false expectations. He had been married, he had been kind to a clumsy gawk of a woman, and the connection Clara had briefly enjoyed was the natural consequence of someone not used to such kindness from a man, married or not.

She wished she could remember more details about his wife's tragic death. There had been a scandal—something about a fire, and an affair?

When she reached the pile of leaves heaped at the back of the garden shed she sank down on the rough bench her brother Willie had fashioned the previous summer.

Clearing her throat, she invested as much cheerfulness into her voice as she could muster. "Good afternoon, Methuselah.

I trust you're enjoying your hibernation. Sometimes I wish I were a turtle like you, especially this time of year. Hibernation strikes me as one of God's most…tidy inventions. So much easier to crawl into a nice hole and close up inside my shell. Do you realize how many homilies human beings have fashioned around the habits of your species?"

Her cat, NimNuan, his coffee-tipped tail swishing, darted past the bench and pounced upon the leaves.

"Nim, you scalawag!" Laughing, Clara shoved to her feet to scoop up the feline, who instantly draped his forepaws on Clara's shoulders and purred in her face. She hugged him, scratching behind his ear while she scolded. "How many times have I explained to you that you're my very favorite companion? Methuselah's a fixture, not your rival. He's turtled around here at least forty years. Granddaddy used to talk to him when he and Grandmother lived here, you know. Methuselah's the perfect listener—unlike the very demanding puss I'm holding."

Talking to a turtle she couldn't see but knew was there, hidden in those leaves, offered Clara a bridge to a faith she struggled with daily to live. Most times, when her mind pretended she was talking to Methuselah, her spirit understood she was actually baring her heart to God. "So behave yourself," she ordered Nim. "No more pouncing in the leaves."

"Clara!" Her younger sister's voice dimmed the crystalline air, sundering Clara's hope of communion with a hibernating reptile and the Lord. "Where are you? Botheration! Your rosebush is attacking me. Clara!"

"I'm behind the garden shed." Clara set Nim down, inhaled a bracing breath. Nim wisely disappeared around the opposite corner. "At least the rosebush was trying to respect my privacy."

Louise peeked around the corner. "I was afraid of that. You were out here talking to that stupid turtle again. Do you realize how bizarre your habits have become over the past years? Bad enough, moving out of the house to this decrepit little cottage, acting like an eccentric—"

"I'm not in the mood for one of your scolding rants." Clara dusted her gloves and gave her sister a look. "Actually, I'm never in the mood for your scolds, but on this day in particular either tell me what you've come for—or leave me alone to my peculiar habits."

Louise blew out an exasperated breath. "Sometimes I have to agree with Mother. Grandfather never should have encouraged your independent notions by bequeathing you this cottage, along with Grandmother's trust fund. If only you could be more sensitive to how others perceive your—your…"

"Don't spare my feelings, now. We bluestockinged spinsters must develop thick skins."

"Clara." Abruptly Louisa reached for her hands and gave them a quick squeeze. "I'm sorry. I didn't mean to hurt your feelings, thick skin or no." They exchanged relieved smiles, the tension between them fading. "But never mind all that. I came on Mother's behalf, to invite you to dinner Tuesday night. There's to be a guest. Would you like to guess who it is?"

"Ha. That doesn't require guessing. I'm sure it will be Canterbury's new physician and ex-congressman, Dr. Harcourt. Albert's been gloating for a month now."

Louise's face fell, her mouth pursing in an unattractive pout while she studied her sister. "I suppose he has. But I'd never heard of the man until last week. You sound almost as though you know him already."

Clara shrugged. "I give piano lessons to children who gossip more than their parents," she began, picking her way through the words. For some reason, she didn't want to reveal the circumstances of the Christmas Gala three years earlier. Her sister would invest more importance in an insignificant event than prudence dictated. Worse, Clara's rebellious heart might tend to believe it.

She began walking back toward the cottage with her sister. "Since you and Mr. Eppling are engaged, I fail to see why you're so excited over having the town's new physician over for a meal."

"I'm excited," Louise stated with exaggerated patience, "because he's asked Albert about *you*. This morning Bertha brought the children over to visit, and she told me Albert mentioned as much."

"Did Dr. Harcourt mention my name specifically, Louise?"

Her sister ducked her head. "All right, no, he didn't mention your name. He knows Albert has two sisters. Bertha did say Dr. Harcourt said he looked forward to meeting them. I thought—I just thought if you thought he was interested, you'd at least…" Her voice trailed away into a thick silence. "I'm sorry, sister."

Disappointment, sharp and bitter, coated Clara like sludge. She'd known, she'd *known* her sister's penchant for tweaking the truth, but that downy feather of hope had persisted in tickling her heart anyway. And the rush of memories about her first meeting with Dr. Harcourt buffeted her until her legs all but trembled. *She'd escaped the crush of elderly statesmen plying her with questions and slipped outside, onto a relatively uncrowded corner of a massive stone terrace. Dr. Harcourt had been sitting on a bench, invisible in the shadows until Clara, still night-blind, tripped. Hard arms had materialized out of the darkness, clasped her waist, gently steadied her. They had shared a* conversation, *not merely exchanged pointless social trivia.*

With an effort she focused on her sister. "Louise, I can no more turn myself into a curvaceous, green-eyed, golden-haired girl like you than I can fly to the moon."

"You could stop thinking of yourself as an ugly old stick. Because you're not, Clara. If you'd look through some of the ladies' magazines, let me help you with your hair, you'd be surprised by how pretty you are."

Disconcerted, Clara brushed off some dead leaves clinging to her old corduroy jacket. Pointed advice for the family spinster had evolved into family tradition. With Louise gazing at her with sisterly shrewdness, subtlety was useless. "Louise. Whatever you're thinking, abandon it at once. Please, for my sake, accept that I am content with the lot God has designed for my life. Some people, like the apostle Paul, are not meant for marriage."

"My aunt Mitty! If we're going to quote scripture, then I'll remind you that the Lord also declared it wasn't good for the man He'd just created to be alone."

"Well, that may be so, but at my advanced age of thirty-one, I'm convinced that God forgot to create the man who would relieve his aloneness with me."

"Perhaps we'll be eating dinner with him Tuesday night."

After Louise left, bearing Clara's reluctant acceptance to put in an appearance ("And whatever you do, please try to dress appropriately for the occasion, just this once."), Clara wandered about the cottage, ruthlessly suppressing the tickling feather of hope. Emily Dickinson should never have written such an evocative poem.

More likely than not, instead of perching on her soul, the feathers would make her sneeze.

On the Sunday morning of his first week as a new resident of the town of Canterbury, Virginia, Ethan Harcourt reluctantly attended the same church as his old friend Albert Penrose, who had also extracted a promise from Ethan to come to dinner at his parents' home on Tuesday. Ethan dreaded the socialization necessary to resurrect not only his former life, but a medical practice. Yet…he craved good friends and food again, he was starving for spiritual sustenance, and he needed to fully embrace what used to be his first calling from God.

Of course, over the past three years he'd fallen back into doctoring in spite of himself, patching up broken miners out west, delivering babies to hardscrabble women, and mopping feverish brows. For two interesting months down in Nevada Territory, his medical skills had kept him alive—a notorious gang of thieves had ambushed the stage he was on. When they saw his doctor's bag, they kidnapped him instead. He spent the next nine weeks patching up gun and knife wounds, and prayed over graves of thieves and murderers with considerably less charity than Jesus had dispensed from the cross. When the gang drank themselves into a stupor one night, Ethan helped himself to a horse and escaped.

The stately little community of Canterbury reminded him of his western Pennsylvania roots, with its neat rows of clapboard cottages and brick homes in Virginia's gently rolling hills and lush woodlands. Despite its proximity to Washington, Canterbury suited him down to the bone. He was weary of roaming the country like a homeless brigand.

Two nights ago he'd finished transforming the first-floor rooms of the rambling old house he'd bought into his medical offices. After this morning's appearance at church, he'd officially be back on public display again. A kernel of dread tickled the back of his throat. Time hurled him backward three years, to the memory of a hotel engulfed in smoke and flames. Thirty-six guests had perished, one of them his wife—found next to the newly elected senator from one of the midwestern states. *Public display…*

His stride slowed as he walked the last block to the church, and he wondered if he would ever be free from his abhorrence of public humiliation. The mysterious letter that had arrived the previous evening hadn't helped:

So…you've returned at last. I knew you couldn't hide forever. How convenient that you've chosen the town of Canterbury.

That was all. Penned with careful precision in plain black ink and plain lettering. No signature and no return address, though the postmark was Washington, D.C.

Ethan spared a few moments puzzling over that note, then tossed it back onto the pile of other welcoming missives. The writer would identify himself eventually; a doctor was almost as public a figure as a congressman. When Ethan made the decision to stop wandering and set down roots again, he'd accepted the associated risks.

All the same, the brief note niggled his mind at odd moments.

When he arrived at the hundred-year-old brick church, the congregation was already singing the second verse of a Christmas carol. Ethan slipped into a pew near the back, beside an elderly couple who gave him their hymnbook.

People rubbed shoulders and shared hymnals in every pew, no doubt because this was the first Sunday in December—Advent, the beginning of the Christmas season. Pine boughs, sprigs of holly and dozens of lighted candles filled the sanctuary with their fragrances. Tensed muscles slowly relaxed as Ethan trained his gaze upon the minister and tried, mostly successfully, to hold bittersweet memories at bay.

The sermon was delivered well, he decided, with enough punch to keep listeners awake without firing off points like a cannonade. Been a long, long time since he sat in a church pew and heard the gospel preached with honesty as well as passion.

"…how we shared in last week's message, the celebration of God's gift of His Son does not always sit well within our private lives. Many of you carry such a heavy sack of burdens you've no room in the inn of your hearts for Jesus. Instead of tidings of great joy, this season prompts naught but despair and resentment and pain. You cannot accept the Almighty's gift, much less present gifts of your own to the Christ child, as did the Magi—the gift of your time, your service. Your very selves. So…" palms planted on the lectern, the minister leaned forward, and a portentous aura filled the church "…how many of you remembered, and brought a symbol of those burdens this week? How many of you have the courage to come forward, leave them at the altar, with the One Who promised to help carry them? Only when you release these burdens can you truly celebrate Christmas."

He spread his robed arms in an inviting gesture. "Come, come, ye faithful yet fearful. Come while the organist plays 'Come, Thou Long-Expected Jesus,' place your symbols in the manger, leave with hope in your hearts, and on Christmas Day, when we sing 'Joy to the World,' the words will resonate with truth…with the birth of your new life in the newborn Christ."

Movement and murmurs rippled through the pews as the organist began to play. Ethan watched, feeling a hollow sense of detachment shadowing his soul again. What would his symbol have been? The wedding ring he'd never been able to throw away? The stiffly formal letter accepting his resignation from Congress? Or perhaps the blank-paged Morocco-leather memorandum still tucked inside his coat pockets that stood for three wasted years wandering about the country in search of a cure for past mistakes?

The elderly couple beside him excused themselves to join the growing stream of people filling the aisles. Ethan slipped out, moving to the back of the church, and watched the progression. The manger rapidly filled with objects. He watched a woman tenderly lay a doll on top of the hay, which was soon covered by a man's shirt…a small string-tied journal…eventually the objects had to be placed around the feet of the manger, spilling across the dais.

"Come, thou long-expected Jesus, born to set Thy people free;
From our sins and fears release us;
Let us find our rest in Thee…"

When the organist launched into the hymn for the fifth time, Ethan's restless gaze fell upon the tall figure of a woman who glided from a side door across to the pile of "burdens." Winter sunlight streamed through the stained-glass windows, highlighting the solemn curve of her cheekbone and a wide unsmiling mouth. Her dark hair was worn in an uncompromising knot on the top of her head. Unlike most of the ladies present, she wore no hat. Something about her struck Ethan as both poignant and proud.

A frisson of memory rippled through his mind.

*He knew this woman.* Someplace, somewhere, he remembered her. Scalp tingling, he followed her every movement, from the soft swaying of her skirts to the slight tilt of her head when she reached the front of the sanctuary, to the taut line of her spine beneath her gaudy green overblouse.

She laid her object down a little apart from the raggle-taggle mound of other objects. Then, still within an invisible pool of isolation, she melted back into the shadows beyond the sunbeams. The music ceased at last, the minister spoke the benediction, and with the conclusion of the service people gathered around Ethan to speak with him, to shake hands with the stranger.

He smiled and responded politely, all the while keeping the corner of his eye on the woman in green. She wove her way across the sanctuary, and the sting of recognition now prickled Ethan like hundreds of tiny needles. She reminded Ethan of—himself. Acknowledged, but apart. Known by all, understood by none. On the surface, serene and confident.

*Her eyes would be deep pools the color of bitter chocolate, a mysterious blend of intelligence and...* He blinked, impatient with the nebulous wisps of memory.

"Do you know that young woman?" he asked Otis Skelton, a merry-faced little man who had introduced himself and for some reason refused to budge from Ethan's side. "The one with the dark hair, wearing the bright green overwaist?"

"Ah, she's wearing the green one today, then?" Otis gave a dry laugh. "That would be Miss Clara Penrose, Albert's sister. She's a strange one, right enough. Seeing as how you've only arrived a week ago, might be Albert wanted you to settle in a bit, before he trotted her out your way. He's a good man, is Albert, but his sister has a way that seems to twist his bow tie in a knot."

Albert's sister? A "strange one"? The revelation teased him with an even stronger sense of déjà vu, almost as vexing as a welcome note from someone who hadn't bothered to identify himself. "What do you mean by *strange?*" he asked Otis.

"Well, now." Otis ran a finger around the bow tie strangling his throat, slid a sideways look as though to see who was close enough to overhear, then jerked his chin once.

Seemed Miss Penrose was the family oddity, a public-spirited young female with a mind of her own, smart as a whip but who dressed more like a floozy than an old maid, much to the despair of her elegantly turned-out family. Never married. Nobody quite knew what to do with her.... "Spends her days teaching younguns piano, and doing good works. Myself and the wife, we always had a soft spot for the girl. Brings us vegetables from her garden, fresh-baked bread. I remember one time when she—"

Someone called Otis's name, and with a faint air of wistfulness the man left Ethan's side. Clusters of parishioners still stood about talking, one of the groups including Albert Penrose. Not wanting to intrude, Ethan debated briefly before making his way to the other end of the aisle. If his calculations were correct, when Miss Penrose finished speaking to a pair of fidgety girls, she would have to pass him to reach the door.

Sure enough, after the two girls darted off, Miss Penrose walked toward him, one hand idly brushing over the ends of the pews, her step brisk and her gaze focused inward.

She would have run smack into Ethan if he hadn't pointedly cleared his throat. "Miss Penrose? We haven't officially been introduced, but—"

"Yes, we have." Startled dark brown eyes searched his face with unnerving intensity. A flicker of some deep emotion stirred, then vanished. "Dr. Harcourt, formerly Congressman Harcourt of Pennsylvania." Her voice was a clear contralto, unforgettable. "We met several years ago, at one of those holiday levees in Washington. I don't expect you to remember."

Like the Red Sea, the veil that shrouded Ethan's life parted in another rush of memories, once again sweeping him three years into the past, only this time to a vast terrace behind a mansion filled with people. He'd been sitting in stupefied misery on a garden bench, and a willowy woman dressed in a plain blue gown had materialized out of the night.

"But I do remember, Miss Harcourt." He smiled down into her wary eyes while the tug of that encounter filled the air with the same brilliant colors as the sunlit stained-glass windows. "Back terrace, Senator Comstock's Annual Christmas Fete. I rescued you from a nasty tumble." Without warning his palms tingled from yet another memory—the feel of that stiff, slender waist beneath his gloved fingers.

"Yes. I don't see very well in the dark."

His gaze swept over her with sufficient thoroughness to infuse the pale cheeks with color. "You mentioned as much that night. I escorted you to a patch of moonlight, and we enjoyed gazing at a moon as round and white as a pearl. We…talked."

"I understand you've lost your wife. I'm very sorry."

"Don't be. It was a long time ago."

She flinched at the curt tone, but to his surprise—and relief—did not retreat. "She was…very beautiful."

"You were more honest three years ago," Ethan returned quietly. "Lillian was also shallow and insensitive." Among other, far more reprehensible flaws. "I apologized on her behalf, and you told me not to, that I was not responsible for my wife's lack of manners."

The flush in her cheeks deepened to rose, and her mouth half parted. "I—I— You really do remember. I never expected, I mean there was no reason… There were so many people— *Fiddlefaddle*." Ethan watched in fascination as her hands clenched into fists, and a vein in her forehead pulsed. Her chin lifted, and before his eyes she transformed from startled doe to a proud lioness on the verge of attack. "This is ridiculous. We shared a brief conversation. That's the end of it. There is no reason to attach any importance to the exchange, Dr. Harcourt."

Lightheartedness, an emotion he almost didn't recognize, sawed at the rusted bars around his heart. "Until a moment ago I would have agreed with you, Miss Penrose. Now…I'm thinking that brief exchange on the terrace might turn out to be one of the most significant in my life."

"Miss Penrose!" A coltish girl of about fifteen bounded up, a mass of curls bouncing around her indignant face. "Molly says you told her she could play 'Jesu, Joy of Man's Desiring' at the recital. I wanted to play that one. I've been practicing…."

"We can continue our conversation Tuesday, over dinner," Ethan murmured. He stepped past Clara and the young girl with a buoyancy he hadn't experienced in, well, longer than he remembered.

Tuesday suddenly promised a lot more than succulent pot roast. A soft chuckle slipped out; Ethan shook his head, then turned his attention to the three sober-suited gentlemen and a plump-cheeked lady who were gathering the last of the "burdens" from the altar. Not until they departed, arms full, did Ethan notice they had missed the object left by Clara Penrose. Keeping one eye on Albert, he strolled over and picked it up— a small pill box holding a dull silver watch charm of...the Capitol Building.

A charm of the Capitol?

He didn't know what precipitated the impulse, but instead of following the gather-uppers and handing over Miss Penrose's offering, Ethan tucked box and charm inside his vest pocket. When Albert Penrose finally extricated himself from a clutch of parishioners and turned with effusive apologies to Ethan, the same inexplicable impulse restrained him from handing the charm over to Miss Penrose's brother.

She had left this burden at the altar, her private symbolic gesture of renunciation, and Ethan could not betray that privacy, especially to a family member. By confiscating it he had already trespassed enough, though anticipation dulled the sting of guilt.

He hoped that over dinner on Tuesday he would gather more insight into the personality of a woman he suddenly wanted to understand—very much.

# *Chapter Two*

$\smallsmile\!\!\circlearrowleft\!\!\!\!\sim$

Clara wore her scarlet shirtwaist with her black watered silk evening skirt for the Tuesday dinner with her family. She convinced herself the bold red was her acknowledgment of the holiday season, and when uncertainty wove hairballs she defiantly tied an equally bold red ribbon around her topknot. Then, to prove her nerves weren't strumming over seeing Dr. Harcourt again, she spent half an hour revising her latest treatise on the efficacy of setting aside vast tracts of land for national parks.

As usual, the distraction made her late.

The Penrose family was famous for its hospitality. Though this particular meal was considered a "family" dinner, Louise had reminded her that a half dozen other guests were invited along with Dr. Harcourt. "Don't worry. I've made sure you're seated beside him. But do please try to remember this is a dinner party, not a debate."

Her sister's heavy-handed matchmaking usually elicited a barbed retort on Clara's part. But it was disingenuous to protest when her heart whirled and her mind spun at the prospect of seeing Ethan Harcourt again. She had even made a stab at flirtation, with Nim as her masculine representative. Since the cat already adored her and, being feline, considered himself master of their small domain, the exercise only proved how silly she could be over a man. Pragmatism nagged her to quit weaving dreams out of dandelions.

One puff of reality would blow them away.

When she reached the stately Georgian brick house three blocks from her cottage, her mother was waiting.

"Clara, dear! Late as always, but I'm grateful you've at least— Oh." The flow of words ceased as Mavis Penrose took Clara's hat and cloak. Lips compressing into a straight line, after a final motherly perusal she gestured toward the hallway behind her. "Well, you're here now. Everyone's in the drawing room. You might want to rescue Dr. Harcourt. I'm afraid Patricia Dunwoody's monopolizing his attention."

*Patricia Dunwoody,* Clara thought, determination faltering. "Where's Willy? He's been panting after her for a year now." The mayor's daughter was a dainty debutante with lustrous black tresses and a helpless air that seemed to attract men the way navy serge attracted cat hair.

"Your brother is amusing himself with Mr. Pate, arguing the opposite political view. Ever since he joined the debating team, he's become almost as obnoxious in his public discourse as you."

"I've trained him well."

Her mother sniffed, but a rueful smile flirted at the corner of her mouth. "All this intellectual energy must be from your father's side of the family. Sometimes I despair of the two of you, at least in a social setting. If only you…" She stopped, waved a graceful hand. "Never mind, let's join everyone before the dinner bell rings."

Clara's first task upon joining the fray in the drawing room was to rescue Mr. Pate. When she waded in, he was thumping his ivory-handled cane on the parquet flooring while he berated her youngest brother.

"...nothing but a glib-tongued young whippersnapper! You listen to a lecture delivered by some musty professor who hasn't left the classroom in forty years, then consider yourself knowledgeable enough to tell me how this country can recover from the Panic?"

Willy grinned down at the elderly gentleman. "Yes, sir." At fourteen, Willy had been a mischievous brat; at twenty-one, his lanky frame might be elegantly draped in a black dinner jacket and striped trousers, but the mischievous brat remained. Clara inserted herself between him and Mr. Pate, one elbow administering a sisterly jab to Willy's ribs. "Welcome home. Still arguing about free silver, are we?"

"Still insist on wearing garish colors, do we?" Willy lifted her hand and gave it an exaggerated kiss. "As always, you brighten the room just by walking into it."

Clara gave his cheek a sisterly pat. "Trifle warm in here, isn't it? May I fetch you a glass of the famous Penrose Christmas punch, Mr. Pate? Mother's given it a new twist this year, adding grated orange peel to the cloves and cinnamon in the cider."

"I'm fine," the man retorted testily. "If I want to be coddled, I'll fetch Mrs. Pate. I'd rather hear your opinion on Secretary of State Olney's accusation that the British violated the Monroe Doctrine in British Guiana."

Across the room, Clara saw Dr. Harcourt say something to Miss Dunwoody, then begin weaving his way through the crowd, directly toward Clara.

Her hands turned damp, and a tight sensation squeezed her middle. "I know England...ah...feels we're overstepping our sovereignty," she began, distracted by the approach of the man who would now be comparing her to Patricia Dunwoody.

"If you want to talk foreign affairs, addressing the problem of Spanish oppression in Cuba is more important, I'd say," Willy put in, his chin jutting.

"Whole world's headed for a fiery destruction," Mr. Pate grumbled. He peered around Clara. "Dr. Harcourt. You're looking fit as a fiddler's fiddle tonight, young man. And that tonic you insisted I take seems to be doing the trick. Mrs. Pate won't let me hear the end of it, I tell you."

"Glad to hear it. Are you taking those daily walks I mentioned?" Tall and imposing in his evening wear, the town's new physician ran an alert gaze over Mr. Pate before turning to Clara and wishing her a pleasant evening. Instead of replying in kind, Clara's throat locked, and every polite social response drummed into all Penrose children from the time they could sip cider from a cup vanished in a fog of uncertainty.

Willy was staring at her strangely. Worse, Dr. Harcourt looked as though he were—bored? Amused? Contemptuous?

"No need to bother spouting pleasantries with this young woman," Mr. Pate broke the awkward silence. "Don't know if you've noticed, Doctor, but Miss Penrose here's possessed of a mighty adroit mind. In fact, last time I was here she trounced me at a game of chess."

"Dr. Harcourt." Patricia Dunwoody floated up beside him, a vision in peach-colored silk and lace, her shining ebony tresses artfully piled in cascades of ringlets interwoven with strings of seed pearls. "I've come to rescue you."

"From what?" Willy challenged.

"From you and your sister," Patricia returned, smiling a white-toothed smile as sincere as a panhandler's. "The two of you do like to go on and on, about matters much too serious for a dinner party." She turned back to Dr. Harcourt. "I'd very much like to finish telling you about the Christmas Festival this coming Saturday. I'm sure you're used to fancy galas, having been a congressman, but we acquit ourselves quite adequately here in Canterbury. Miss Penrose and I are on the planning committee, of course." She laughed lightly. "It's quite the battleground on occasion."

Clara exchanged glances with Willy, and wondered if her own emotions were as easy to read as her youngest brother's. *She's not worth it,* she longed to warn him, love and the instinct to protect finally unlocking her throat. "My brother and I believe God endowed human beings with the ability to think, and to make reasoned decisions. We enjoy lively debates, even when it's over a seemingly simple issue, such as whether to include Sousa and Stephen Foster melodies along with Christmas carols at the town's annual Christmas Festival, in an effort to allow unbelievers as well as believers to feel that they're part of the community. I love Christmas carols, but I'm also partial to a lively march or a nostalgic folk melody."

"Clara, really, the matter was settled weeks ago!" Patricia glanced up at Dr. Harcourt. "Do you see what I mean? She's always so serious, one can't enjoy a simple tête-à-tête without Clara Penrose turning it into a verbal jousting match. Besides which," she added, "the committee agreed with me. Sousa and Foster are more suitable for the Fourth of July, not Christmas. How like you, to keep badgering an issue when you've already lost."

Losing did not necessarily equate to being wrong, Clara almost whipped out—except she would only prove Patricia's point. Stung, she lifted her chin and forced her lips to curl up in a smile. The couple looked good together, Ethan Harcourt's restrained virility the perfect foil for Patricia's dainty femininity. Clara might have been whisked backward to Senator Comstock's party, when Dr. Harcourt's wife stood impatiently beside her husband, her gaze passing through Clara as though she were invisible. Which was worse, she wondered bleakly—invisibility or condescension?

*Why did beauty always win over intellect?* "Willy, why don't you and I go find Albert?" She finally patched words together to form a sentence. "I haven't been able to annoy him in almost a week now. How about you?"

Willy managed a laugh. "I told him just last night I always thought the word *pettifogger* was coined because lawyers fog the facts with petty notions. I annoyed him just fine then, but I'm always open for more opportunities."

Ethan Harcourt emitted a deep-throated chuckle that caused Clara to gape at him in astonishment. "No wonder Albert warned me about you," he told Willy. "Frankly, I think I might prescribe a daily dose of brother *and* sister."

His eyes twinkled down at Clara, and for the first time she noticed their color—green, with flecks of amber when they twinkled. Surrounded by dense black eyelashes, and attractive laugh lines at the corners... Willy loudly cleared his throat. "I beg your pardon," she mumbled. Her cheeks burned like chilblained skin. "I'm afraid I didn't catch that."

"I said," Dr. Harcourt responded congenially, "your older brother's a good friend and a conscientious attorney, but—" he stepped close enough for his coat sleeve to brush against Clara's shoulder, and finished in a conspiratorial whisper, "I'm afraid Albert's a bit stuffy, isn't he?"

Overhearing, Willy grinned. "Like the moose head hanging in Father's study. Well, doc, since you brought it up, I'll go administer another dose. Tell you what, Miss Dunwoody, how about if you join me? You can make sure I don't slip up and administer an *over*dose."

"I need to speak to your father about a, ah, matter," Mr. Pate announced. Cane thumping, he effectively herded Patricia and Willy along ahead of him, Patricia with a backward look of ill-concealed vexation, Willy with an irrepressible smirk.

Clara and Dr. Harcourt were alone.

"Smile, Miss Penrose," he commanded her softly. "And stop comparing yourself to Patricia Dunwoody."

"How did you—" Clara bit her lip, then gave up and allowed a pent-up sigh to escape. "It's an exercise in futility, at any rate, isn't it? Comparing oneself to another person?"

"Yes, but I've done so myself," Dr. Harcourt admitted. "Usually to my disadvantage…except for the time when I was a reluctant member of a gang of outlaws."

"Are you trying to divert me from wallowing in self-pity, Dr. Harcourt?"

"Absolutely, Miss Penrose. From personal as well as professional experience, I guarantee that self-pity is not conducive to good health." His expression turned reflective. "You have no need for such feelings toward yourself, you know."

There it came again, that disorienting sensation of being flung into dizzying mist. She fiddled with the ruffles on her basque, stalling, then gave herself an impatient mental pinch. "Do you talk with such familiarity to everyone you meet, Dr. Harcourt?" The breathlessness in her voice made her wince.

"Not for a very long time, Miss Penrose." The melodic tinkling of the dinner bell sounded behind them. He offered his arm, and after a panicked internal skirmish Clara laid her hand on it. "I'll share some particulars over the meal, if you like. I've had it on good authority that you're to be my dinner partner."

"My younger sister Louise." Clara sighed. "I'm sorry. My family is famous for many admirable traits, but subtlety is not one of them. I'm their thorn in the flesh, a spinster of independent means who scribbles prose nobody reads. They all think if they could procure a hus—"

"You're a writer, Miss Penrose?"

Loose-tongued, empty-headed…*twit*. Nobody outside her immediate family knew about her secret pastime. "Not really.

Please forget I said that. I'd really rather hear about that band of outlaws you mentioned."

For some reason the twinkling green eyes had turned frozen as hoarfrost and his expression— No. She realized as she pondered his face that it was wiped clean of any expression at all. "Dr. Harcourt?"

"Mmm? Oh, sorry." With a dismissive headshake he resumed speaking, and the skittish fingers scraping down her spine disappeared. "The outlaws. Yes. As Albert may have told you, for the past several years I've been wandering about out west. Last summer I was on a stage, bound for some tumbleweed town in the Nevada Territory. Gang of bandits ambushed us. Killed the drivers, threw open the doors and started on the passengers—an old miner, seventy-four years old, on his way to visit grandchildren he'd never seen…a young couple from Missouri. Homesteaders—they shot them dead, every one."

The quiet words spoke of brutality and horror, of actions inflicted by humans upon fellow human beings. "I read a lot," Clara murmured, self-consciously glancing around the room. In its hundred-year history, this dignified old Virginia home had survived war, financial chaos and illness, yet somehow retained its atmosphere of Christian charity and decency. "I've seen greed. I've witnessed poverty and hopelessness and helplessness in tenement housing. But I've never witnessed coldblooded murder. I won't even try to pretend to understand." Dr. Harcourt's story reminded Clara anew of her privileged circumstances, rekindling the lifelong tussle between pride and inadequacy. "Why didn't they kill you as well?"

"I happened to be holding my doctor's bag on my lap. I was searching through it for some ginger drops for the young woman, who was feeling ill. One of the brigands realized the significance of that black satchel. Their leader had been shot a week earlier, so they kidnapped me. If he died, they promised after I dug his grave they'd hang me, and leave my body for the buzzards." He paused, adding dryly, "According to the U.S. Census, as of 1890, the Western frontier no longer existed. Someone forgot to tell those villains."

"Dr. Harcourt," her mother spoke from the entry to the dining room, "I see you've found my older daughter. I trust she'll allow you to enjoy the meal, and not try to monopolize the conversation."

In her pearl-gray evening gown, Mavis Penrose epitomized the Penrose heritage. The diamond pendant she'd received for her sixtieth birthday gleamed against the *poult-de-soie* fabric; matching earrings—an anniversary gift—perfectly complemented her silvery-blond hair. How could this vision of sophisticated elegance inhabit the same world as a band of soulless murderers?

Mavis pointedly cleared her throat, and with a start Clara pulled herself together. "I'll try to be on my best behavior," she promised. "Confine my remarks strictly to the weather."

"Clara, really…"

"I'm afraid I'm the one who has been monopolizing the conversation," Dr. Harcourt interposed with the suavity of a seasoned diplomat. "We were reminiscing about old times."

Her mother arched one eyebrow. "I see. Well. The holiday season does seem to evoke feelings of nostalgia, does it not? I hope you enjoy the decorations as well as the meal, Dr. Harcourt." With a final lingering glance she turned to a sprightly couple in their seventies whose property abutted the Penroses'.

"Mother loves to decorate for holidays," Clara murmured as everyone was seated. She gestured to the centerpiece—a footed silver bowl brimming with fruit, sprigs of holly and gilded pinecones, all trimmed with red ribbon streamers which drifted around a matched pair of silver candlesticks. "Every

Sunday in December she creates a new centerpiece for the dining-room table. The one for Christmas Day is the most extravagant. Some years ago a ladies' magazine wrote an article about them. Ever since then the centerpieces have grown more elaborate and outlandish."

"Did you notice that the ribbons match the one in your hair?"

Clara made a production out of arranging the lace-edged napkin in her lap. Her appearance had never been compared to the centerpiece on a dining-room table, particularly one in which her mother had invested weeks of preparation. "It wasn't deliberate. Are you still seeking to divert me from self-pity? If so, I'd rather hear more about your saga with outlaws."

Unexpectedly he laughed, a rich, deep sound that attracted attention from the entire assembly of twenty-four guests. Clara's father immediately reclaimed control with an authoritative announcement that everyone bow their heads for the blessing. But in the respectful silence that descended before he spoke, Dr. Harcourt leaned sideways, toward Clara. "I can see," he whispered next to her ear, "why you're able to beat Mr. Pate in a game of chess."

So while her father thanked the Lord for His bounty and the food they were about to receive, Clara offered a quiet addendum, asking God to protect her heart from a man who was dangerously close to stealing it completely.

# *Chapter Three*

That night Ethan had trouble falling asleep. The quantity and quality of the four-course meal he had consumed at the Penrose home was only partially to blame. At three o'clock in the morning, with a stifled imprecation he threw aside the covers, snatched on a Turkish smoking jacket foisted upon him by a grateful saloon girl whose life he had saved in Leadville, Colorado, and stalked down the hallway to his study.

After dropping down in the creaky old rocking chair in front of his desk, he turned on the banker's lamp, then moodily rocked for several moments while he contemplated a small locked drawer. Finally, his gut knotting, he unlocked the drawer and retrieved two envelopes and read the notes yet again. But no definitive proof that Clara Penrose was *not* the author revealed itself.

Clara Penrose, who liked to write yet who didn't want anybody to know she…"scribbled prose."

Clara Penrose, whose relations with her family contained inexplicable overtones of disapproval.

The rocker groaned as Ethan leaned back, his hands absently shuffling the notes. All sorts of welcoming missives had been delivered over the past weeks, some several pages long, others merely a line or two of greeting—"looking forward to meeting you," "relieved another physician available to help old Doctor Witherspoon," etcetera, etcetera. But at least the senders signed their names. All right, yes, his reaction to these anonymous notes stemmed from an admitted hypersensitivity to intrigue of any sort. Between backdoor politics and an adulterous wife, Ethan had choked down a bellyful of human deceit. If the stupid notes had been signed, he wouldn't be sitting here at three o'clock in the morning, stewing over the motives, their mysterious tone or the sender.

Which brought him full circle back to Clara Penrose.

After running a weary hand around the back of his neck, Ethan sat forward, snagged a magnifying glass and spread the sheets across the desk.

> So you've returned at last. I knew you couldn't hide forever. How convenient, to have chosen the town of Canterbury.

The letters were written with a steady hand and a good pen. No blobs of ink, no dribbles or scratched-out misspellings.

The second one, which he'd found tucked inside the curved brass handle on his front door when he returned home this evening, was shorter, only a single line:

> This Christmas will be one you'll never forget.

Was the ink darker, were the letters broader? Or was his mind manufacturing the threat?

Ethan was no detective; based upon the quality of the stationery and the cryptic messages, however, he felt confident they'd been written by a woman.

Clara Penrose, the elderly Mr. Pate told him, was possessed of a fine mind, which Ethan had seen for himself during the course of the evening.

Well, she did have a fine mind, a mind sharp enough to win at chess and carry on intelligent conversation. But secretive? Devious? A short laugh rumbled in his chest. A woman who wore a scarlet overblouse to a dinner party could not be accused of subtlety, much less deviousness…unless her design had been to capture Ethan's attention.

*Like writing anonymous letters.*

Of course, over the past week he'd learned that Clara's love of bright colors and indifference to fashion was the bane of her family. Clara dressed to please herself, not others. It would be the height of arrogance for Ethan to assume her eye-popping attire had been designed solely to attract his attention.

Clara Penrose was not Lillian, he reminded himself. She was not the sort of woman who would stoop to subterfuge, who would— With a snort of disgust Ethan sat up straight. All women resorted to subterfuge when it came to men. He had learned that dismal truth through the crucible of humiliation.

And yet… With a groan he propped his elbows on the desktop and rested his head in his hands.

The Clara Penrose he'd met three years earlier had been different from any woman he'd ever known. Forthright in manner and word, she had also projected an aura of uncertainty that appealed to every one of Ethan's chivalrous instincts. Unlike tonight's, three years earlier her evening costume had been forgettable, drab and dark. If she hadn't tripped over his feet he might never have known she existed at all. Lillian, he remembered in a sharp stab of recall, had tossed out some contemptuous remarks, though her character assessments tended more toward character assassination.

Within the quiet yellow lamplight more memories sprang forth, as vivid as they were painful.

*"You always were a stick, preaching compassion and common sense, when if you possessed an iota of either you'd tell Albert Penrose he should have left his sister at home, knitting socks for orphans. She's pathetic, Ethan."*

*"The woman I chatted with on the veranda is far from pathetic, Lillian. On the contrary, I found her well-spoken, with a rare sense of humor. You could learn a thing or two."*

*"I've found a much more agreeable sort to teach me a thing or two."* With a final flick of a glance that had the power to break a bone, Lillian strolled off into the crowd, boldly linking arms with the man who burned to death with her forty-eight hours later.

If it weren't for the two notes, Ethan might have thanked God for resurrecting the memory of his first encounter with Clara Penrose, reminding him that something good had happened that bitter night.

All right, these days he was a bit rusty on thanking God for anything. He'd strayed from his faith, not renouncing it, but certainly not living it. Ethan hadn't felt much like *living* for a long time…until Albert had convinced him to settle in Canterbury, and re-establish a medical practice. Until he'd met Clara again.

If he hadn't found the second letter stuck in the door handle, Ethan had been planning to intensify the flirtation he'd initiated at dinner.

*Admit it, man. You enjoyed the evening.* Despite her own heavy-handed attempts to return his flirtation, he enjoyed Clara Penrose's company. Tonight he had discovered another side of this fascinating woman, one he would not have expected—in her own milieu, she was a social lioness. Regardless of her family's ill-concealed disapproval, Clara Penrose transformed dull dinner chit-chat into a broad range of discussions that commanded the respect—and participation—of every guest at the table within hearing distance.

All right, so he enjoyed her company, and admired her. Didn't mean he was planning to offer a proposal of marriage.

Ethan's hand closed in a fist.

He despised the needy part of his heart Lillian hadn't succeeded in killing, the part stubbornly tempted to risk that bond of connection again.

Eventually fatigue coated his brain; he fumbled the notes back into their envelopes and relocked them inside the drawer. Either the notes were innocent, or they were threats. Eventually he would discover which and who. For now, he was finally too spent to care.

The wall telephone in the hallway rent the silence before he reached his bedroom. "Dr. Harcourt?" The operator's tinny voice was threaded with urgency. "Mrs. Brown's gone into labor, and Mr. Brown told me to tell you the pains are three minutes apart."

"I'll be there in twenty minutes."

In an instant his exhausted mind clicked into place; in eight minutes he was on the way, all thoughts of Clara Penrose and mysterious notes banished.

The following Saturday a snow squall dusted Canterbury with two inches of powder-fine flakes, then blew out to sea. Distracted, for most of the day Clara flitted around the cottage, baking pies in the kitchen, tying red ribbons around white peppermint sticks and cutting out the last of the paper bells to hang around the Meeting Hall for the Annual Christmas Festival.

Sometime in midafternoon her best friend Eleanor Woodson arrived to help load everything into baskets.

"Brr! It's nippy outside. Good thing this snowstorm seems to have passed. Maybe we should have the Christmas Festival in September instead." She glanced around the parlor, her merry brown eyes widening. "For heaven's sake, Clara. Are we having it here instead?" Shaking her head, she turned to give Clara a brisk hug. "You do realize you're supposed to look like an upstanding member of Canterbury's finest families, not the local washerwoman?"

"I still have time to change. I've spent most of the day in the kitchen. Mrs. Brown's baby came a week early, and her mother couldn't make the pies she promised." Dr. Harcourt had performed the delivery, which from the little bit Clara gleaned had been a difficult one. CoraMae Brown and her baby daughter were alive only through the skill of the attending physician. Ethan Harcourt, it seemed, was fast replacing Clara Penrose as the favorite subject of Canterbury conversations.

Clara gratefully ceded him the honor. She was befuddled, however, over the discovery that her heart gave a little jump every time Ethan's name was mentioned. Best not mention that weakness to Eleanor. "I volunteered to make the pies," she explained. "I don't have a husband or children."

"Spinsters are so convenient to have around, aren't we?" Unrepentantly plump, cheerfully accepting of her status, Eleanor maneuvered her way around a stack of evergreens woven into long ropes, pausing by the chair to give Nim a pat. "You do realize we're society's slaves, relegated to any and every task nobody else wants to do?"

"There's not enough time to engage in one of our discussions, Eleanor. Frankly, I'm too weary to care one way or the other."

"What?" Eleanor charged back across the room, her heavy serge skirt hem narrowly missing a stack of cookie tins. "Clara? Are you ill? No, of course not. You're never ill. Wait…oh, no. Tell me what I've been hearing isn't true."

Clara offered a vague smile. "There's always gossip. Some

of it might actually be true. Um…if I'm going to make myself presentable enough to prevent more of it, would you mind organizing everything? Everything is labeled, decorations are all on the sofa or stacked here on the hall tree, except for those tins full of gingerbread men. I'd just brought them out when you arrived. The rest of the food is in the kitchen by the picnic baskets. Gifts for the orphanage children are by the fireplace. Willy's supposed to be here at five to be our pack mule, but if you—"

"As usual, Willy's late. It's five-twenty, Clara."

Clara threw one appalled look at the prosaically ticking wall clock, then fled toward her bedroom with Eleanor jabbering at her heels.

"Bathe your face and hands in scented rosewater, you'll feel better and smell clean even if you're not. I'll weave a sprig of holly in your hair. Why don't you wear your red overwaist?"

"I wore it for dinner on Tuesday." Stupid mistake, one she wouldn't make again. If she'd been thinking properly instead of like a besotted schoolgirl she would have saved the red for tonight. "The green will do. No—wait. When Louise dropped by yesterday, she mentioned something about leaving me a dress. I was up to my elbows in flour at the time, and haven't bothered to look. If she did what she threatened, a totally unsuitable gown, dripping with geegaws and ruffles and lace—" something Louise herself preferred "—will be in my wardrobe."

"She can't help it, Clara. Louise has succumbed to the concept of femininity preached in *Godey's Lady's Book,* in part because she's undeniably lovely."

"I know. Everyone loves my youngest sister." Perhaps someday the thorn of wistfulness would not jab so deep.

"Pooh! Half of those everyones prefers stimulating conversations and crowd around you. I'm sorry I missed dinner at your home the other night." A good friend, Eleanor always knew when to change the subject. "Seems I missed more than a good meal and your mother's decorations. What did she do this year?"

"Gilded fruit and pinecones, trimmed in red ribbons." And Dr. Harcourt had told her that her hair ribbon matched the table decorations.

Eleanor followed Clara over to the dressing table and unfastened buttons while Clara tugged pins out of her hair. "Well, underneath the scent of gingerbread your hair still smells clean, at least. Gracious, you have a lot of it." She shoved the unpinned tresses over Clara's shoulder. "No wonder you just stuff it up in a bun. Myself, I'd hate to deal with your horse's mane." Two years earlier, much to her old-fashioned parents' outrage, Eleanor had cut off her baby-fine hair. Now it framed her face in silky ringlets that scarcely covered her ears. "There. All unbuttoned. I'll find the dress, and you tell me about the dashing Dr. Harcourt."

Clara had been waiting for it, and barely flinched. "There's nothing to tell. He came, Louise contrived for us to be dinner partners and, yes, he's a charming gentleman who can hold his own in a conversation. One would expect as much, him having been a congressman."

Eleanor made a rude sound. "You can't do a Methuselah with me, Clara. You may enjoy your reputation as Canterbury's most colorful maiden lady, but I'm the one who knows every jot and tittle about every soul. And, dear one, I've learned from no less than five individuals that Dr. Ethan Harcourt spent most of Tuesday evening watching you. He even, I understand on good authority, leaned close enough on a couple of noticeable occasions that you couldn't pass a hairpin between the two of you."

She plucked an errant pin from Clara's hair, dropped it into the china jar on the dresser. "Besides which, the moment I mentioned his name you colored up like a tea rose. Clara Penrose, please tell me you haven't gone and allowed your heart to sweep away all your common sense. Look at us! We're never going to have husbands, nor should we even want them. You own this charming cottage, and when my parents are gone, I'll own Tavistock Farm and, by jingo, I'll turn it back into a prosperous one."

By jingo? "You've been attending too many lectures, Eleanor." Unsettled, Clara walked over and flung open the old oak wardrobe. Sure enough, a flowing gown of dark blue watered silk hung on a padded hanger. Two wide bands of lace decorated the bodice, overlaid by a strip of velvet ribbon. Surprised, Clara lifted it out of the wardrobe and carried it over to her bed. "Shoo, Nim." With absentminded gentleness she lifted the cat off the counterpane, hugged him a moment, then placed him on the floor.

"Well," Eleanor admitted, "for once I think your sister matched the dress to you, instead of herself."

Nerves made her fingers tremble as Clara lightly stroked the velvet bow set at the waist. "Yes. She did. It's a lovely gown. But all the lovely gowns in the world aren't going to transform me into a vision of grace and sweetness."

"I hope not! The world would be a dull place without you, Clara."

A thunderous knocking sounded on the front door, followed by the sound of Willy's voice.

"I'll go help your brother," Eleanor said. "Pull yourself together. And if you have to wear a corset with that gown, whatever you do keep the stays loose so you can breathe."

She would breathe just fine, Clara muttered to herself, if Dr. Harcourt stayed away from her.

## Chapter Four

He was enjoying himself, Ethan realized with a seismic internal shock as he strolled among the townsfolk at the drafty lodge hall. Red and green crepe ribbons draped from the ceiling, evergreens filled the window ledges, and the band dutifully produced joyful tidings of the newborn King of Kings. Hundreds of paper cutouts in the shape of bells dangled... everywhere.

Clara, he had learned, was responsible for the bells, not to mention half the baked goods and the Christmas-stocking charity bazaar in one corner to raise money for an orphanage.

"Good to see you, Dr. Harcourt. Heard you were a mighty fine replacement for old Doc Witherspoon. Say..." the gentleman pumping his hand leaned closer "...I've got a small matter to ask you about. Won't take but a second..."

Ethan knew better than to succumb. "A good physician never takes 'just a second.' Come by my office, and we'll take it from there. Hours are daily nine until six, except for Tuesday, when I'm off at noon." Giving the man a final warm handshake, Ethan turned to compliment the mayor's wife on her eggnog.

Over the course of the evening he caught glimpses of Clara,

but after three hours he had still found no opportunity to speak directly to her. Either she was bustling around displays, ladling punch and slicing pies, or surrounded by a mostly male crowd, talking animatedly in loud voices. All Ethan glimpsed was her head, with her hair confined in its severe bun.

Eventually he worked his way over to a long row of tables that overflowed with gifts and toys peeping from the top of a bulging red flannel sack. Momentarily alone, Clara seemed to be counting—Ethan watched her lips moving silently as she ticked off numbers with her fingers. Above a flushed face, beads of perspiration slid along her temples. Her ears, Ethan noted, were free of earrings, offering a tantalizing view for any male astute enough to give them a closer inspection. Delicate and pale pink, they were, with a strand of rich brown hair dangling around the left one. Ethan clenched his hands against a tug of yearning strong enough to tempt him to do something too risky to contemplate.

Before he succumbed to her lures, Ethan moved until he stood directly in front of her, his back to the room. "Well, Miss Penrose. You're a popular and busy lady. I was losing hope of enjoying another conversation together."

Her head jerked up, and a plethora of emotions chased across her face. "Dr. Harcourt."

"May I say you look quite fetching this evening?"

"Why ask permission when you've already said it?" She turned scarlet, and bent her head to straighten one of the huge red velvet ribbons fastened to the table's edge. "But…thank you. You should compliment Louise. She's responsible for my costume."

"You're the one wearing it." He'd learned that any compliment, however deft, flustered her, so Ethan changed the subject. "Charming party. I like Canterbury very much, and you've done a wonderful job with this Christmas Festival. I think everyone in town is in attendance."

"Except for the Browns. I heard about the delivery. You saved Mrs. Brown's life, and the baby's. Albert was right. You're a wonderful doctor, and everybody I've talked to is mighty glad to have you hang your shingle outside old Mr. McLean's house."

Unlike Clara, instead of shyness Ethan tended to respond to compliments with suspicion, particularly ones proffered by women. On the other hand, Clara might simply be telling him the truth. Weary of the incessant internal battle, he shrugged. "Most of the time I think God is the primary healer. Good doctors just offer a bit of assistance." Bad ones, on the other hand, usually ushered their patients along to the pearly gates, and blamed God's will for the patient's demise.

"A humble attitude in a physician. But if everyone left the healing up to God, you'd soon be out a medical practice."

He studied her curiously. "You sound more like a skeptic than a believer, Miss Penrose."

"Only occasionally, Dr. Harcourt. I no longer blindly believe anymore. No matter how hard you pray for healing, people die. No matter how faithfully you follow the tenets of your faith, eventually you'll feel…" she hesitated, then looked him in the eye "…betrayed, or the fool."

"Mmm. It's a tightrope, isn't it—trying to find a healthy balance between life's cruelties and faith? Jesus was the Great Physician, but even He didn't heal everyone." He paused. "My early years as a doctor, back in Pennsylvania, I struggled a lot, especially with cases where neither prayer nor all a physician's skill reversed an inevitable course."

Clara was looking at him strangely. She opened her mouth, shut it, then shook her head as she gestured toward the room behind them. "This is much too serious a conversation for the occasion. But…I wouldn't mind pursuing the topic, some other time." Her next words emerged far more rapidly. "When the band starts playing 'O Come Little Children,' Reverend Miggs brings the children in through the front door, and St. Nicholas will arrive through the back door, to dispense these gifts to all our orphaned little ones. It's loud and confusing and great fun. I...ah...I need to finish counting these gifts, make sure we have enough to go around."

Ethan nodded. "I'll help." Without giving her an option to refuse, he strode around behind the table to join her. Warning bells clanged in his head, but he couldn't ignore this compulsive need, a need that intensified with every encounter. He wanted to find out who had betrayed *her*, and whether her life was fueled by courage—or a bitterness tightly restrained beneath a personality that, if pushed beyond measure, would erupt, destroying everyone in its path.

*Like Lillian.*

Stubbornly he reached for one of the wrapped boxes. "Where did you leave off?"

For several moments they worked without speaking, until the awkwardness between them gradually settled into comfortable congeniality. Occasionally they exchanged pleasantries with passers-by, and one time Ethan even caught Clara humming beneath her breath. The blue gown flattered her, he thought, casting a surreptitious appraisal over it as he handed her the last gift to stack around St. Nick's sack of treasures. She was not a beautiful woman, nor would she command instant attention in a crowded room. But the more he was around her, the more he wanted to know about those contrary flashes of wistfulness that clashed with the sharp-edged wit, and blunted the edge of bitterness she'd let slip earlier.

"What do *you* want for Christmas?" he inquired casually just as she intercepted a young boy dressed from head to toe in Scottish plaid, complete with Tam o' Shanter, as the sprout sidled around the table.

"You know better, Charlie," she scolded the child with a smile. "These gifts are for boys and girls at the Home—those with no families. You're helping St. Nicholas hand them out this year, aren't you?"

"Yes, ma'am. I was…um… I just wanted to see…"

"Never mind, Charlie. Here." Clara produced a peppermint stick tied with a red ribbon, and winked at him. "Don't tell anyone where you got this." Grinning, the boy departed, and she turned back to Ethan. "What were you saying?"

"I asked what you wanted for Christmas."

Bewilderment flickered across her face. "What *I* want?" she repeated, shaking her head. "Why would you ask? I'm not a child, expecting a stocking full of goodies to magically appear Christmas morning."

Ethan glanced around; the orphans had arrived, and the din practically set Clara's paper cutout bells to ringing. Several adults herded the children into place while everyone's attention focused on the door at the end of the hall, where old Vladimir Cherkorski, the town blacksmith, would momentarily appear. Clara promised Ethan the blacksmith would look the spitting image of the Santa cartoonist Thomas Nast first created for *Harper's Weekly,* during the War Between the States. After Vladimir and the town children handed toys out to the orphans, he would recite *'Twas the Night Before Christmas* in a splendid bass voice.

For the Christmas Eve pageant in the town square, however, Vladimir played the part of Joseph. "A lovely harmonious blend of faith and tradition," Clara finished before adding with a twinkle in her solemn eyes that "Most of the children here believe Santa Claus speaks with a Polish accent."

She needed to smile with her eyes more often.

Ethan leaned close, his lips almost brushing the delicate ear. "You're wonderful at giving to others, Clara. But have you ever stopped to consider that an equally significant portion of the Christmas message is learning how to receive?"

To his astonishment she flicked him a raw look bristling with hurt, then half turned her head to stare blindly across the room. "Too much is made of gift-giving. The custom may have originated from those gifts the Magi offered the Christ Child, but it seems to me that every year more attention is focused on presents than on Jesus' birth." Abruptly she hugged her narrow waist. "I beg your pardon." One hand briefly fluttered toward the bulging sack. "Considering what I'm—what we're doing at the moment, you must think me the worst of hypocrites."

The door at the end of the hall burst open, cheers and delighted shrieks erupting as a great hulk of a man dressed in cherry red, with a flowing white beard, ho-ho-hoed his way into the room.

Clara's hand, Ethan noticed, had balled into a white-knuckled fist that pressed against the midnight-blue velvet bow at her waist. Turning slightly to screen his actions, Ethan reached for that fist, cupped the chilly curled fingers inside his. "I think a lot of things about you, Clara Penrose." He ran his thumb over her knuckles, then lifted his other hand to prise her fist open, gently spreading the cold fingers across his palm. "But a hypocrite is not one of them. You do have more facets than a prism, so what I'm thinking is that I want to see every one of them in the sunlight."

"There's nothing colorful about me, other than my choice of attire. I can't imagine why you'd think otherwise." Her fingers trembled. Guileless brown eyes reflected honest confusion.

"I don't understand all the whys," Ethan admitted honestly. "And I know neither of us is ready for me to admit this." She did not return his crooked smile, nor even blink. He resumed stroking the trembling fingers because he couldn't quell the need to soothe. "When I look at you I see a woman of extraordinary strengths, but I also see questions and loneliness and...well, something that strikes a chord inside me. I see a reflection of myself." He no doubt sounded idiotic, and if she told him so he'd no one but himself to blame.

Instead she stared at him, looking both confused and sympathetic.

The noisy mass of humanity would be upon them in less than ten seconds. Ethan gently squeezed her hand, then with a lingering caress slid his fingers free. "Time to be Santa's helpers. But we will definitely continue our discussion later."

"You might discover that familiarity breeds contempt, Dr. Harcourt."

"Ah. Since you're familiar with Aesop and his fables," Ethan replied, "perhaps you recall his observation that it is not only fine feathers that make fine birds."

# Chapter Five

What to do, what to do? Clara spent most of the Sunday service alternatively trying to determine how to respond if Ethan approached her after church, or how to approach him herself if he didn't. Frequent mental whacks of self-disgust could not discipline the tenor of her woefully girlish dreaming.

The previous Sunday, heeding Reverend Miggs's sermon, she had renounced her prideful longing to be Someone of Significance—grand hostess for a literary group, or the benefactress of a much respected Washington philanthropic organization—endeavors suitable for the eldest daughter of Clarence Penrose. The family old maid. Until today, that solitary walk up to the dais with the little silver charm of the Capitol Building clutched in her hand had been one of the most painful experiences of Clara's life. But now... *Lord? You must know I never intended to cultivate a prideful heart, or a silly one.* Had she unwittingly become a coward as well, unable to admit her attraction for a gentleman?

She should write an article about it: "Death of a Spinster's Sensibilities."

No, what she should do was focus on *worship,* set her mind

and heart on things above. On the moment in time when the course of history changed forever because God transformed Himself into flesh, and moved among the flawed human creatures with whom He longed to connect.

People constantly hovered around Dr. Harcourt, vying for his attention. Not only was Ethan Harcourt an attractive, erudite, respected man—he had a past. Thus, being a widower of marriageable age, a former congressman *and* the town's physician, every single female in Canterbury, from Clara's giddy piano students to several widows in their early forties, fluttered about him in hopes of making a favorable impression. *You're just another flutterer, Clara.* Last night signified nothing—he was merely being courteous, helpful.

Patricia Dunwoody had twice now inveigled his presence for tea. "He was quite impressed with our Festival, and made a point of complimenting me on the smoothness of the arrangements," she preened before the service. "By the way, Clara…a teensy bit of advice? Last night, I couldn't help but notice your attempt to monopolize his attention, when Vladimir was giving out gifts to the orphans. Nothing annoys a gentleman more…"

Her friend Eleanor was probably right. The prospect of courtship rendered all participants desperate, or diabolical. "So you need to watch yourself with this one, Clara. All you're doing is making yourself miserable. Life's too short to squander on a man." For all her cheerful demeanor, Eleanor tended to prefer persimmons to plums, and pragmatism over romance.

The congregation rose to sing "Break Forth O Beauteous Heavenly Light." Fumbling the pages, Clara ignored the surreptitious glances the family cast her way. She fought an irreverent smile: in a desperate attempt to include the Almighty in her mental meanderings, she began to pray. *Lord, You did create male and female. Contrary to Eleanor's opinions, You indicated they are better off together. But as of course You also know, everyone seems to have made a fine mess of things these past few thousand years. I don't seem to be able to do much better, Lord. I'm not an Eleanor, and I don't want to be a Patricia. Frankly, Lord, I don't know who I am these days.*

Louise tugged her skirt. "Clara, sit down!" she hissed. "The hymn is over."

After Reverend Miggs pronounced the benediction, her sister immediately launched into speech. "You've been behaving strangely ever since last night. Willy said when he took you home you acted—and this was the word he used—*moonstruck.* He told me he couldn't even provoke you into a quarrel." With an impatient wave of her hand, she grabbed Clara's arm and pulled her to the end of the pew, out of the way. "The dress worked, didn't it? Everyone in town saw the way Dr. Har—" hurriedly she lowered her voice "—Dr. Harcourt's attentiveness. Tell me, what did he say to you?"

"Louise, I've admitted the gown turned out very well, and I thank you. But if you think that entitles you to pry into any conversations I might have with Dr. Harcourt, I'll tell you—again—they're none of your business."

"Piffle. Of course they are. I'm your sister. You like him. Don't even try to deny it."

"Of course I like him. So does every other woman in town, and all the men with whom I've chatted. Every person in Canterbury likes Dr. Harcourt. For once Albert deserves to gloat." She smiled at several ladies from the missions committee, thanked them for their contributions to the Festival.

"Clara— Oh, botheration. Now Eleanor's headed this way. I might as well try to stop a steamship. Very well. Mr. Eppling's waiting for me, anyway."

"Honestly, Louise. You're marrying the man in four months. Can't you refer to him as Harry, at least with me?"

"You know what Mother would have to say about that level of familiarity."

"I know that for all our lives Mother has used convention and manners to distance herself from any form of familial intimacy with her children." Frustration with everything—her sister, her family…with life—pushed through Clara in a strong gust of rebellion. "As a matter of fact, I think of Dr. Harcourt as Ethan. I might even ask him to call me Clara, since I'm thirty-one years old and quite capable of establishing my own set of conventions."

For a moment Louise gaped at her, then she reached up and pressed a quick kiss against her cheek. "Good for you, sister. I shall take courage from you, and promise to at least call my affianced Harry when I'm alone with you." After a brief but fierce hug, she slipped past, smiling at Eleanor but not stopping to speak with her.

Before Eleanor managed two sentences, several piano students surrounded Clara, followed by more townsfolk wanting to compliment her on the success of the Christmas Festival. By the time Clara extricated herself, promising to visit Eleanor later in the afternoon, Ethan was nowhere in sight. Hurriedly she fastened her coat, all but running down the now-deserted aisle to the church's front doors, and almost ran smack into him.

"Whoa! Is the sanctuary on fire, then, Miss Penrose?" he teased, his hands steadying her shoulders. In her flustration Clara probably only imagined that his grip lingered before he set her free and stepped back. Eyes narrowing, he examined her with what Clara thought of as a physician's analytical intensity. "Is something wrong?"

"I thought you'd left," she stammered, stupidly. "I wanted to… I wanted to, ah…thank you for your help. Last night, at the Festival. With the gifts. It's always a melee, as you saw…" Finally she corralled her tongue and lapsed into silence. Regrettably she could not corral her thoughts. Even now the memory of their closeness the previous night produced a surge of warmth. Under cover of all the joyful confusion she and Ethan had shared an unnervingly personal conversation. *He had held her hand.*

"It was my pleasure," Dr. Harcourt commented easily. "Miss Penrose—Clara? Are you sure you're all right? You're flushed, and—" he hesitated, then added with slight smile, "—you're not acting like yourself."

"I know, and I despise myself for it."

Flirting, she had instructed Louise since her little sister first let down her dress hems, was degrading to both parties. Honesty was preferable to artifice. Since Clara had spent the past twelve hours rehearsing the latter, either God wanted to administer a dose of humility, or He was indulging in a bit of divine comedy. Very well, then. She would try her hand at both honesty *and* artifice. "I did enjoy your company, last night—Ethan." She fluttered her eyelashes as much like Patricia Dunwoody as she could manage, and summoned what she hoped was an inviting smile. "I look forward to seeing you this coming Thursday. Bertha told me that you're joining the rest of our family for dinner with her and Albert. She tries hard to emulate my mother's formality, but with my nephews and niece you're more likely to feel like you've tumbled back to last night at the Festival."

"I'll try to look forward to the experience." Perhaps it was only a cloud passing in front of the sun, but to Clara his face seemed to darken. "I must go. I promised to stop by the Browns' after church, to check on Mrs. Brown and the baby." After touching the brim of his hat, he turned and rapidly departed, disappearing around the corner of the church.

"So," Clara murmured aloud, shivering a little in the nippy winter day, "was I too obvious, or too subtle?"

\* \* \*

Scowling, Ethan climbed into the buggy, his scowl deepening because he was forced to shove aside several more envelopes, along with a brightly wrapped mason jar full of pickled cucumbers. He had never been the kind of man who believed he understood women, except from a medical perspective, and Clara Penrose was tempting him to go search out that band of outlaws in the Nevada Territory.

Last night she had been everything he'd ever wanted in a woman—and he'd come dangerously near to making a fool of himself again. He had felt safe with Clara. Free. Unlike most women, including and especially Lillian, Clara did not dissemble, or batter him with admiring glances and honeyed words.

Until today.

Ethan seldom swore, but he was tempted to now. What was she trying to do, anyway, batting her eyelashes like a professional floozy, flashing him those bright and utterly artificial smiles? On the church steps, of all places! And to think he'd been entertaining the notion of courting her. Angrily he rifled through the scattered missives beside him, thinking with the only portion of his brain still capable of rational thought that he needed to calm down before he visited the Browns. After sucking in a deep breath and holding it for a moment, he picked up the note on top and read the cheery Christmas greeting. By the time he made it through another two unpretentious notes he felt his pulse slowing down to a healthier rate.

Then he opened the envelope with the fourth note, and the hair on the back of his neck lifted as he removed the neatly folded vellum: *Somebody plans to give you something special this Christmas.* As with the other two notes locked in his desk drawer, there was no signature, no other greeting.

Had Clara been running because she'd slipped out the side door, left the note in his buggy, then dashed back out the front door to waylay him? The prospect sickened his gut. He wasn't sure which of them suffered from a mental malfunction—Clara or himself—for believing she was capable of such aberrant behavior.

*Enough,* Ethan vowed to himself. He'd endured quite enough. On Tuesday afternoon, when he closed the office at noon, he would pay Clara Penrose a visit. In his thirty-seven years he had suffered enough from the clandestine intrigues of females to last thirty-seven lifetimes.

Tuesday, in the way of weather in this corner of Virginia, dawned mild, with skies the color of aged pewter.

"Rain by tomorrow," Mrs. Gavis pronounced stoutly when Ethan finished his examination. "My shoulder's set to aching. It's never wrong when I get that ache."

"Mm…" Ethan had learned which patients to coddle, which to lecture, and which few to simply agree with because he would never change their minds.

"You're a bit down in the mouth today, Dr. Harcourt. Something besides my lumbago troubling you?"

"I'm fine," he lied, courteously cupping her elbow as he escorted her down the hall to the door. "But I will take my umbrella tomorrow, when I do my rounds."

After Mrs. Gavis departed, Ethan turned off all the lights and, eschewing the buggy, set off for Clara Penrose's cottage at a brisk walk.

A block away a woman watched from the one-horse trap she'd rented at the livery stable. Her hands, slippery and trembling, clutched the reins too tightly; the livery horse backstepped, his tail swishing. The woman spoke to the animal, apologizing, then nervously edged the trap closer to Dr. Harcourt's office after his tall figure disappeared around a corner several blocks down the street. Her movements clumsy with haste, she set the brake, secured the reins and, after climbing down, turned to pick up a large basket from the floorboards. The putrid odor of rancid fruit brought tears to her eyes. She darted several glances around to ensure that nobody was in sight before carrying the basket down the brick path, up onto Dr. Harcourt's wraparound porch. One of the broad planks squeaked when she stepped on it. She froze, holding her breath. She'd never seen a servant loitering about the place on Tuesday afternoons. The daily maid he hired to clean and cook meals was allowed Tuesdays off, she'd discovered.

She was safe, if she hurried.

Carefully she set her gift down directly in front of the door, where he'd be sure to see it—or, perhaps better, to trip over if he returned after dark. After wiping her eyes, she reached into the pocket of her long overcoat and tugged out the note, which she placed between two brown-specked, soggy apples to ensure a breeze wouldn't blow it away.

All the way back to the livery stable she sang, her heart pounding with victory and grief.

# Chapter Six

Clara lived in a quaint stone cottage with tall brick chimneys at either end. She didn't answer Ethan's knock, but as he turned away from the door a slender cat with the most unusual markings he'd ever seen materialized from beneath a pruned-back rosebush at the corner of the cottage. Wide, myopic blue eyes appraised Ethan unblinkingly. Fascinated, Ethan knelt, stretching out his hand. "Hey, fella. What kind of feline might you be?"

As though his voice was a signal, the cat strolled over, sniffed Ethan's hand, butted its head against the fingers, then commenced purring.

"You sound like a sawmill," Ethan remarked, obliging the animal by scratching its seal-colored ears and then under the chin. "Where's your mistress?"

The cat turned and whisked with silent grace around the corner. Slowly Ethan stood, dusted the knees of his trousers and followed, telling himself that the animal was *not* responding to the question, but for whatever reason had decided to run off. When he turned the corner he stopped, his mouth dropping open. Though it was winter, he could still see the gifted hand of a loving gardener everywhere he looked. Beneath several massive oaks, an English-styled garden had been laid out, with neatly pruned-back shrubs and mulched flower beds lying dormant, waiting for spring. The grounds were tidy, as scrupulously tended as Ethan's examining rooms.

The cat waited for him in the center of an ancient flagstone path. When Ethan approached the friendly feline greeted him with a meow that was part growl, part purr and part an indescribable conglomeration of sounds that nonetheless emerged as though the cat were, well, speaking to him. Then it darted down the path, chocolate-tipped tail waving.

"Lewis Carroll must have used you for his model in *Alice in Wonderland.*" Smiling despite himself, Ethan trod along the uneven stones half buried in the ground to the rear of the cottage. An immense thicket of lilacs crowded the back corner of the structure. Peering around the branches, Ethan glimpsed a small shed, a large pile of composting leaves—and Clara Penrose. Her back was to Ethan, but he could hear her talking, and assumed it was to the cat until the animal burst from the lilacs, streaked across the dead grass and leaped into the pile of leaves.

"Nim! You are such a spoiled-rotten boy! Bad kitty. You know this is the first time I've been out here in a week." She picked up the cat—Nim?—and despite the scolding hugged him close. "Go along now, and let me have a few more moments. Methuselah was about to provide some illumination, I believe. I haven't perfected turtle talk, so you're just going to have to be patient."

Methuselah? Turtle talk?

Head shaking, Ethan stepped around the lilacs. "I'm afraid Nim's not the only one you'll need to scold."

She'd been sitting on a crude bench, and sprang to her feet so rapidly the cat panicked. With a hiss and a yowl Nim catapulted from Clara's arms, then vanished behind the garden shed.

"Sorry I frightened everyone," Ethan began as he walked over to her. "I knocked on your door first. You didn't answer, but your butler showed me back here."

"I don't have a butler. Oh…you mean NimNuan." She grimaced. "He'd be insulted if he heard himself relegated to the status of a servant. He's a new breed of cat known as Siamese. It's my understanding they were originally bred by royalty to guard the temples of Siam. A friend of our family knows the British Consul General. The King of Siam gave him a breeding pair of the animals. Nim's descended from them, and he takes his royalty seriously."

"I'll humbly beg his pardon the next time I see his majesty. Here—what's this?" He dropped the banter and reached for Clara's arm. "Don't flinch away. I'm not initiating an improper advance. But you have a scratch on your neck, courtesy of your royal cat Nim—Noon, did you call him?"

"Nim*Nuan*. It means *supple and graceful* in Siamese, despite what you just witnessed." She drew in a sharp breath as Ethan took hold of her chin and turned her head so he could examine the scratch. "I— It's nothing, I'm sure. He's usually very careful not to use his claws on people."

The skin beneath Ethan's fingers felt soft as a newborn's. The chin he held, however, was an uncompromising one and her eyes, the same dark bitter chocolate as her cat's paws and ears, searched his with alert wariness. He reminded himself forcefully that this woman might have left him three very disturbing anonymous notes over the past two weeks, and the purpose of his visit was to have a serious conversation with her, not only as a man, but as a doctor.

He dropped her chin and stepped back. "You're right. Skin's a little puffy from the scratch, but unbroken. You still ought to clean it before bedtime. Cat scratches can turn nasty—they're actually more open to infection than a dog bite."

"Unless it's a rabid dog. Why are you here, Dr. Harcourt?"

Ethan contemplated his answer, finally countering with a question of his own. "Do you often talk to piles of dead leaves, Miss Penrose?"

"Only when a box turtle is hibernating in them."

A box turtle? "You're telling me you were talking to a *turtle?*"

A faint blush dusted her cheeks. "I inherited this place from my grandparents. My grandmother loved gardening. When I was a child, I helped her plant over a thousand daffodils imported from Holland. Come spring—"

"Clara…" he emphasized her name deliberately "…answer the question."

"I'd rather not. You might conclude I'm dotty, not eccentric."

Despite his suspicions, Ethan smiled. "Possibly. But I'd like to know about Methuselah anyway. That's what you called him, isn't it?"

"He's a biblical and godly man in the Bible who lived for a very long time." The color in her pale cheeks deepened.

His mouth twitched, but Ethan clamped down the laughter. Her evasive manner might be shyness, but it could just as well be shrewdness. Thoughtfully he studied her. She was tall for a woman, slender—almost bony, her skin pale as alabaster. As usual, her hair was scrunched up in the unattractive bun. More unusual was her attire. In stark contrast to the bold jewel tones to which he'd become accustomed, and especially to Sunday night's elegant gown, today she wore a plain gown faded to an unattractive gray, with only a shawl woven in equally depressing shades of gray over it.

There was nothing about her of glowing beauty or curvaceous femininity or elegant sophistication.

Yet Ethan didn't care a flea's whisker about her appearance, fashionable or not. He did care about self-preservation, which seemed to evaporate around Clara. Something about this maddening, confusing woman appealed to him on such a visceral level he was rapidly losing any semblance of control. He needed to reclaim his objectivity, immediately. After finishing his appraisal, he folded his arms and drawled, "I have the afternoon off. I'm quite content to stand here until dark. Since I'm blocking the path, we might as well indulge in a useful conversation. Learn a bit more about each other."

Her gaze flicked over her shoulder.

*Uh-uh. No escaping like your cat.* "Don't bother dashing around the garden shed," he warned. "Come now, Clara. You were more intrepid three years ago, not to mention the other evening. Here—I'll start. I'm intrigued—and irritated—by you. And I'm not feeling noble. I came to have an honest conversation without interruption. Now it's your turn. Tell me about the turtle."

For a moment she stood in silence, hugging the shawl closer around her shoulders, her hands restlessly smoothing over its fringe. Finally she shrugged. "Box turtles can live half a century or more. The one hibernating under those leaves was already a permanent resident thirty-odd years ago, when my grandparents moved into the cottage. I named him Methuselah. Sometimes I need to—to clear my head. After I moved here and started gardening, I used to meet up with Methuselah quite a bit. Some years ago, when I was having trouble praying…" she stopped, searched his face, and finished simply "…I started talking to Methuselah instead of God. I've come to believe neither of them mind." Her chin jutted out. "I warned you that you'd think I'm dotty."

Not a single individual out of all the people Ethan had ever known—not one of them—would share such a bizarre confession, even with their physician. A decade earlier, he might have been smug and insensitive enough to label that person as mentally deficient.

Life, however, tended to beat the starch out of a body; he was also coming to accept that while God usually didn't prevent the beating, He at least dispensed grace to make it possible to survive it. "I don't think you're dotty," he told Clara, his voice gruff. Because she stood there as unmoving as one of the old oaks around them, he reached for her hand and looped it through his arm. "Introduce me."

"I assume you mean to Methuselah, since you've indicated at least a passing acquaintance with the Lord."

"Let's say I'm interested in pursuing a deeper understanding of both."

Her tart response sparked the fire that had been smoldering inside Ethan for weeks. The woman might be unpredictable as a dragonfly, but regardless of her evasiveness and his own wariness, she always made him feel alive. At this moment his doubts seemed more the product of an embittered mind than the observations of a man honed in the world of political chicanery.

Watching her, he lifted the hand resting on his forearm and pressed a kiss against her knuckles. "Perhaps talking to you and a turtle will provide it."

Clara yanked her hand free. "Are you making sport of me, Dr. Harcourt?"

"I only make sport of ladies who talk to goldfish, not turtles." In a quick move he recaptured her hand and tugged her over to the leaves. "After Saturday night, I was hoping you'd think of me as Ethan."

"I did, until you provoked me. Frankly, I don't know what to think. You're not acting like the congressman I met three years ago, nor the thoughtful gentleman who helped me with gifts the other night. You—well, you're acting more like my brother, the way you're—"

"Clara—" he bent so his lips brushed the shell of her ear "—this is not how brothers behave toward their sisters."

"The last time Willy nibbled on my ear he was eight months old and teething."

Her voice had gone breathless. Ethan could hear the light rapid exhalations, feel the pulse skittering beneath his fingers. And the way she looked at him…

*If she kissed him, he'd be lost. For months Lillian enticed him with bashful gazes and half-parted lips until he would have followed her off the edge of a cliff. After that fateful evening when she'd pulled him behind an urn bursting with greenery and pressed those lips against his, he'd asked her to marry him the very next day.*

He'd been twenty-three, and an idealistic fool.

"Ethan…you're hurting my fingers—"

"Sorry."

He dropped her hand as though it were a bundle of thorns. Silence thickened between them until he finally scraped up the courage to meet her bewildered, half-angry gaze, the eyes grown dark as the dregs at the bottom of a cup of very bitter coffee. Swallowing hard, he ran his hand around the back of his neck and prepared to abase himself. Then Clara spoke.

"She really hurt you, didn't she? Your wife?"

In three years, no one had dared broach the subject, even indirectly. Yet this indefatigable woman, a woman he had just manhandled and frightened, sliced through all the polite social fabrications to offer him something he'd forgotten existed—honest empathy.

"Yes, she did." The admission still stung. In a flash of insight Ethan realized how much he'd needed to talk about Lillian with someone, instead of immersing himself in mindless flight to a place where nobody knew him from Adam's house cat.

Festering wounds to the heart required lancing as much as boils on the skin. "Can we sit down on that bench? Perhaps Methuselah will listen in, and have some helpful counsel."

"I've learned that most times, just listening is enough."

# Chapter Seven

They sat on the damp wood bench, shoulders almost touching. Thin silver-gold sunlight washed over the yard, and a stray wisp of breeze twirled a couple of leaves. Somewhere a bird twittered. Clara sat quietly, her mood contemplative, her gaze steady on the pile of leaves. She kept her hands folded in her lap, and didn't speak or even clear her throat because she didn't want to distract Ethan. He had indicated a need to clear the air between them. While her heart might palpitate with fearful hope, his behavior toward her was erratic; one moment he was tender, solicitous—the next moment he was crushing her fingers, his expression cold as a winter wind.

She could not afford to trust this troubled man.

All of a sudden he began to talk, the words halting at first, then escaping in a geyser, and Clara forgot about the need for caution. "The adulteries were humiliating enough—but what hurt more was her vindictiveness. I wasn't the man she'd wanted me to be, I refused to turn a blind eye to her infidelities, so she delighted in making them as public as possible. I think by the time she died, I—" he turned slightly, watching Clara with fierce intensity "—I think I hated her. I wouldn't have wished her to die like she did, but I was glad I wouldn't have to deal with her anymore. It's a desecration of the spirit, allowing that poisonous emotion to take root."

"Oh, Ethan... Even if you did grow to hate her, you never acted on your feelings. Based on what I saw at Senator Comstock's party, and what I've learned since, you're a private man with a reputation for personal integrity. Of course you'd need to build a wall around yourself to try to cope with a wife who possessed neither. I'd say your hatred was over the circumstances and your wife's behavior, not a reflection of your true feelings toward—her name was Lillian?"

"Yes."

He chewed over that a while, then shook his head. "I never should have gone into politics. I'm afraid I've spent the past three years avoiding the whole blamed mess because I don't want to forgive either her, or myself for being relieved that she's dead."

"Obviously I've never been in your position. If anything, at times I know all too well *I'm* the embarrassing weed in the Penrose family garden. But..." she relaxed her guard, even as common sense stridently warned against it "...but Ethan, I can tell you I'd probably feel the same way you do—did, if I'd had to step into your shoes." He flashed her a grateful look, and Clara told her common sense to hush and go sit in the corner. "She betrayed you, in every way, publicly and repeatedly. I'm so sorry."

"A lot of people said that to me, back then. You're the first one I actually believe."

Oh! His compliment sang through her. "One of my more awkward flaws is my inability to dissemble to spare someone's sensibilities. You may have noticed?"

"The trait has manifested itself upon occasion."

She had always appreciated dry humor. "I've tried to...

ah…control it by…by writing." A nervous gulp of air shuddered through her body as she confessed details of her most closely guarded secret, one she had not shared even with Eleanor. The sense of fellowship with this man was a potent elixir, and Clara had been thirsty for a long time. "I spent most of my childhood with a leaky pen, holed away in nooks while I scratched ponderous thoughts on papers I scrounged from my father's study."

Pausing, she glanced up at him, wondering vaguely about the aura that seemed to have gathered around him like a cold gray mist. *Don't dry up now, Clara. He's listening closely to you, not searching for ways to shut you up.* "The habit's never changed," she plowed ahead. "Writing, I mean. I believe I mentioned nobody outside the family knows about my eccentricity? My parents never approved—my mother deplored my ink-stained fingers. Father was annoyed every time I pilfered through his desk looking for paper, even more so after he gave me an allowance and I spent most of it buying journals and foolscap instead of hairpins or hat pins or other feminine fribbles. When it became apparent that I—that I…" she stumbled a bit, then finished matter-of-factly "…that I was destined for spinsterhood, they sent me off to college, mostly because they hoped it would at least retrain my energies on something of value, like teaching or nursing. I disliked both. I now have a useless degree gathering dust in a trunk, and my parents have given up hope of reforming me into a proper Penrose. It was a relief, moving here to the cottage, where I can indulge myself to my heart's content."

"So you've never outgrown your…writing habit?"

"Well, no. And I probably wouldn't have told you, except I'd already mentioned it at my parents' dinner party." Self-conscious now, she forced the rest out before fear froze her tongue. One bared heart deserved another. "I wondered…you might want to try writing yourself? It's very therapeutic, you know. Actually, most of what I write these days are letters to editors, offering unsolicited my opinion on, um, everything. I've always admired the courage of men like you, who sought public office to proclaim their platform. Albert told me you were one of the few men he knew who believed women should have the right to vote. I've wished ever since that night we'd been able to discuss the subject. Of course, I don't have the courage to flout *that* much convention, so I write letters." After clearing her throat, she finished sadly, "Even then I use a pen name so I won't embarrass the Penrose family name."

Letters. *She wrote letters, using a pseudonym.* Despite his unwillingness to accept the obvious—Clara possessed the time, the convoluted mind and now, the predilection for the medium—he did not want to believe she was the author of the notes. It required a tremendous effort of will for Ethan to keep his voice uninflected, stripped of emotion, yet warm enough to avoid spooking the young woman sitting beside him. "So you have no secret ambition to emulate the Brontë sisters or Jane Austen? Write charming stories of life in American towns instead of English villages?"

"Heavens, no! I've little use for fiction. Why waste all your energy making something up, when real life offers more challenges?"

"Point conceded. But if you write make-believe stories, you retain all the power of the creator, where with the stroke of a pen you bless, or curse, your characters."

"A rather Machiavellian-esque touch in your mind, Dr. Harcourt? Well, I already know I'm too opinionated. Whatever characters I might create in a work of fiction would be held hostage to my own will, so I don't create them at all. Letters, on the other hand, leave the option to be blessed, or cursed, upon the reader."

Feeling trapped, Ethan casually shifted sideways. "So what do you write about, in your letters to editors?"

"Hmm?" She blinked several times. "Lots of things. Political, religious, social issues—sometimes I chastise them for their abuse of their responsibilities as journalists to, well, strive for objectivity and truth. The written word holds power, would you agree?"

Ethan managed a short nod, and Clara continued, her pale face lightly tinted with apricot. "Since I use a pseudonym, I'm fearless. My family of course would be horrified. For them public decorum and private discretion are nonnegotiable. I have a dear friend, but I've never shared this secret with her. She's a born debater and we engage in lots of lively discussions. But I don't want her reading over my shoulder. She'd argue about every phrase."

An awkward pause ensued until Clara finished lightly, "You're the only one who knows my secret vice. You'll have to promise either to be Methuselah, who certainly knows how to keep a secret, or Nim, who thinks paper was intended to be scrunched into balls and chased."

"I don't know whether to feel honored or intimidated."

Beside him Clara stiffened, and Ethan couldn't blame her; his response sounded as friendly as a trapped wolf. He wanted to bang his head against the garden shed. This was neither a stupid nor a silly woman; her candor left her particularly vulnerable, through no fault of her own. He felt like a clod, being angry with her when he was still unwilling to confront her with the suspicions that fueled the anger. Obviously she sensed something of his internal violence. Tone of voice, his expression…women possessed a sensitivity to atmosphere God had not seen fit to pass along to the male of the species. Or perhaps God just wanted to teach Ethan Harcourt a lesson in—what? Hadn't he eaten enough humility pie?

Inside the pocket of his trousers, the tiny charm of the Capitol Building seemed to scorch through the layers of fabric to burn fresh shame on his soul. *Be a healer, Ethan, not a blasted judge and jury. You've learned that at least over the past three years.*

"I've bored you, haven't I?" Clara announced. Her hand jerked in a half-abortive gesture. "Made you feel awkward, prattling away about a girlish habit I should have outgrown years ago. Forgive me. Would you like some apple cider? I still have some leftover Sally Lunn bread from the Festival I can offer as well. The cottage is woefully untidy, but you're more than welcome. Don't worry about the lack of a chaperone. I'm too old and too contrary to care. If you're uncomfortable being alone with me, Nim's pretty efficient at the task of maiden aunt." Her quick laugh emerged too high. "Which of course I am already. You needn't feel confined by convention, Dr. Harcourt…Ethan."

She stood, forcing Ethan to follow suit. *What do I do here, Lord?* "Convention is pretty necessary, under some circumstances," he returned slowly. "But not between us, hmm? We've never been conventional, have we, Clara, even three years ago? Some cider sounds pretty good."

Clara nodded without looking at him, then set off toward the front of the cottage. When they reached the door, Ethan quickly stepped in front of her to open it. She was correct—the cozy rooms on either side of the minuscule entryway *were* a mess. Comfortable horsehair furniture feminized with lace antimacassars was covered with dozens of embroidered and needle-point pillows; sheet music spilled onto the floor out of an opened music cabinet by an ebonized grand piano; stacks of newspapers and periodicals bulged from several walnut stands. A faded oriental rug covered the wide-planked floors. To Ethan's left, the other front room bulged with bookcases filling two of the walls, and a ladies' desk in the far corner. Wads of crumpled paper littered the floor, and a colorful paisley shawl draped forgotten over the spindle desk chair.

Not a single sign of Christmas, not even a sprig of holly, was on display.

Clara wandered across the parlor to the right, surprisingly turning on a pair of electric floor lamps before she lit the fire in the fireplace, laid with old-fashioned wood. With more force than finesse she gathered up an armful of sheet music and stuffed the pages into the music cabinet before finally returning to Ethan.

"Well? Would you like to sit by the fire while I prepare a tray, or shall I invent an engagement I've forgotten and allow you a graceful exit?"

He had hurt her. Now he could either inflict the coup de grace and level his accusation—or he could heed the remnant of idealism still clinging to life in a corner of his soul. "Clara…" Her name emerged on a long sigh as he surveyed her carefully expressionless face. "How about if we flout all the rules further, and I follow you to your kitchen? While you serve us up some cider, you can tell me why there's no evidence of the Christmas season inside your home."

Some indefinable emotion flickered across her face, and her erect posture seemed to droop. Then her chin lifted. "Just because I don't decorate for Christmas doesn't mean I don't celebrate the occasion."

"You have lots of habits I'm coming to know. One of the more annoying is avoiding a direct answer when you don't like the question."

"Why should you care one way or the other? Is your home fragrant with ropes of evergreens? Do you have heaps of gifts all wrapped in ribbons and sprinkled with stardust, waiting to be delivered on Christmas Eve? Is there a crèche on display in your waiting room?"

"Perhaps you should come see for yourself."

"I'm not sick."

Ethan cocked his head to one side while he sifted through the passionate outburst. "You feel you can't compete with your mother or, for that matter, your sister-in-law? Is that what this is all about?"

Clara swiveled on her heel and marched over to poke at the fire. "Don't be ridiculous. I don't decorate because it's a distraction, a sentimentalization of what should be a reverent, holy celebration."

"Hmm. I suppose a manger full of straw, surrounded by smelly cattle in a dark stable, does lend itself to reverence."

"Now you are mocking me."

"Only a little." His mood turned contemplative as he chewed over thoughts that had jigged about in his brain for a while. Here with Clara, they finally settled into place. "I've always considered the birth of any baby a miracle, worth celebrating whether the birth takes place in a stable or a castle. Perhaps all the lavish decorations folks like to display for Jesus' birth merely reflect their inadequate attempts to acknowledge what God gave up when He squeezed Himself into human form. Doesn't matter whether they live in a castle or a stone cottage, it's a way of saying, 'Welcome to the World, we're glad You stopped by.'"

"It's not the decorations God looks for, Ethan. It's how people decorate their hearts."

"Well said. Point conceded. Ah…I enjoyed the decorations you made for the Christmas Festival."

"Since you obviously enjoy debating, perhaps you shouldn't give up on running for public office. For the record…*Congressman,* I do enjoy decorating—for others." She stabbed at a log with enough force to send a shower of sparks shooting up the chimney. "For the present moment, however, let's leave it that the dearth of decorations here is because I simply don't have time, and this cottage is cluttered enough."

"You may rest assured I won't run for public office. I'm not interested in debates—except with you." The quip elicited nothing but silence. His voice gentled. "I think I understand more than you realize, Clara. A year ago I barely noted the Christmas season at all, much less sang 'Joy to the World' in a church."

Floorboards creaked as he made his way to the fireplace. The flames cast brooding shadows over Clara's face, accentuating the strong bones of her cheeks, the straight uncompromising line of her nose. But the wide mouth was trying not to tremble. Compelled by a force he no longer wanted to ignore, Ethan waited until she hung the poker on its hook, then lifted her to her feet and clasped both her hands in his. "This year, I'm finding my way back to Christmas. Your family, this town—and you—are part of the reason. Grace seems to be a concept we human beings have trouble accepting, as well as dispensing—except at Christmastime. Your outside is full of grace, Clara. Over the past weeks I've watched you scatter it freely over everything and everyone, except yourself. A little bit ago, outside, I felt that grace when without any censure you allowed me to share secrets that have festered inside for years. Trouble is, I think you're nursing a secret pain or two of your own, hiding it deep, somewhere inside where nobody can see."

"I don't want you to believe I—"

"But you let *me* see it." He talked over her, ignoring the interruption. "Clara…you let me see a part of you I've never known." Before he could regret the impulse, he lifted her hands and brushed a kiss over the backs of her knuckles. "I'll take you up on your offer of refreshments another day. I've some thinking to do, about you, about me. About…" he released her hands so he could trace the furrow between her brows with his index finger "...things." When Clara opened her mouth he shook his head at her, adding softly, "While I'm thinking, perhaps you would write a letter—to me? Only sign your real name, this time. Write me a letter, Clara."

## *Chapter Eight*

Write Ethan a letter. For the next two days Clara crammed so many activities into the hours between sunrise and midnight she scarce had a moment to eat, or even scribble a recipe for Eleanor. Nim padded after her whenever she was home, meowing pitifully and snuggling close, the tilted eyes reproaching her for her neglect.

At one o'clock on Thursday morning, after lying sleepless while the cat kneaded her shoulder and groomed her face with his rough tongue, in order to salve her conscience Clara got up and darted through the cottage, robe and gown flapping as she pulled a piece of string for the cat to chase until they both collapsed back into bed.

She could find time to placate her pet, but Ethan Harcourt was another ball of string entirely.

No matter how busy she stayed, the string *he* had cleverly dangled kept tickling her nose, no matter how many times she pushed it out of the way. Tonight she would see Ethan again, at the dinner with Albert and Bertha. Sure as oaks dropped acorns Ethan would find a way to bring up his bizarre notion that she should write him a letter.

Write Ethan a letter... How about: *Dear sir, your request for a letter, sharing personal intimacies similar to those you confided out by my garden shed on Tuesday past, exceeds the bounds of social convention even for someone who prides herself on ignoring them. If you desire written correspondence—you go first.*

Her imagined sauciness prompted Clara's first laugh in days, and she dressed with a pinch less trepidation for the evening. Her peacock-blue dress costume further bolstered her confidence—with its oversize leg-o'-mutton sleeves and figured silk skirt she might light up the room brighter than Albert's hundred-light chandelier, but nobody could accuse her of looking like a drab mouse with a drippy nose.

Words possessed such power. A soft tongue, Proverbs warned, could break a bone. And a careless tongue could wound a heart forever. *You're nothing but a dull, skinny, brown beetle, and your pointy nose always drips...I'd rather kiss a mouse in a mud hole than Clara Penrose.* Her first introduction to boys, Albert's best friend Petey Fitzsimmons, should have offered sufficient warning. But at thirteen... Clara absently smoothed her fingers down the bright blue sleeve, over and over. At nineteen, older but no wiser, the man her parents selected for her husband should have cured her forever of all romantic notions.... *No man will ever want a bag of bones with a tongue like a cheese slicer...* Those had been Mortimer's parting words. The taunts had lost their sharp sting, but even now the memories could not always be silenced.

And apparently she still hadn't learned to accept what couldn't be changed.

Defiantly Clara pulled on her cloak, pinned her hat over her topknot, then dashed out into the cold December night to the carriage Albert had sent to fetch her.

By the time the coachman turned the ostentatious brougham

into the equally ostentatious drive leading to the three-storied masonry mansion Albert had had built five years earlier, an idea had sprung forth in Clara's mind to counter Ethan's suggestion that she write him a letter.

Come morning, she would set her mind as well as her feet to the task.

"Clara! How colorful you look!" Bertha greeted her with plump, moist hands and a bosomy hug. "I've always envied a woman who could carry off that shade of blue— Nan! Come out from behind that urn at once. You know your papa warned you about slipping downstairs after bedtime."

"Want to see Auntie Clara." At six years, the youngest daughter, Nan, with her flaxen hair and blue eyes, bore an uncanny resemblance to her aunt Louise. Yet she was a studious child who preferred reading to dolls. Clara adored her.

"Hello, sweetkins." She knelt and cuddled the slight form. "You should obey your parents," she whispered in her ear, "but I'm very glad to see you."

"Papa says you wear clothes that re-resemble Joseph's cloak of many colors," Nan whispered back, and above them Bertha choked. "But I think you're beautiful, like a rainbow." After pressing a damp kiss to Clara's cheek, the child scampered back up the wide staircase. *The power of words...*

"Don't look so mortified," Clara reassured Bertha. "I rather like the comparison to a rainbow. Might even pass that one along to Albert."

Confidence intact, she sailed down the hall toward the salon, and the sound of Ethan's deep baritone voice.

Dinner was a disaster.

For some inexplicable reason Ethan was remote, even austere, not revealing by word or expression his visit with Clara on Tuesday. In fact, for most of the evening they scarcely exchanged a sentence. Because he was seated beside Louise's fiancé, Mr. Eppling, on the same side of the table as Clara, little opportunity arose at dinner to engage him in conversation, intimate or challenging. After the meal Albert promptly herded the men into the library. Bertha was summoned by the children's nanny to check on three-year-old Abner, who had woken up and refused to go back to sleep without his mama.

Clara's mother and Louise pounced upon her the moment Bertha disappeared.

"Really, Clara, challenging your brother and Mr. Penrose on pro bono counsel for the poor and elderly? Must you always trot out the radical bent of your mind and beat us over the head with it?"

Louise smacked a dramatic hand to her brow. "Mother, for goodness' sake let it rest! Why not brag about her generous heart instead. Despite her peculiar personality and 'radical mind,' she still has one, you know."

"Hmmph. And people are forever taking advantage of that as well." Mavis Penrose lifted the lorgnette she'd taken to wearing the past year and examined Clara. "Are you eating properly? You look as though you've lost weight. I'll have the cook send over some chicken soup, but you really should consider curtailing some of your charitable activities. I won't have you sicken with a cold or something more unpleasant, like influenza, for Christmas, Clara."

"I wouldn't dream of it, Mother."

"You know Clara," Louise observed dryly. "The more charity work she does, the healthier she grows." She gave her mother a brief peck on the cheek, then stepped back. Mavis Penrose discouraged affectionate displays of any kind. "At this point there's little we can do to change her inclinations. However—" in a gentle swirl of rose-colored taffeta Louise turned to Clara "—I do refuse to give up trying to instill at least a paragraph of style sense in your book-crammed brain. This evening offers the perfect illustration. I don't know how many times I've explained to you that that shade of blue—unlike the gown I picked out for you to wear at the Festival—is not good for your complexion. Turns it frightfully sallow." Louise shuddered. "Remember how Dr. Harcourt couldn't take his eyes off you last Saturday? That's hardly been the case this evening. He's not even looked your way. I wanted to kick Har—um, Mr. Eppling, for prattling on about the best fishing spots on the Potomac. We can't do anything about your costume, but let me at least refashion your hair, and I promise you'll command the doctor's undivided attention. You'd look stunning with a simple Grecian knot, sister. It would soften your face, possibly even help with that sallowness."

Clara batted her sister's hands away. "Don't touch my hair. I know you well. The last time I submitted to your pleas I looked like a—"

She stopped, her mind churning. Hadn't she decided on the drive over here to call Ethan's hand, by pursuing *him* with the same disregard for decorum he had displayed? Already her head was full of plans—baking him gingerbread men, leaving a basket full of Christmas greens anonymously on his porch, and yes, she planned to write him some kind of note on the most over-romanticized Christmas card she could buy at the stationer's. Perhaps he regretted his display of affection on Tuesday. Equally possible, however, Clara had not adequately signaled her reciprocal feelings, hence his distance this evening. Men, Louise reminded her frequently, might avoid overtly flirtatious females, but they still required sufficient encouragement to fan the flame. "What's the point in striking a match to wet wood?" she'd pointed out several days earlier.

*Time to prove you're* not *a coward, Clara.* Swallowing hard, she lifted her hands, tugging out combs and pins until her hair unfurled down her back and shoulders. "There. Do your worst. Consider this a Christmas gift."

For a humming span of time her mother and sister gawked at her as though she'd…well, as though she had announced her intention of playing the part of Delilah, with Dr. Harcourt an unknowing Samson.

"Hurry up," she said, thrusting pins and combs at Louise. "The gentlemen won't linger in the library indefinitely, suffering through Albert's and Father's ponderous speeches. Imagine the scandal, all of them trooping in here and me with my hair down." Her mother would suffer apoplexy for sure if she knew Ethan Harcourt had held her hands in his, had even brushed a kiss against her knuckles when they'd been at Clara's cottage, alone. Unchaperoned.

Or that Clara longed for more.

Fifteen minutes later, the sound of masculine voices swelled, echoing down the hall into the sitting room. Louise frantically stuffed the last pin in place. Clara had no idea what her sister had fashioned, since there was no mirror available, but she figured her hair now looked as different from her usual topknot as Louise could manage. The stage was set. She would maneuver herself close enough to force Ethan's attention, then commence whatever appropriate feminine behavior her panicked brain divulged, to indicate her reciprocal interest.

The gentlemen filled the entry, resplendent in their black tie and tails, Dr. Harcourt in the middle of the group. The hard planes and angles of his face looked more relaxed than when he first arrived. He half turned to her father. "…and I look forward to speaking with you on the matter soon."

"Anytime, sir," Clarence Penrose replied, clapping a hand on Ethan's shoulder. "Canterbury's fortunate to have acquired such a knowledgeable healer of bodies. But I must say again,

Doctor, that Congress has lost a powerful voice. Perhaps in a few more years, you'll reconsider."

Bertha rejoined the party. Chatting and smiling, she wove her way through the men, urging them to partake of dessert and coffee. Then she spied Clara. Her mouth dropped open in dumbfounded silence. Close to bolting, Clara fixed what she hoped was a congenial expression on her face.

Dreamlike, she watched Albert frown when he glanced down at his wife, watched Harry hurry over to Louise, Willy to the plate of Christmas petit fours on the sideboard.

Watched Dr. Harcourt finally turn away from her father to face the ladies—and Clara. His eyes flared wide, then narrowed to slits that reminded Clara more of a rattlesnake's stare than an admiring gentlemen struck dumb by a lady's beauty. A muscle in his jaw twitched. "Ladies." Ignoring Clara as though she had melted into the wallpaper, he bowed to Bertha. "Thank you for opening your home to a newcomer, Mrs. Penrose. Mr. Penrose is fortunate to have so accomplished a hostess for a wife."

"Clara?" Holding a delicate china plate piled with confections, Willie elbowed his way past the other men. Though twenty-one, he had not perfected the fine art of dissembling. "What in the name of Abe's aces have you done to your hair? You look like—you look…"

"Absolutely lovely," Mr. Harcourt finished smoothly, his eyes darkened to a fiery emerald green. "And now, I must beg your leave. It's late."

He turned on his heel, nodded to the others, and strode down the hall, leaving behind him a widening pool of silence.

## Chapter Nine

Friday morning, before he opened his offices for morning patients Ethan paid a visit to the sheriff's office. After the rotten fruit basket Tuesday evening and Clara's transformation the previous night, he could no longer justify a private investigation on his own. But as he drove the buggy through the almost deserted streets he continued to second-guess himself.

He should have tried harder to secure a few moments' privacy with Clarence Penrose, subtly pick his brain about Clara's childhood.

He should have conducted the Tuesday afternoon visit with Clara like a medical visit, not a blasted confessional.

If only he knew *why* she'd transformed herself the previous night—a joke on him, for ignoring her most of the evening? A ploy to force his attention? Prove he was as helpless against feminine wiles as the next man?

He had spent another sleepless night, fighting all those 'if onlys,' shadows he couldn't touch, feelings he couldn't ignore.

Whatever alchemy Clara had contrived with her hair, the result had taken his breath away. She had looked…beautiful. Bewitching.

And he was questioning her sanity.

*God help me,* he prayed the last four blocks to the town hall, where the sheriff's office resided.

Canterbury did not have a jail; on the infrequent occasions when confinement was required, law enforcement transported miscreants to the jailhouse in the town of Fairfax. Ethan pulled the horse to a stop in front of the sturdy redbrick building, for several moments staring blindly between the horse's ears before he heaved himself out of the buggy. Sheriff Millard Gleason's office was on the first floor, where tall windows allowed him to survey the busiest blocks of Main Street. When Ethan pushed open the door, the sheriff had just poured himself an earthenware mug of eggnog.

"Morning, Dr. Harcourt. What brings you to town so early in the morning?"

"My first appointment's at nine, so I'll need to head back shortly. But I…" he fought, and lost, the final battle with his heart "…I need to alert you about a…I'll call it a situation."

The sheriff's congenial expression disappeared. "What are you saying here, Dr. Harcourt? I take it this is an official call, then?"

Ethan crossed his legs, fingers hovering at his waistcoat pocket before he reluctantly pulled out the notes. "I might have a problem. But my, ah, dilemma, seems to have progressed from mischief or medical, to legal, and I don't like my conclusions. Someone's been leaving me these notes." With a sinking sensation hollowing his gut, he handed them to the sheriff. "No signature, no return address. Only the first one was postmarked."

Gleason swiftly read them, shaggy eyebrows drawing together. "Hmmph. By themselves, benign. Read all together, I can see why you're concerned. One with the postmark's from Washington, D.C. Inconclusive as far as tracking it down. What happened to this one?" He held up a discolored, rumpled note.

"Tuesday night when I returned home from evening rounds, I almost tripped over a basket of rotten fruit. That missive was stuck between two rotten apples. There were also rotten potatoes, moldy bread—and two rotten eggs. The stench was so bad I had to hire a man to scour the entire porch."

"I can imagine. Note still stinks a bit, too." Scowling, Gleason read through all three again, grunting a bit over the last one. "'More will be coming, because you deserve more,'" he read, his frown deepening. "Considering the mode of delivery, I'm inclined to agree with you, Doc. This constitutes more of a threat than a malicious prank. So why didn't you bring this to my attention first thing Wednesday?"

Ethan shifted. The back of his neck felt as though an iron spike was shoving its way to the base of his skull. "Because until the rotten fruit, it was just the notes, and they're phrased very…ambiguously. I tried to fob them off as trivial incidents, annoying rather than posing any sort of problem. When I was a congressman, this sort of thing happened all the time—the price one pays for serving the public. You learn to ignore most of them unless a specific threat is tendered."

"You're no longer a congressman." The sheriff's fingers, thick as cigars, were nonetheless nimble as he spread each note out on the desk. "So. I think the reason you've waited until now to bring those notes to me is because you have an idea who's behind this."

"I do." Ethan sat forward, while inside the sickness swam in tightening circles. "Evidence is circumstantial, a bit of conjecture. The last thing I want to do is impugn the reputation of a lady."

Gleason rumbled an agreement. "Handwriting's definitely female. From what I hear and see, there's not an unattached woman in Canterbury who hasn't eyeballed you for potential husband material, you being a fine-looking fellow and a widower. You don't strike me as a man who deliberately tramples a lady's delicate feelings, but it appears you have ruffled a feminine feather or two?"

"Not intentionally, except for…one."

"Ah." The sheriff picked up his mug of eggnog. "Well, get on with it, then. Do what you came here to do. Who's the suspect, Doctor?"

Ethan closed his eyes, braced himself, then faced the sheriff and stated flatly, "Clara Penrose."

"What!" Gleason choked on the eggnog. "Clara Penrose?" he spluttered after he quit coughing. "Clara's about as sly and secretive as a brass band. Woman's got a mouth on her, that's a fact, and she's never been shy about stating her opinion. But she's a *Penrose*. I mean, the family helped found this town. Their roots go back to the Revolution. Her father's law firm is one of the most respected on the east coast."

"Don't you think I know all that?" Ethan stood, paced the room. "Albert Penrose is my friend. I've eaten meals with the family, I've observed them in social settings. I worship with them." He whirled around and pounded his fist on top of Gleason's desk. "I feel like a Judas! But she's…she's… There are indications. Habits—"

He couldn't do it. He simply could not break confidence, not with Clara. *Even her family doesn't know.* Yet she'd bared her heart's passion for writing…with him. *But why? God? Why?* "I'm a physician," he ground out. "Regardless of the improbability, if Clara Penrose wrote those notes, my first priority is to determine the motivation. To diagnose whether her actions are malicious rather than medical. Then, if possible, to help her. But without proof, provided by trained officers of the law, I can confront neither her nor her family with any authority."

"Take it easy, Dr. Harcourt. I see your point. You're in a difficult position. Come on, have a seat. Drink some eggnog. I'll tell you what I'm going to do." The sheriff snagged a second mug from a shelf, then poured some eggnog out of a large mason jar. "I won't mention any names, but I'll have a word with Donald Fitzwalter—he's Canterbury's postmaster. Ask him to keep an eye out for any correspondence mailed to you without a return address. Also, either myself or one of my deputies will immediately commence keeping an eye on your place. Discreetly, mind you. No names will be mentioned to anyone but my two deputies. If anyone comes snooping around, we'll catch 'em in the act. But I can pretty much guarantee it won't be Clara Penrose."

By Saturday afternoon, while carefully packing fruitcake, snickerdoodles and two jars of preserves into a basket, Clara finally admitted the truth—she had fallen in love with Ethan Harcourt. Instead of the heavens opening with golden trumpets, her eyes stupidly teared up.

Her fingers fumbled with a silver ribbon she was weaving around the handle of the basket; twice she had to wipe her cheeks with the back of her hand. Despite Louise's overly romantic soul, despite the evidence in literature, poems—even Bible stories—Clara had never believed love rendered a person brainless. Yet what else could account for her stubborn refusal to scrap her "counter-courtship campaign" after Ethan had left the dinner party Thursday night with that barely civil departure?

"Intolerably rude," her mother had pronounced after the door shut behind him. Then she turned a glacial stare upon her two daughters. "As for you and your sister, I trust there will be no repeat of this ill-timed and inappropriate conduct."

"But, Mother, did you see the look on Dr. Harcourt's face?" Louise unwisely pointed out. "I think Clara poleaxed him. That's why his leave-taking smacks of rudeness."

After her mother had excoriated Louise for her vulgarisms, she'd swept out of the room. Clara had hugged her sister and escaped to the sanctuary of her cottage.

Miserably, she finished her first "secret gift" basket by covering it with a bright red tea towel, newly decorated with green holly leaves embroidered in each corner. She'd stayed up until three in the morning doing the needlework, her eyes burning along with her heart.

She wanted to believe Louise was right about Ethan's expression; it was difficult, however, when Clara felt more like the ugly duckling who had grown into an equally ill-favored duck instead of a swan. Here she was, thirty-one years old, supposedly content to be the erudite spinster of the family. *Quit lying to yourself, Clara.* Ethan's ice-tipped comment, shorn of any emotion—*She looks lovely*—had wounded her deeply. If she hadn't cared so much, if his earlier honesty and tenderness had not tricked her into trust, she wouldn't have cared two figs about his indifferent reaction to Louise's handiwork.

Love. One either soared on its wings, or sank like a stone into a bog of self-pity.

*Rubbish.* Next she would pen bad poetry instead of competent prose. Sigh over sunsets, weep by a window—a reluctant smile at last brightened Clara's mood.

Well, then. Tonight she had promised to join a group of carolers, comprised mostly of members of various church choirs, along with other townsfolk who, like Clara, possessed some level of musical training. Unless she quit mooning over her basket of goodies and instead set about delivering it, she wouldn't make it to the meeting spot on the front steps of the town hall by seven o'clock.

Moments later she let herself out of the cottage and set off down the street. The afternoon was cold, but not unpleasant. With sunbeams slanting sideways through the elms, Clara made her way to the livery stable on the edge of town, basket clutched firmly in her gloved hand. She could have walked the mile or so to Ethan's house, but she risked being seen by too many people, all of whom would ask too many nosy questions. She also refused to borrow the family runabout, because a family interrogation was worse than good-natured nosiness. Amos Todd would rent her a hack, no questions asked. She would simply tell any loiterers who perpetually gathered around the stable to gossip that she had walked to town, then decided to follow up on some duty calls which required a buggy.

Truth sometimes served better than sleight-of-handing explanations.

By the time she pulled the trap to a halt a block away from Ethan's house, streaks of red-orange and salmon pink fingered across the western sky; shadows had lengthened, allowing Clara to dart from tree to tree as she approached the house from the side opposite the door to his offices. A fine sense of the absurd fluttered beneath her breastbone, along with a recklessness that throughout her life presaged nothing but trouble.

She ducked behind the screen of some unpruned English boxwood, waiting for a carriage to roll by in the street, then two schoolboys furiously pedaling bicycles to disappear around the corner. Perhaps she would write her next letter to the editor of a ladies' magazine, warning about the irrational behavior precipitated by a heart in the throes of love.

Her family and friends...heavens, the entire community, would never believe that Clara Penrose could skulk through the bushes outside a gentleman's home. Grinning now, she hurried across to Ethan's front porch. It was half past four, and she knew his Saturday hours ran late, usually until almost six. He would still be busy with patients, all of whom would use the door on the other side of the house, leaving the front porch nicely deserted.

After some swift internal debate, Clara deposited the basket in the middle of the porch, beside the afternoon paper. The recklessness shimmied through her in a delicious shiver; she dashed back toward the boxwoods, her mind on her next "Ethan Project" until from the corner of her eye she spotted movement in the shadows off to her right. Seconds later Deputy Michael O'Shea stepped out from behind the trunk of a white pine. Arms dangling, mouth half-open in disbelief, he gawked at her as though he couldn't decide whether to socialize—or flatten her with his billy club.

Thoughts scattered, Clara gathered her skirts in her hands and ran for the rental buggy.

## Chapter Ten

$\sim\!\!\!\curvearrowright\!\!\!\bullet$

Saturday proved to be a viciously long day for Ethan. First patient of the morning was Saul Porter, who had to be told the pain was due to an incurable cancer. After that he treated seven cases of chicken pox, two of mumps, set one broken arm and two broken fingers, then puzzled over an inexplicable rash. A little past five o'clock he was about to draw his first deep breath of the day when Patricia Dunwoody dropped by with a trumped-up complaint about a dry cough.

"Tonight I'm going caroling. I was afraid not to see you, in case there's something wrong."

Ethan avoided the sweetly smiling eyes, examined her, and pronounced her in perfect health, the cough likely due to dryness in the air. "Suck on some peppermint drops," he suggested. "Take in as many fluids as possible. Nonalcoholic, of course."

She colored up prettily, and a coy smile tipped the corners of her mouth. "Of course, Dr. Harcourt. Um…would you like to join us with the caroling this evening?" she tried next. "We're always in desperate need of gentlemen who can carry a tune, and I've heard on good authority that you've a fine tenor voice."

Now his face heated. "I don't think so, Miss Dunwoody."

"Please reconsider. There's something wonderful about singing Christmas carols on a clear winter's night, bundled up with all your friends and neighbors, strolling the streets." She paused before adding casually, "Clara will be there. She doesn't have much of a voice, but she does have a good ear. You know she teaches piano?" Ethan managed a nod. Patricia finally picked up a fur-trimmed wool coat and slid her arms into the sleeves. "It's none of my business, of course, but I've known Clara all my life. Underneath her bluestocking ideas and annoying habits is a very nice person, Dr. Harcourt. She and I butt heads a lot, but…I wouldn't want her to be hurt by misunderstandings, or expectations fueled by erroneous gossip."

"I don't know, or care, about town gossip." Teeth grinding, Ethan restrained his temper. Barely. Protestations and denials would only fan the flame, so he mustered up a smile. "I'm pretty rusty at it these days, but I used to enjoy singing. Perhaps I'll join you after all, Miss Dunwoody. Thanks for the invitation."

Surprise flared in her face. While he maintained the upper hand Ethan, plying her with questions about the caroling, managed to usher her out to her waiting runabout. Dusk had fallen, the air turning colder. Streetlights threw out yellow smears of light against a darkening sky. Shivering a little, Ethan waited until Patricia expertly backed the horse, and waved as she drove away.

*Clara will be there,* Miss Dunwoody had slyly informed him. Might as well slice open a vein and let his blood drip down the middle of Main Street, since apparently nothing about his life passed unnoticed. In a burst of unspent fury he scooped up a couple of acorns, and hurled them across the street. He was no longer a politician—he was a physician, for crying out loud. What gave these people the right to poke about his private life, speculate on his personal relationships with others? Skin crawling, Ethan stalked around to the front porch to fetch the afternoon paper, and found Mick O'Shea, the deputy sheriff, sitting in one of the old cane-bottom rocking chairs the previous owner had left with the house.

O'Shea tipped his bowler back and nodded to Ethan, a grim look carving deep lines on his weather-beaten face. "Dr. Harcourt. Been waiting for you a spell." Lackadaisically he struck a match on the bottom of his shoe, lit a kerosene lantern sitting beside the chair. Light spilled across the porch, limning a wicker basket covered with a red cloth, sitting beside the paper some six yards away from Ethan. "Saw the person who left that there basket, I did. And I wouldn't be wanting to alarm ye, but 'twould seem you had the way of it. Miss Clara Penrose left it, and she wasn't wanting to be seen committing the act."

If O'Shea had punched him in the solar plexus with his billy club, Ethan couldn't have felt more sickened. With a feeling of unreality he walked across to the basket. A perky silver ribbon had been wound around the handle, ending with a fancy bow at one corner. The faint aroma of some kind of spice tickled his nose when he hesitantly picked the thing up.

He supposed he should be grateful that she hadn't left rotten fruit this time.

"You wanting me to examine that for you first, Dr. Harcourt?"

He hadn't even noticed that the deputy had approached, and now hovered at his side. "No, thanks. I'll do it. Put the lantern on the railing, if you don't mind, so I can see." Fingers numb, Ethan fumbled the cloth aside, then stared at the contents, a lump swelling in his throat. Silently he carried the basket back over to the rocking chairs and sank down in the one O'Shea had vacated. One by one he lifted out the objects, holding them where the lantern light fell. A sack full of cookies, dusted with sugar sprinkles. A loaf of fruitcake, which he quickly set aside, his stomach turning over. Fruit… Two jars of preserves.

No note.

"Thanks for waiting," he told the deputy. "I'll come by in the morning to talk to the sheriff. I'd appreciate it if you wouldn't mention this to anybody."

"I'm to stay hereabouts till midnight. If you're of a mind, I'll ask the sheriff to send along a replacement. Don't be needing mischief to befall ye, Doc."

"That won't be necessary. And you may as well go home to your wife. I'm…not going to be here this evening. I'm going caroling." Bitterness lapped over him at the prospect of singing merry Christmas melodies elbow to elbow with Clara.

Bitterness, however, was preferable to despair.

After the deputy reluctantly clumped down the porch steps and vanished into the gloom, Ethan carried the basket inside. In the silent house, the steady tick-tock of the handsome cherry wall clock he'd inherited from his father only magnified his isolation. Ignoring the time—he needed to leave in half an hour to make it to the town square by seven—he dumped the contents of the basket on the kitchen table. For some moments he sat, chin resting on the heel of his hand while he contemplated the condemnatory evidence.

Eventually he gave in and selected one of the cookies, sniffed it. If she'd laced it with some kind of poison, or any of several noxious substances designed to incapacitate but not kill, he wanted to find out now. Memories danced in ethereal will-o'-the-wisps around his head—Clara, talking to a pile of leaves with a real or imagined turtle buried in them; Clara, walking in graceful solitude to the front of the church to lay the charm on the corner of the dais; Clara, listening to him bare his soul…. *Dear God. I don't know what to do.* He had no choice but to believe O'Shea, yet he could not abandon entirely his own observations, or yes, blast it, his feelings, which insisted that Clara Penrose was not capable of this level of deceit. All the evidence accumulated against her remained circumstantial, not definitive enough to convict her of any crime but driving *him* crazy.

If amoral thieves and murderers hadn't hanged him in the southwestern desert, surely God did not intend him to perish at the hands of a spinster who talked to cats and turtles. A spinster whose personality shone with the brightness of the North Star... His free hand fumbled inside the pocket of his vest, closing around the tiny silver charm.

Abruptly he bit off half the cookie, chewed and swallowed.

Flavors exploded in his mouth—of nutmeg and sugar and vanilla, a delicious concoction too irresistible for a man who hadn't eaten since breakfast, not to mention a man who stood on the brink of destruction. Five minutes later he'd eaten every one of the cookies. As he poured himself a glass of tepid limeade from the bottle the housekeeper had left in the icebox, he finally faced a truth far less palatable than the cookies.

He'd fallen in love with a woman who baked like an angel, yet who might very well be clinically insane.

Clara shifted from foot to foot, shivering a little despite the smothering confines of coat, hat, muff and a muffler wound at the moment over half her face. It was five past seven and Jeremiah Fiske, choir director at the local Catholic church, was, with limited success, attempting to arrange the milling carolers.

"...so that each group of four comprises a harmonious whole. Please remember this endeavor will offer much more musical satisfaction to the listeners when sung in harmony."

"I only know the melodies," one of the men called out.

"Can I stay with my aunt? She sings off-key if I don't help her..."

"I have to leave by nine...."

Finally everyone was collected to Mr. Fiske's satisfaction. Clara was paired with another alto because her voice, though true, possessed little carrying power. The other three members of her little ensemble worshipped at the Methodist church; Clara had a nodding acquaintance with them but set off gamely despite learning on their first carol—"Lo, How a Rose e'er Blooming"—that Mr. Klausner, the tenor, sang with more force than purity.

It looked to be a long, chilly night.

Halfway through "O Little Town of Bethlehem" she sensed movement in the darkness to her left, and Mr. Klausner's voice faltered. She heard the rumble of a whispered exchange as another man pressed against her shoulder close enough that she felt him inhale a deep breath before he joined the carolers with a magnificently pure tenor that tripped Clara's heart. Almost unconsciously she angled her head to better blend her light alto with the new man's voice. *"No ear may hear His coming,/But in this world of sin,/Where meek souls will receive Him still/The dear Christ enters in..."*

She lost herself in the sheer joy of singing beside a man who surely must have Irish in his blood, so reverentially soaring was his voice. When Mr. Fiske signaled the carolers to move along, Clara twisted her head to compliment the newest member of her little ensemble. "You've a marvelous tenor," she began, except the group passed beneath one of the wreath-decked streetlamps, and she caught a glimpse of the singer's face. The rest of the words caught in her throat.

"I'm glad you think so," Ethan returned, light and life now stripped from his tone. "You're a marvelous cook, Miss Penrose. I ate every one of the cookies, which is why I was late arriving. I, ah, persuaded Mr. Klausner that his services had been requested for a section lacking a strong tenor voice, because I wanted to let you know my feelings about your anonymous gift."

The cookies? He must have discovered the basket, then. Should she be warmed or piqued that he had instantly divined the identity of the giver? "How do you know I left the basket?"

Above her head a sound like a hiss escaped. A strong hand clamped down on her shoulder. Even through the thick wool caplet draped over her long coat she felt the commanding strength of his grasp. "I'd like to say I recognized your handi-work. But the truth is—"

"All right, everyone," Mr. Fiske announced. "For our next song, 'It Came Upon a Midnight Clear,' we'll start with just the ladies. Gentleman, join in on the second verse."

He hummed the starting note, and all female voices save one launched into the song. Ethan's hand slid down her arm, burrowed beneath the cape so that he could grasp her elbow. "We're going to have a little chat," he whispered into her ear as he relentlessly herded her away from the carolers.

## Chapter Eleven

"**W**hat are you *doing?*" Heart thumping hard enough to make her dizzy, Clara stumbled over a crooked brick, and Ethan's hand tightened. "Ethan, I can't see well in the dark, and you're walking too fast—oomph!"

He stopped with a suddenness that made her smack straight into him. But even as she tried to pull back, his arm wrapped around her, coat and all, then he half guided, half carried her past the Gordons' house, Mrs. Brenders's boardinghouse and a packed-dirt cross street until they reached the livery stable, now deserted. Obscured by the night, a horse and buggy waited in front of the hitching post.

"Get in," Ethan ordered, his hands insistent as he virtually shoved her up onto the narrow cloth seat.

Clara might have leaped out while he walked around to untie the horse, except she was almost as curious as she was furious. The seat springs squeaked when he climbed in beside her. He jiggled the reins, setting the buggy in motion. "I've never dealt well with officiousness," she began levelly enough.

"Right now, I'm not dealing well with anything." While Clara sputtered her way through that retort he tossed a heavy wool lap robe over her. "Bundle up. I'm the only physician around Canterbury these days, and in my present mood you wouldn't want to fall sick."

"I never get sick of anything but surly high-handed males." She was grateful at the moment for the thick shroud of darkness, otherwise Ethan would be able to see her face. Surely the hurt would show—how often had he told her about her expressive face? Worse yet, tears stung her eyes.

Clara was not a weeper. One more reason she never should have fallen in love with this difficult, confusing man, she decided as one of the puddled tears finally slid down her cheek. If it wouldn't have involved fighting her way free of muff, coat and heavy lap robe, she would have swatted his arm. "Now that you've successfully abducted me, where are we going?" she asked instead.

For a sickening moment Ethan didn't respond. The horse trotted along, its hooves and the jingle of the harness the only sounds other than the rattle of the buggy wheels. Clara's vision blurred no matter how many times she blinked the moisture away.

Without warning he swung the horse to the side of the road, under a bare-branched elm whose immense trunk, when combined with the starless night, plunged them into invisibility. "I don't know where we're going," he growled before muttering some inaudible phrase. "For three years I've been doing my best to go nowhere. When I finally scrape together the courage to try living again, you come along and resurrect feelings I thought atrophied a long time ago."

"So sorry to hear you have feelings. Since you've trampled all over mine, I'll try to return the favor." Struggling furiously, Clara worked one hand free of all encumbrances, swiped her face, then attacked the lap robe. "Ever since we met again you've behaved like an India-rubber ball, bouncing helter-skelter in all directions. One moment you're a charming gentleman, the next you act as though I'm a noxious insect in need of squashing. You compare me to a *table arrangement,* but when I try to alter my appearance to look more…more womanly you storm out of the house without a word. You call unannounced, bare your soul, and now you're dragging me off in the night like a pirate! So to reassure you, *Dr.* Harcourt, I will abandon all the plans I've made, and promise to pretend you don't exist even if we have the misfortune to sit beside one another at a dinner party. And if I'm ever unfortunate enough to need a physician, I'll find one in Washington!"

"You want to talk about erratic behavior? Very well, let's look at yours. You're an educated, intelligent woman, yet for all intents and purposes your family acts as if they're embarrassed by you. You're also a striking woman, yet you seem set on hiding the beauty. You live alone, you write anonymous letters to editors that you don't want anyone to know about. You talk to me with perception and sensitivity, then turn around and…and— *Dear God in heaven.*" His voice turned hoarse, even anguished. "This is too much. I can't—"

All of a sudden his hands burrowed beneath her cape to clamp over her upper arms. "Clara, why didn't you include a note with the basket?"

She passed her tongue around dry lips and tried not to cringe. "What difference does it make? You apparently knew instantly I was the giver. I planned to include a note with my next surprise." When Ethan jerked as though she'd jabbed him with a hatpin, Clara couldn't control a reflexive flinch.

Thick silence froze the air between them.

Then slowly, his movements almost caressing, Ethan slid his hands up her arms to her face. Like Clara he wore gloves. The faint scent of expensive leather burned her nostrils and the careful touch burned her heart. "I've frightened you, haven't

I?" he asked in a voice gone soft as kidskin. "I'm sorry. Shh...don't say anything. It's all right."

"No, it's not." She sniffed loudly. Where had her righteous indignation disappeared to? "I don't understand you."

"The feeling's mutual." There was a pause. "Clara? Why, you're crying, aren't you?"

"What if I am? You drag me off into the night, hurt my feelings, then you—you..." The words dribbled to a halt because he removed his hands long enough to tug off the gloves, then skimmed her cheeks with his bare fingers. Though chilled by the winter night, his touch set off torches that heated Clara's skin and shot Chinese sparklers along her veins.

But his gentleness intensified her confusion. More tears spilled over. She heard Ethan's breath catch. "Here." He pressed a handkerchief into her hand.

Silently Clara mopped her face, and wondered if she possessed the strength to maintain her composure until she reached the privacy of her cottage. "I'm cold. I'd like to go home. Please."

"Will you at least answer a question? I know I don't have the right to ask, but...I need to. Badly."

She peered through the darkness, but could scarcely discern the faint glitter of his eyes, much less his expression. But she sensed the desperation rolling off him in waves, desperation and a profound weariness that mirrored her own. Love, Clara decided, truly left one's soul too vulnerable to pain, and all the joys promised in the Bible were not strong enough to counter it.

Yet she could not refuse Ethan's plea. Perhaps that in itself was from God—this longing to dispense reassurance, to offer comfort despite the fear of enduring further hurts. *Comfort ye, my people...*

Hesitantly, Clara allowed the tenuous emotion to fill her up, praying that her own fractured faith would still be heard with compassion.

If Ethan asked her something improper or salacious, however, she'd wallop him with the buggy whip, assuming she could find it in this ink-blot darkness. "What do you want to ask me, then?"

A short laugh was the response, followed by another moment of strained silence. "I'm probably shooting myself in the foot, but at this juncture I don't care anymore. Clara…over the past several weeks have you sent me other notes? Anonymous ones?"

Mystified, she tilted her head, straining to catch at least a glimpse of his expression. "No. I know you asked me to—" and she'd spent days fretting about it "—but I've never sent you any sort of note, anonymous or otherwise. It might sound contradictory, considering the basket I left on your porch, but it would be rude to send an unsigned note, don't you think? I don't write many personal letters—don't have time."

"You do write letters to editors, using a pseudonym."

"Which is why I don't have time to write personal notes. As you pointed out, I'm already an embarrassment to my family. They would be—I'll call it indignant—about the tone of some of my letters."

"I never should have said what I did, about your family. Will you forgive me? My sister harped about my stupidity in marrying Lillian. My dad never understood why I wanted to leave medicine for politics. But they still loved me. So does your family." He paused, then heaved a long sigh. "Never mind. I know you're still confused. I'd like the chance to explain. Actually, if you're willing to trust me enough, I'd like to show you something."

Gathering fortitude about her like chain mail, Clara cautiously responded, "I trust the man I met in a garden three years ago. I trust the doctor my brother convinced to open a practice here. As for anything else…"

"That will do for now. Whether you believe it or not, I understand. You might say I'm not the trusting sort myself, when it comes to women." He gave another bitter little laugh. "You tell yourself you'll heal, that time and God's grace will eventually do its work. You finally lower your guard—and get thrashed."

"What have I ever done, that you believe I could deliberately hurt you, Ethan?" The question burst forth, but she no longer cared a fig what emotions she revealed. Later she would work through any regrets—much later, when she was a tottering old lady who only faintly remembered what it felt like to have been seared by unrequited love. She would write her memoirs, then burn them to ashes.

"God help me," Ethan said, "but I hope the answer to your question is nothing at all." He gathered the reins and they continued down the street. "What I want to show you is in my desk drawer. If you prefer, we can stop by the sheriff's office, and have him or one of the deputies accompany us."

The sheriff's office? A niggle of alarm quickened her pulse. "Does this have something to do with Deputy O'Shea lurking around your house?"

"Yes."

"So he's the reason you know who left the basket."

"He saw you leave it, yes."

When he didn't elaborate, Clara leaned her head back against the seat and closed her eyes. Sometimes, picking at the scabs of a person's hurts left deeper scars. Lord only knew she bore a heart full of them herself. "Do whatever you want," she told Ethan.

He murmured something in response. She wasn't sure, but she thought it sounded like *If only I could.*

# Chapter Twelve

On the short and silent journey to his house, Ethan tried to pray. His thoughts had scattered like windblown snowflakes when Clara claimed she'd never written him any notes. She'd even offered an explanation, one quaintly Clara-esque, and because he wanted to believe her so badly he'd behaved like the most boorish of clods.

He had frightened her. What sort of man bullied the woman he loved into a buggy and drove off into the night with her?

*Don't ask the question if you can't face the answer.*

After securing the horse, he assisted Clara down, unsurprised when she marched down the brick walkway without once looking his way. Fortunately a streetlight illuminated the path to his front porch. Once inside, he hung their coats and mufflers on the coatrack, then led her down the hall to his office. "This won't take long," he promised, reaching for a scrap of paper and a pen. "Please sit down." She stiffly perched on the edge of the chair while he dipped the pen in ink, then handed it to her. "Would you write a sentence, anything you think of—a line from a Christmas carol, a poem? Even a shopping list will do."

"You want to see if my handwriting matches the notes, don't you?"

He nodded, noting absently that his blood pressure had given him a headache, and his insides felt as though he'd ingested an entire block's worth of bricks.

"What on earth do those notes say?" She stared blankly at the pen, then up at Ethan, comprehension draining her complexion of color. "Someone's *threatening* you, aren't they? That's why Officer O'Shea was here. He's guarding you. So where is he now? If you've been threatened, what are you thinking, to wander around without him? Ethan, why haven't you— Wait. Wait." Her gaze slid back to the pen, then the paper on the desk.

When she lifted her head again, Ethan planted his feet square on the floor and stood unmoving, shoulders braced for the killing blow. A hurt, angry woman inflicted more injury with words than any hurled stones. His hands, sweating now, curled into fists, and he could feel the nervous tic in his left eye he'd developed the year Lillian began her first affair. *God, I don't want to run anymore. Help me face her like a man.*

So he stood still while she searched his features with excruciating thoroughness. Stood while she wrote several lines on the sheet of paper, then solemnly thrust it out.

Their fingers brushed; he watched in stupefaction as color rushed into her pale cheeks, and the pen dropped with a clatter onto the desk. A blob of ink splashed onto the blotter like drops of blood. Slowly Ethan forced himself to look down at the words.

It is easy to go down into Hell…but to climb back out again, to retrace one's steps to the upper air—there's the rub, the task.

"It's from Virgil's *Aeneid*. I could have written it in Latin, but I was afraid you'd think I was showing off. Well?" She stood abruptly, chin tilted imperiously. "What do you have to say, Dr. Harcourt?"

Ethan tossed the paper onto the desk, then carefully reached for those cool, slender fingers. "I say thank God, and will you forgive me?"

"Amen. And…eventually."

A gust of pure relief weakened his knees. He brought her hand to his mouth and pressed a fervent kiss against the inside of her wrist. "Would it help if I confess that I love you, that these past few weeks have been eating me alive…and your quote could not have been more accurate if you'd been inside my head?" He smiled, loving the sight of her rapid descent into flustered confusion.

"I… What did you say?" she stammered out. "Is this another trick?"

"No, dear one. It's the declaration of a man teetering on the verge of destruction, because he was terrified the woman with whom he'd fallen in love had instead fallen into a mental abyss where I couldn't save her." Wrapping his fingers around her delicate wrist, he tugged her closer. "Not only are you inside my head, you're inside my heart."

Because he'd come to better understand her, Ethan quietly held her hand against his thudding heart and waited for her to sort everything out. The wait was not devoid of pleasure; for the first time he felt free to absorb her features—the line of her jaw, the shape of her ears and the soft tendril of seal-brown hair that had escaped to dangle along her temple. Her incredible eyes brimmed with intelligence and uncertainty and shyness.

After a while the prolonged silence began to erode his nascent confidence.

*God, I don't deserve her. But I can't bear the thought of*

*her turning away.* He should have waited, should have kept his fool mouth shut until he gained her trust again. He should have—

"Ethan?"

"Ask anything you want, sweetheart." He brushed his index finger, which trembled slightly, to the pulse throbbing in her temple. "I understand why you're confused, and I can only apologize—the rest of my life if necessary—for ever believing you'd be capable of writing threatening notes, no matter how vague the threat."

Unbelievably, Clara shrugged. "If I'd been married to a man who repeatedly betrayed me, I'd feel the same suspicion toward all other men. Without evidence to the contrary, of course you'd wonder if I'd written…whatever was written in those notes. Then for Mr. O'Shea to witness my delivery of a basket—" her eyes crinkled at the corners "—which I'm afraid was carried out in a noticeably clandestine manner, well, I'd be suspicious of me, too. You don't have to apologize. You've made it…ah, abundantly clear that I'm no longer a suspect."

Abruptly the wisp of humor vanished. "I just can't believe… I never dreamed a man, especially someone like you, would…would…"

Her voice trailed away and her eyelashes swept down to screen her expression. When she started shaking, Ethan with scant ceremony tossed convention aside and drew her into his arms. "Shh…" he whispered, pressing her head against his shoulder. "Shh…"

Her hands clutched fistfuls of his waistcoat. "You're a former congressman, a respected physician. You can't possibly lo—" She stopped.

"Love you?" he finished it for her. "Well, now that I'm convinced I'm not going to have to have both of us admitted to St. Elizabeth's Asylum, how about if I spend between now and

Christmas convincing you that, if you'll have it, my heart is yours, Clara Penrose?"

"You don't know me!" She thumped her hands against his chest. "That's why you suspected me in the first place. I'm eccentric. I live alone. I love animals and treat them like people. I have absolutely no fashion sense as you know, and I never know what to do with my hair. That's why I just stuff it in the bun. What you saw that night at Albert's house is impossible for me to duplicate. My fingers can play a Bach fugue but they don't know what to do with hairpins. And…and I believe that women really should have the right to vote and that— Mmph."

He stilled the panicked flow of words with a kiss, a brief but thorough kiss that ripped through his wavering control like a scalpel slicing cheesecloth. When Clara turned boneless in his arms, he forced himself to lift his head. "I refuse to apologize for my gross impropriety."

"Mmm. Me either," she mumbled dazedly, then blushed a lovely shade of rose.

Charmed, he cupped her chin. "As for your character condemnation—a trait we'll have to work on—I happen to believe God knew precisely the sort of woman I needed to clear the scales from my eyes. And that woman, dear one, is you."

"I always heard love was blind." Her fingers crept up to his face. "I've never been kissed like that before," she whispered. "Is it different, when you love someone?"

All the breath sucked out of his lungs. Throat tight, Ethan hugged her, dropping soft kisses to her eyelids, her nose, forehead, then finally eased her back down into the desk chair to avoid the temptation of her tremulous mouth. "What are you saying, Clara?" he asked, the words husky.

She swallowed several times, but the dark brown eyes didn't so much as flicker. When at last she spoke, the words emerged soft yet clear as a cloudless winter night. "I'm saying that I love you back, Ethan Harcourt. I'm not sure what we're supposed to do about it, though."

All the Christmas bells in the world could not equal the joyful clanging in Ethan's heart. He wanted to shout, wanted to sweep this precious woman back into his arms and never let her go.

Instead, because she was Clara, he knelt on the floor beside her, lost himself in those great dark eyes, and allowed himself one last kiss, repeating his avowal of love against her lips.

Tomorrow he would address the unknown woman's identity, and contact the sheriff. But for tonight, he needed to embrace the one he was convinced had been heaven-sent, at just the right time, for all the right reasons.

*Thanks for the best Christmas present You could give me, Lord.*

Outside, a dark figure slowly sank to the cold ground, one fist pressed against her mouth to stifle the scream clawing to escape. How could he? How *dared* he bring a woman to his house, late at night, without even a butler or housekeeper in residence? He knew better. And the woman—she knew that woman. She'd seen her face in the streetlight when the doctor helped her out of his buggy. Of all the women in this self-righteous little community, Clara Penrose should know better than to engage in such scandalous behavior.

Except she *was* Clara Penrose, who, despite her unconventional ways, was considered practically a saint. Oh, she'd heard all the stories in the boardinghouse. It was Miss Penrose this and Miss Penrose that. They might talk behind their hands about her eccentricities, but they still thought she set the moon and stars in place.

Well, perhaps Clara Penrose's reputation deserved a readjustment.

Her previous warnings to Ethan Harcourt had not achieved the desired effect. She had been too cautious. Too…squeamish.

Huddled on the bone-chilling ground, she rocked back and forth, awful memories swirling around her in shades of scarlet and orange and black. It wasn't fair, wasn't fair, *wasn't fair.*

Gradually a thought formed deep inside, gathering force until it dispelled the ugly memories. A slow smile spread across her cracked lips and chilblained face.

Yes. The idea offered a perfect solution, though she didn't have much time to gather everything. She risked one last peek through the window, which revealed two silhouettes still at the desk. The Penrose woman looked to be reading something while the doctor stood close by her side, his hand resting on her shoulder.

The woman slipped away from the window and melted into the night.

# Chapter Thirteen

Despite the chilly December night, Clara decided she felt like an icicle in sunshine. Shiny but brittle, soaking up the warmth, and melting into a blissful puddle. No wonder Louise wandered about with a glow on her face.

Love might be worth the painful uncertainty after all.

After they left Ethan's house, he drove the buggy back to the town square, where other carolers had parked their conveyances, instead of taking her directly home. When he lifted Clara down, the tingling warmth from the firm touch of his clasp around her waist permeated all the way through the layers of heavy fabric. Clara Penrose, the skinny town spinster, was strolling down Main Street with a man, a man who was *holding her hand*.

A man who claimed to love her.

Her heart skipped a beat, and so did her feet.

"Easy." Ethan's grip slid to her elbow, his voice murmuring low in her ear as he steadied her. "Remind me not to take you on a hiking expedition at night."

Clara stifled a laugh. "Disastrous," she whispered back.

A dozen yards away the carolers launched into the first

verse of "As with Gladness Men of Old." Without a word of communication both she and Ethan began singing along. By the time the first verse ended, they had eased into a clutch of singers at the back of the group, Ethan's hands now clasped behind his back, Clara's burrowed deep inside her muff.

Perhaps it was only her imagination, but—did the singing sound richer, the harmony a perfect balance of voices proclaiming the good news of Jesus' arrival? The delicate icicle feeling melted into the gladness of men of old as Clara blended her voice with Ethan's and those of the smiling carolers around them.

Two songs later, after a rousing chorus of "Joy to the World," with effusive expressions of gratitude for their splendid performance, Mr. Fiske dismissed everyone. Clara and Ethan were immediately surrounded, and spent several chaotic moments fending off invitations to thaw out in friends' homes while everyone wandered back to the town square. Finally only a handful of people remained, most of them choir members from another church who were noisily piling inside an old wagon.

"Did you walk from your home, Miss Penrose?" Ethan inquired politely.

"Why, yes, I did, Dr. Harcourt," Clara responded with reciprocal cordiality. "Every year I remind myself that I'll regret the decision by the end of the evening. But when the weather's clear and not too frigid, I enjoy being out in it." She had to bite the inside of her cheeks to keep from breaking into a fit of giggles.

"Miss Penrose." From behind Ethan, Mr. Fiske loomed out of the darkness. "Might I have a brief word with you, please? I would be more than happy to offer you a ride home in my trap while I discuss my plans for an ecumenical hymn sing on the twenty-third. I was hoping you'd be the accompanist, since my organist is unavailable."

"I...I..." Her usually nimble brain seemed to have frozen like her fingers and toes.

"I'm afraid Miss Penrose has already accepted my offer to take her home," Ethan declared, pulling her hand through his arm.

The streetlight illuminated Mr. Fiske's face. He looked from Clara to Ethan, and a little smile softened the disappointment in his eyes. "I see. I won't keep the two of you any further then." His smile broadened, and before he turned away Clara thought he winked at Ethan.

"Oh, dear." Clara laughed. "The gossip will ignite now. Mr. Fiske loves to talk about folks almost as much as he loves singing with them."

"Good. Let the whole world know." He lifted her back into the buggy, tucked the lap blanket around her, and after settling beside her on the seat his arm came round her shoulders. For a moment he didn't move, just hugged her in the darkness.

"Ethan? What is it?"

"Nothing, my sweet. No," he corrected, and his lips pressed a soft kiss against her temple, "no more evasions between us. I was loving the lilt in your voice, and wondering how many years it will take for me to get over feeling guilty for thinking *you* were..."

Ah. The notes again. "I know about guilt." Sighing, she settled back against the seat, the warm but unfamiliar weight of his arm more comforting than the most luxurious of fur stoles. "It never solves anything. I told Methuselah once that guilt reminds me of mildew. No matter how hard I scrub the floor, there's a corner near the back door where I can never seem to get rid of it. The odor permeates everything. I try not to put anything on the floor there."

"An apt metaphor." For a little while they rode in silence, the steady clip-clop of the horse's hooves beating with metronome precision. "What guilt are you wanting to scrub away?" Ethan asked finally, the arm around her shoulders tightening again. "It's not writing letters to editors, is it?"

"No." She'd wondered when he would ask, but until this moment she had not been sure of her response.

"Will you tell me about it?"

Because God had apparently decided to give her a man who said he loved her for Christmas…and because she loved the man back, Clara told him. "When I was nineteen, my parents informed me they had arranged for me to be introduced to the man I was to marry. After sifting through a number of candidates, they'd picked a state senator with congressional aspirations. I was young, with grand ideas of my own. I didn't fret overmuch about love. Marriage, we Penrose children were informed frequently, was about suitability, not sentiment." A little laugh more close to a sob escaped and she hurriedly finished, "I agreed without a fuss. I was… I had my own dreams…"

"We all do," Ethan observed, his voice comfortably matter-of-fact. "What happened to you and your perfect candidate for the office of husband?"

"Oh!" She rubbed her cheek against his forearm, the only part of him she could reach. "I've always believed a sense of humor offers one of God's most effective tinctures against life's hurts. One of the reasons I eventually refused Mortimer was because he didn't have one. He considered laughter a 'vulgar expression of the bourgeoisie,' was how he phrased it."

"Met a few of those myself. Insufferable snobs, aren't they?"

"My parents didn't see it that way. He was wealthy, attractive and willing to overlook all my flaws. I was, of course, expected to overlook all of his, which, along with advanced snobbery and no humor, included an insatiable thirst for liquor. I never saw him drunk, but I also never saw him without a drink of some sort in his hand. When I queried him on the matter, he reminded me that only one opinion counted—his own." After a brief internal debate she added sadly, "But the main reason I finally couldn't agree to the marriage is one I never told my family, because I…because…" She swallowed hard, annoyed that even after all these years the raw spot hadn't completely healed. "It's a silly reason, I expect. I don't know why I can't just spit it out and be done with the subject."

"I doubt *silly* is the appropriate application," Ethan said. "It's all right, Clara. You don't have to tell me anymore right now."

"Yes, I think I do." She stared straight ahead, into the silvery-black night that no longer made her feel safe. "Because it's one of the reasons I struggle with guilt. You see…I discovered Mortimer was a—a mean-spirited hypocrite. Quoted scripture, prayed unctuous prayers and promised my parents that our children would grow up in a Christian home. I discovered the truth by accident. Overheard him tell one of his friends he was marrying a bony Christian chit with too much virtue and not enough vanity. He supposed he'd have to attend church, but faith in God was a waste of time. Jesus might have existed, but He was no more the Son of God than Mortimer's valet, who at least knew the difference between a Windsor knot and a four-in-hand. I tolerated the slurs against me. But I challenged him about his faith, and was again ordered to keep my mouth shut, or after we married he'd turn my life into— Well, never mind what he said. I ended the engagement. Six months later he married a debutante from Richmond. For months Mother badgered me about her disappointment or ignored me completely. My father shrugged, told me to ignore my mother back and proclaimed to everyone he talked to that he was resigned to his eldest daughter's status as the family old maid."

Without warning Ethan pulled the buggy to a halt, right in the middle of the road. "We'll see about that," he snapped, the arm around her shoulders hauling her so close she felt the huff of his breath on her face. "I've had a bellyful of people inflicting their warped opinions on others, particularly the ones they're supposed to love. I wish Mortimer and my wife had met. They certainly deserved each other." Once again he cupped her face in his gloved hands, his thumb brushing the sensitive skin beneath her jaw. "I think it's time we both let the past go, don't you?"

His touch soothed, yet set every nerve to jumping. "Yes." Her voice broke on the word. "I don't care about Mortimer, and I've made peace with my parents, Ethan. It helped when I moved out, and Louise has softened my mother's attitude. It's just that…I don't want to be a hypocrite myself. I believe in God, I do. I believe Jesus is His Son, that He willingly sacrificed His life for me. But sometimes…sometimes I feel like I'm only saying words, especially at Christmas. I wouldn't marry a hypocrite—I'm terrified I'll become one."

"Mm. So…no decorations in your home. No dreams of Santa filling your stocking with oranges and nuts and candy canes…"

"Yes. I know it's silly, but—yes. It's just I…I have all these questions without answers. I feel when I should be thinking, and think when I should be feeling."

She pulled her hand free of the muff and blindly reached to lay it against *his* cheek, drawing strength from the beard-roughened skin, the firm line of his jaw. "It's exhausting, trying to live my faith. Some days, I'm tempted to stuff it in a box, because no matter how many letters to the editor I write, no matter how many 'good works' I perform to help people, there's all this pain in the world. So much evil. Yet right now…"

The words trailed away in confusion and she paused, astonished at herself, a little afraid of Ethan's reaction. But his head merely shifted against her hand and, rumbling vague encouraging sounds, he brushed a kiss against the palm resting on his cheek.

No condemnation, no condescension, not even a lecture.

Drawing in a grateful breath, Clara shared the last of her thoughts, one in particular that had churned in her mind these past few hours. "The woman who's writing you those letters? I recognize the implied threat, and I'll do everything I can to assist you in discovering her identity. But she hasn't physically harmed you. If she did I…well, I'd drag her by her hair to jail myself—ooh, *this* is what I was trying to explain! There's this unruly piece of my heart that isn't very Christ-like toward this woman. But the rest doesn't want her in jail, particularly over a few malicious letters. I—I want to help her."

"I believe what that makes you is human, not a hypocrite, Clara. I've struggled with similar thoughts myself, and some worse. Want an example?" When Clara nodded her head he continued, his voice wry, "How about…I used to believe that service to my fellow man—whether as a doctor or a congressman—was sufficient for God to overlook my less-than-pure attitudes and behavior. See? My badge of faith is every bit as dented and tarnished as you perceive yours to be. What's more, if this unknown woman hurts *you*, I'd be tempted to dispense with jail altogether, and administer my own brand of justice." The arm around her shoulders jostled her a little. "We both know that we'll do the right thing, in the end. Sin isn't the temptation—it's giving in to those base urges and impulses."

A feeble star twinkled to life inside her. "You're right. You make a much better confidant than a turtle, Dr. Harcourt." When he laughed, the starlight burned even brighter. "I feel much better. And when we discover the identity of this unknown woman…? I think…I think perhaps that's how to live our faith when we don't feel the words. Help someone else who's hurting inside."

"I think you're right, and that I should buy you a camel, Miss Penrose." He dipped his head and pressed the lightest of kisses against her half-parted lips. "But instead of offering gold, frankincense or myrrh, I recommend some of those cookies like the ones you left on my doorstep. I love you very much, Clara," he continued. "All of you, especially the struggling parts. I understand why you don't quite trust my love, that you don't quite believe it's going to last. That's all right. I've squandered a good many years of my life, so I figure I can invest some time in pursuing what I believe is God's personal gift to me for Christmas this year—you."

He released her and set the buggy in motion once more.

"But…that's how *I* feel!" Clara exclaimed. "While we were singing those carols to the townsfolk of Canterbury, I was really singing them to God, because I wanted to thank Him for giving me the most wonderful gift I've ever received for Christmas. For the first time in a very long time, I was feeling the words as well as singing them."

"I know exactly what you mean." Ethan pulled the horse to a stop by the path that led to the cottage.

Wrapped in wonder, Clara floated out of the buggy onto the frost-stubbled grass, one hand inside the muff, the other nestled securely in Ethan's.

The stench assailed their noses before they walked half a dozen paces down the flagstone path to the front door.

## Chapter Fourteen

An unnatural pall hung in the air. The noxious odor flooded Ethan's senses even as warning pumped through his veins. "Get back in the buggy," he ordered, stepping in front of her.

"I will not!" Clara shot back, the words crackling in the still night. "This is my home. What *is* that horrid odor?"

"Rotten garbage, among other equally putrid things. Dumped on the path just inside your gate." Muscles taut, he peered through the stygian darkness, searching for movement, ears straining for sound. "Clara, I haven't told you everything about the woman. Last week, she left one of those notes in a basket on my front porch, only, unlike you, she'd filled hers with rotten fruit. So please, love, get in the buggy. Let me search—"

"No wonder you've had such a miserable few weeks, and don't be ridiculous." When Clara stubbornly shoved past him he grabbed her even as he conceded the battle. "At least hold my arm so I can guide you. I don't want you stepping in the mess."

Gingerly he led her around it, his skin prickling. "There's more, I'm afraid. Looks like it's all over your front stoop."

"It's her, isn't it? Only this time I'm the victim, not you. She must have been spying," Clara hissed the last sentence from the side of her mouth. "When you took me to your house, to show me the notes, she—" A gasp choked off the words. "Ethan, *what if she went inside?* I never lock my door. Nim… NimNuan!"

Frantically she struggled against him, her breath ragged with fear. "I have to find him. Nim. P-please, God. Please…"

His own heart slamming against his rib cage, Ethan clamped both her forearms, trapping her inside her cloak against his chest. He pressed his face close against hers. "We'll find Nim. But you have to calm down. You told me you have a back door?" He barely made out her nod. "All right. We'll go inside that way. Hold my hand, there you go…shh. He'll be all right, Clara."

"You don't know that." She choked on the words, and Ethan could hear her teeth chattering. Even through their gloves he could feel the pulse galloping in her wrist at breakneck speed.

No, he didn't know what might have happened to Nim. But he did know Clara was on the verge of shock, and the last thing he wanted right now was to confront a deranged woman when he was administering aid to an ill one. Grimly he lifted her completely off her feet, swinging her over a stinking mass of garbage, then led her down the flagstones to the back of the cottage.

The door gaped wide-open.

A whimpering cry burst from Clara's throat. Ethan forced her behind him, and used his body to block the entrance. He could see a bit of light coming from the kitchen, and his nostrils stung with the mildewy odor Clara had described earlier. Slowly, one arm stretched like a bar across the threshold, he eased into a minuscule mudroom, his gaze swiftly searching the dark corners for movement.

"Ethan. Please…" Clara pushed against his arm, her hands digging into the wool of his overcoat. "I can't bear this…"

Grimly he stepped forward and forced himself to peer into the kitchen, dread and fear and determination tangling his own insides into knots.

A square oak kitchen table with four press-back chairs sat in the middle of the floor. An oil lamp had been lit and placed atop the table. A woman dressed in black widow's weeds sat in one of the chairs. Another oil lamp sat beside the sink, its light shining on a pile of damp rags from which the putrid odor emanated, though less strong.

Purring noisily, NimNuan sat on the widow's lap, his blue gaze trained upon Ethan.

Suddenly Clara shoved her way past him to charge into the kitchen, where she came to a dead halt. Ethan came to stand beside her.

"Nim!" she cried brokenly. The cat leaped down and streaked across the floor. Clara scooped him up into her arms and buried her face in the cream-colored fur.

Ethan scratched behind one chocolate ear, then skimmed his fingers soothingly down one of Clara's tear-dampened cheeks; all the while his gaze remained trained upon the other woman.

"I wouldn't have hurt him," she spoke into the charged silence, her voice surprisingly refined.

"That's good." Approaching her carefully, he watched her eyes, which after a moment flickered before she turned her head away. Her hand, reddened but scrubbed clean, lifted to her throat. Ethan pulled out one of the chairs and eased down beside her. "What's your name?" *Stay casual,* he repeated to himself, while his trained gaze noted the gaunt, paper-white cheeks, the tremor in her hands and the eerily calm rise and fall of her breathing.

"Velma Chesterton."

She met his gaze, and even as he sifted through his memory he automatically catalogued the dilated pupils in her light blue eyes—and the expression of shame. Deranged individuals did not manifest an awareness of inappropriate behavior.

"You don't remember me, do you?" she asked, her voice resigned. She lifted one hand to wearily press her fingers to her temple, and the lamplight caught on the dull gold of her wedding band.

Shock jolted Ethan's heart as the name finally clicked into place. "Chesterton," he repeated with lips gone numb. An amalgam of memories poured through him. "Your husband was Senator Chesterton, from…Indiana?"

"Iowa." The haunted gaze moved beyond Ethan to Clara, then returned to Ethan. "I've always loved animals. I grew up on a farm. When we moved to Washington, my husband promised I could have a pet to keep me company, because he would be gone so much. But he died. *He died and it's your fault.*"

Ethan's muscles tensed, instinctively ready to defend Clara, or himself, from physical attack.

Seemingly impervious to the seething atmosphere, with Nim draped over her shoulder in a limp purring bundle, Clara sat down opposite Mrs. Chesterton, then transferred Nim to her own lap. "What do you mean, it's his fault? Why have you committed all these acts of vandalism against Dr. Harcourt?" she demanded. "What has he ever done to you?"

Clara was not a woman to beat about the bush.

"He didn't control his Jezebel of a wife!" The words spewed across the table. "He stood by and watched while she seduced my husband. Never lifted a hand, never made her leave him alone. If he'd done his duty by her, I wouldn't be a widow, haunted to this day by the scandal of it all. I'd still be a wife. I'd have a husband who loved me."

Tears glazed the fever-bright eyes, their gaze locked on Ethan. "I heard when you returned, heard all about the congressman who went back to doctoring in this idyllic little town in Virginia, only an hour's ride from where you failed your wife and turned your back on your duty to your country. It wasn't fair. Your wife ruined my life, and here you are, cool as you please, setting up a medical practice, buying a home." The long fingers curled into fists. "And then…and then you have the audacity—*both of you*—to engage in the same sordid behavior that robbed me of my husband."

Rage scorched Ethan's body in a conflagration. "Madam, you may level any attacks at me and I'll answer to them. But you will not impugn the character of Miss Penrose." He planted his palms on the table and stared the woman down until she turned her head aside. "May I remind you that my wife, like your husband, is dead. I am legally and morally free to pursue any unmarried woman I choose. And if that woman accepts my attentions, you *will not* accuse either of us of less-than-honorable behavior."

Clara soothed an alarmed Nim with one hand while she stretched her other across the table, resting it on Ethan's forearm. "Mrs. Chesterton, I think you should be careful about painting a scarlet letter on my back, when you're the one who's guilty of trespassing, not to mention vandalism."

The other woman's face crumpled. She fumbled a black hankie from her sleeve and dabbed her eyes. "You're right. I'm sorry, so sorry. I don't know what came over me. Ever since that awful night when my husband perished, I haven't been myself." She glanced at Ethan with streaming eyes. "I couldn't bear returning home to Iowa in shame, nor could I stand the gossip and the looks of pity. For the past three years I've been living in a one-bedroom apartment, so full of anger and bitterness I could scarce swallow a bite of food. The day after I learned you'd returned to Virginia, I took the train here. Took a room in a boardinghouse. I s-saw when you put out your sign.

Watched all week how patients flocked to see you. It was as though you had erased the past, while I..." she twisted the damp handkerchief into a gnarled rope "...I couldn't escape from it."

"So you decided Dr. Harcourt deserved to be as miserable as you?" Clara asked, though her tone remained mild. The hand stroking Nim never wavered. "Hence the letters?"

A sigh shuddered through Mrs. Chesterton's body. "I never intended any real harm. I was just... The anger... It was choking me alive. Writing those notes—it seemed harmless enough. It...helped."

"And the basket of rotten fruit?" Ethan put in, eyeing her without sympathy. "The garbage all over Miss Penrose's front porch and path?"

"I shouldn't have done that. I do realize now. But the feelings... For the first time I was focusing on something other than my own suffering. I even slept at night. Except the notes...after a while, they weren't enough. I knew I needed to stop, but I couldn't. I...couldn't."

"Why did you come into my house?" Clara suddenly blurted. Nim stretched his front paws up on her shoulders, as though he were embracing her, and let loose a plaintive meow. Clara's eyes teared, and she tucked the cat against her like a small child. "Thank you for not hurting my cat," she whispered. After clearing her throat, she finished more strongly, "My house—why *did* you stay?"

"I'd frightened your kitty, when I was—" Her shoulders hunched, and her feet shuffled nervously. "He came up behind me, out front, and meowed. I was so startled I dropped the, um, well, the sack, and your kitty ran off. I felt so bad. I followed him, and he was there, at the back door. Sh-shaking." She covered her face with the handkerchief, but after a moment managed to continue. "I opened the door for him, and he ran inside. I wanted to reassure him, but my hands were filthy. So I washed them in your sink, and while I was washing them he came over and sat at my feet. He's so beautiful, and he started purring, and making strange sounds, almost as though he were…"

"As though he were talking," Clara finished. "He was. Nim's not your ordinary barn cat. He's from Siam, and he thinks he's supposed to converse with humans. He's also discriminating about his company. Normally he doesn't take to strangers, particularly ones in the process of slinging garbage all over my yard."

"After I washed my hands, he let me hold him." She glanced from Clara to Ethan, deep lines scoring her forehead and cheeks. "I know what I've done is dreadful, unforgivable. But you must believe me about the cat. I would never hurt him, or any other animal. And even when I wrote those notes, I knew it was wrong. I knew, but I couldn't stop. I'm sorry. So sorry."

A strange sensation feathered through Ethan, like the brush of warm invisible fingers. The outrage seemed to swell like a cresting wave before it receded into a widening pool of…peace. "I know a thing or two about guilt, and lack of forgiveness," he said, and had to clear his throat before he could finish. "I've spent the past three years hating my wife, feeling guilty because I wasn't the man she wanted me to be. Those injurious emotions almost cost me the love of a good woman."

When Clara's hand lightly slid over his shoulder, he turned toward her—and instead found himself inches away from a pair of myopic blue eyes. A smile that started deep in Ethan's belly whooshed up and tugged at the corners of his mouth. "Not to mention the love of a good cat." When Nim more or less poured his agile feline body into Ethan's arms, all Ethan could do was accept the lithe bundle and grin. "Tell you what, Mrs. Chesterton. Tomorrow morning you clean up the mess you made out front, then you come with me to the sheriff. I think we'll be able to clean up the rest of the mess you've made of your life without too much trouble. As for the past—" over Nim's head he and Clara exchanged a warm look "—perhaps Miss Penrose and I can help a bit with how to let it go. Some things aren't worth hanging on to."

For the first time he looked at Velma Chesterton with compassion, and saw enough of himself to realize Clara was right—sometimes living one's faith simply meant helping a hurting person, regardless of the state of your own emotions. "I've also rediscovered the love of God," he confessed, his skin suddenly prickling with that indescribable sensation of warmth infusing his heart—his soul, his spirit. "I'd say it's long past time to quit toting the coffins of our respective spouses on our backs. I believe, with God's help, I can dump mine in the grave where it belongs. Then between the two of us, not to mention the help of a good woman and her cat, we ought to be able to do the same with yours."

"I don't deserve… I don't understand." As though she couldn't help herself, Mrs. Chesterton reached a trembling arm out, her fingers barely skimming Nim's furry belly. "You have no reason to be kind," she whispered.

Clara rose and walked around the table. "It's Christmas," she said, leaning down to give the other woman a hug. "It's the perfect time of year for kindness. Forgiveness. And new hope. Some weeks ago our minister gave the congregation a task. We were to bring symbols of our burdens, and lay them in the manger, renouncing them in order to celebrate the Christmas season. I had broken dreams, just like you, dreams that were never realized. So…I listened to our minister, and I let them go—and God supplied me with something infinitely more wonderful."

"After we take Mrs. Chesterton home," Ethan commented, gently depositing Nim on the floor, "I have something to share with you about that Sunday and the symbol you left at the altar."

# *Epilogue*

On a blustery afternoon two days before Christmas, Clara was busily writing when someone pounded on the door. When Clara opened it, Ethan stood grinning on the freshly scrubbed stoop, his thick hair wind-tossed and a glint sparkling in the clear green eyes. "Good. You're not busy. I've brought something, and I'll need your help with it."

"Ethan, what on earth—? And I am busy. I'm writing."

"Your letter to the editor can wait."

"It's not a letter," Clara began, but he had turned aside and leaned down. When he straightened, his arms were full of a fragrant little fir tree.

"You'll need to clear off that table under your window. I think this tree will look quite nice on it." And with Clara dazedly trailing after him he proceeded into her parlor, set the tree on the floor, then strode back outside to return with a large gift-wrapped box tied with a huge red ribbon. "Here. Open this while I clear the table."

"You brought me a Christmas tree."

"I've always known you were an intelligent, observant woman. Open the box, sweetheart."

A whoosh of sentimentality gummed up her throat, paralyzing her vocal chords. Clutching the box to her middle, Clara watched while Ethan cheerfully cleared the tabletop and plonked the tree—to which two strips of wood had been attached crossways, forming a stand—right in the center. A fresh, resiny fragrance permeated the air.

Nim strolled in from the bedroom, instantly going over to strop himself against Ethan's legs before rising up to sniff the tree. Smiling, Ethan gave the cat an affectionate pat before walking back over to Clara. "Looks perfect, doesn't it?" Gently he removed the box from her unresisting hands. "Like Christmas has finally arrived at Clara's cottage."

"You're impossible, and I love you." She reached for the box, her heart fluttering at the same time the rest of her seemed to be dissolving like the sugar glaze she'd applied to a batch of cookies she'd made that morning. "Your present isn't ready yet."

"This isn't a present, it's decorations. Hurry up and open the box. This will take some time."

So Clara ripped off ribbon and paper and lifted off the lid, to discover dozens of tissue-wrapped objects nestled inside. The objects turned out to be tiny charms, like the one of the Capitol Building she'd relinquished weeks earlier. Only these charms were made of gold. "Ethan… You… I don't know what to say." Eyes filling, she held up the first one, a long-tailed cat with a mischievous smile. Bright blue-colored glass eyes winked in the December sunlight pouring through the window. "It's Nim!"

"Keep going. Methuselah's in there somewhere."

Until this moment, Clara had never experienced the childlike joy possible only at Christmas. Each charm elicited a happy gasp, a delighted laugh, a sigh of contentment. Ethan helped her tie them to the tree with strands of red ribbon—a turtle, as promised, a piano, a key…

"The key to my heart," he told her as he brushed a circumspect kiss against the nape of her neck, sending a wave of goose bumps all over Clara's skin.

"I love you, Ethan Harcourt," she replied. "And I'll cherish my Christmas tree forever. But don't delude yourself for an instant if you think I plan to consider any garlands, or gilded angels, or magnolia leaves and sprigs of ivy, or— What's that?" He had reached inside his waistcoat to tug something out, which he shielded from Clara with his other hand.

"I thought I'd defer negotiations on appropriate Christmas decorations until after I gave you your Christmas present."

"But…Christmas is still the day after tomorrow. You were supposed to wait. I told you I haven't finished—I mean, I'm not ready to give you— Oh, padiddle!" Eyes narrowed, she lunged for his hands. "What is it, then?"

Ethan held his hands up high, way beyond her reach. "Are you sure you don't want to wait for another forty-eight hours?"

"If you'd wanted to wait, you shouldn't have teased me." Exasperated, she picked Nim up, then turned her back on Ethan, ostensibly to study her lovely tree, proudly displaying the dozen gold charms amongst its fragrant branches. "I can't wait for everyone to see this. Albert will take all the credit for introducing you to me in the first place. Eleanor will probably kiss you—no, she'll shake your hand, firmly. Willy will offer to take you to his favorite fishing spot and Louise will enlist your aid on the sly, to hang a few greens and some mistletoe."

"I like the mistletoe part. What about your parents?"

For a second the old defensive misery dimmed the present glow. But as she absorbed the kindness in Ethan's eyes, the defensiveness transformed into an extraordinary lightness. "Mother will rearrange the charms to her liking. Father, as he comments every visit, will suggest I either rid myself of half the furniture, or move someplace where he won't trip over a footstool or something. They might congratulate you on re-forming their daughter."

"Well, their daughter *transformed* me." Slowly he returned whatever he'd been holding to the pocket of his waistcoat. "Perhaps I'll wait until Christmas Day after all. I want your whole family to witness how much I love you."

"Ethan…Louise has been matchmaking from the first time she heard about you. Our feelings for one another, especially after you and Mrs. Chesterton talked with Sheriff Gleason, by now fuel every conversation in Canterbury from dawn until dusk." After putting Nim down, she approached Ethan, grateful when, without asking, he took her hands and tugged her closer. "Speaking of Mrs. Chesterton…I learned she was a church organist before she married. Oh, and she's no longer wearing widow's weeds."

"I know. She stopped by yesterday to offer me another basket, this one filled with fresh oranges, nuts and a mince pie." He grinned down at Clara. "She's not as good a cook as you, but it was nice seeing her looking the way a woman ought to look, delivering food fit for human consumption. She also included a formal note of apology, on the same stationery, only this time she signed it."

"Feels good, doesn't it, watching her bloom?"

"Mm. Not as much as watching the woman I love bloom." His gaze wandered lazily over her. "Your hair looks nice today. I like the way you moved the bun from the top of your head to the back of your neck. I especially like the strand of hair dangling by your ear. Have I told you how much I love your ears?"

Clara blushed and took refuge in a geyser of words. She wasn't sure she would ever entirely believe Ethan's effusive blandishments, but she hoped he'd never cease giving them. "I, um, I took Mr. Fiske to Mrs. Chesterton's boardinghouse after church this past Sunday. They developed an instant rapport. She's playing for the community hymn sing tonight. From the gleam in Mr. Fiske's eye within an hour of meeting her, I've a hunch he won't be inquiring about my services as an accompanist much longer."

"Good."

They stood together in a puddle of sunshine, listening to the wind rattle the shutters and the fire crackle in the parlor fireplace, holding hands and basking in a transcendent peace.

"Ethan?"

"Hmm?"

"I don't want to wait for Christmas Day."

"I know. I don't either." He reached back into his waistcoat, and withdrew a small box. "Here."

Fingers suddenly unsteady, Clara took the proffered box and fumbled it open. Nestled in a bed of midnight velvet was the small charm of the Capitol she'd laid on the altar. "I don't understand." She lifted uncomprehending eyes to Ethan's.

"The first Sunday I went to church was the Sunday when the minister asked you to leave your burdens. Yours was accidentally left behind, so I picked it up. I've been carrying your secret burden ever since. Now I think it's time for us both to follow Reverend Miggs's counsel, and lay this at the foot of the manger."

As he spoke he produced a slender red ribbon, took the charm out of the box, threaded the ribbon through the hole and handed it back to Clara. "There's a nice spot on that branch, just below the manger charm."

Feeling as though she were dreaming, Clara carefully looped the ribboned ornament so that it dangled close by the charm depicting a manger with the Christ child sleeping peacefully in the hay. "I had no idea," she whispered. "All this time…"

"Even back then I found myself needing to protect you, wanting to discover all your secrets. Though I didn't comprehend God's fine hand at work, I couldn't shake you loose from my mind. Now that I understand why…" he plucked the box from her hand, removed the scrap of velvet, then handed the box back to her "…I'm hoping to replace your old burden and lost dreams…with this."

Speechless, Clara stared up into his face until with a little laugh he clasped her chin with his thumb and index finger, gently forcing her to look down into what she'd thought was an empty box.

Instead of a tarnished silver charm of the Capitol Building, a ring holding a diamond surrounded by sapphires lay in the bottom, waiting in splendid silence.

"Is that for me?" she stammered.

"Well, I suppose it might fit Nim's tail, but I'm not sure it's his style." Laughing, he waited with more patience than Job until Clara finally scraped together the wit to gingerly clasp the ring.

"Does this mean—?"

"Yes. Now it's your turn to say the word. Would you like some help with the placement? Custom dictates that you slide it onto the fourth finger of your left hand…shall I help?"

Like a flock of birds freed at last from their cages, joy and happiness and hope soared upward, filling the small cottage with heavenly light. She could almost hear the angels singing. "Yes," she managed, and held up her hand. "Yes and yes and yes!"

She watched with an overflowing heart as Ethan slid the ring onto her finger. Almost reverently he bestowed a kiss upon her lips. "Merry Christmas, sweetheart."

"I love you." In a rapture of emotion she flung her arms around him and hugged him fiercely, then stepped back. "Wait here." Whirling, she dashed across to her sitting room, over to her desk. Before she lost her nerve, she gathered everything up in a messy bundle and returned to her—to her fiancé.

Shyness tugged, but she thrust it aside and handed Ethan her offering. "It's very rough," she told him breathlessly, "and will take a lot more work. But—I've already sold it." A pang of sheer nerves turned her palms hot, filmed with perspiration. She watched in an agony of suspense as Ethan accepted the pages and began to leaf through them.

"'Joy of Every Longing Heart. A Story of a Spinster. Why a Believer Should Never Lose Hope in the Power of Love. By Clara Penrose,'" he read the title aloud.

"I started it weeks ago, when I knew I'd fallen in love with you," Clara said, quivering inside because she wasn't sure whether the light blazing from his eyes was a reflection of her own joy, or—

He snatched her into his arms, crushing her and the manuscript against his chest. "You used your real name! Clara…you used your name. I love you, love you, love you."

"Ethan…I just thought of something," she managed between the intoxicating kisses he pressed to her brow, her temple, her lips. "Wait…" Laughter wove through the breathless words in an effervescent tumble. "The editor tells me the book won't be published for well over a year."

"Doesn't matter. It will be worth waiting for, like you." He stole another kiss.

"I can't use my name!"

When he froze, she grabbed the manuscript, smoothed the crumpled pages, and laid it on the table, beneath the Christmas tree.

"Clara…"

"When were you thinking to marry me?"

"I thought…Christmastime next year? It seemed appropriate. My love, you should be proud to use your name. I know I am. I'll announce it from the rooftops, on every street corner."

"By the time this book is published, I won't be Clara Penrose. I'll be Clara Penrose *Harcourt*."

Ethan threw back his head and shouted with laughter. "So you will be. So you will…" Then he wrapped her back in his arms, and sealed her lips with a thorough kiss.

NimNuan watched unblinking beside the tabletop Christmas tree, a loud purr proclaiming his satisfaction with the arrangements.

\* \* \* \* \*

Dear Reader,

The working title of *The Christmas Secret* was *Long-Expected Love,* which came from an old Christmas hymn "Come, Thou Long-Expected Jesus." I still can't think of this story without humming that melody in my head and repeating those comforting words—*"From our fears and sins release us; let us find our rest in Thee…"* That's what music, especially Christmas music does to me, sticking like colorful Post-its in my mind and heart. I love the reverence of all the ancient hymns, the soaring magnificence of Handel's *Messiah,* the irrepressible fun of Frosty and Rudolph (except when the tunes are blared over store speakers in September), the sing-along nostalgia of *White Christmas*—so the very day after Thanksgiving our home is filled with the music of Christmas.

However, like Ethan and Clara in the late nineteenth century, our family has also struggled through difficult holidays, where our twenty-first-century radios and CDs remained silent because our hearts were grieving, and joyful holiday music only drove the pain deeper. Life during the dark times of the soul is somehow harder to bear in the Christmas season. Yet God steadfastly reaches out until He captures your attention. Through that mysterious process called faith, He can heal the soul and lift the heart. For me, most often His Voice speaks through the music. That's why *The Christmas Secret* is filled with references to Christmas carols. My heartfelt hope for each of you who reads this story is that you may experience an hour or two of lightness, that one of the carols mentioned rings a chord within and allows you to look up—and hear the heavenly choir proclaiming joy to the world.

*All ye, beneath life's crushing load,/Whose forms are bending low,/Who toil along the climbing way/With painful steps and slow,/Look now! For glad and golden hours/ Come swiftly on the wing:/O rest beside the weary road,/And hear the angels sing.*

Regardless of circumstance, may your hearts this Christmas sing with joy,

*Sara Mitchell*

# QUESTIONS FOR DISCUSSION

1. Though they love her, Clara Penrose's family consider her an oddity, and they don't understand her. Why do they feel this way about Clara? What does Clara do or not do that perpetuates this view?

2. Ethan's reaction to human betrayal is to turn his back on God as well as his country and his calling. What significant event occurred to change his mind?

3. Both Clara and Ethan try to "prove" their faith through good works, and discover that merely doing good is not enough to enjoy lasting peace with God. What problems do Christians with this perspective encounter? In your life how do you reconcile this issue?

4. Clara's pet cat NimNuan plays a significant role in her life. How do pets influence our lives? Do you believe God can speak to us through animals?

5. The minister of Clara's church challenges the congregation to leave symbols of their burdens at the altar, in the manger. What message was he trying to convey? What symbolizes a burden in your life that may have robbed you of the joy of Christmas?

6. Like Christmas itself, *The Christmas Secret* is full of symbols. How many did you discover when reading the story? What did they represent?

7. Throughout the story Clara and Ethan create Christmas memories they can cherish the rest of their lives. Which

scenes did you find the most "memorable"? What Christmas memories of your own do you hold most dear?

8. Ethan tells someone "...it's long past time to quit toting the coffins of our respective spouses on our backs." What does he mean? Did you think this was an accurate metaphor to describe their circumstances?

*Here is an exciting sneak preview of*
*TWIN TARGETS by Marta Perry,*
*the first book in the new 6-book*
*Love Inspired Suspense series*
PROTECTING THE WITNESSES
*available beginning January 2010.*

Deputy U.S. Marshal Micah McGraw forced down the sick feeling in his gut. A law enforcement professional couldn't get emotional about crime victims. He could imagine his police chief father saying the words. Or his FBI agent big brother. They wouldn't let emotion interfere with doing the job.

"Pity." The local police chief grunted.

Natural enough. The chief hadn't known Ruby Maxwell, aka Ruby Summers. He hadn't been the agent charged with relocating her to this supposedly safe environment in a small village in Montana. He didn't have to feel responsible for her death.

"This looks like a professional hit," Chief Burrows said.

"Yeah."

He knew only too well what was in the man's mind. What would a professional hit man be doing in the remote reaches of western Montana? Why would anyone want to kill this seemingly inoffensive waitress?

And most of all, what did the U.S. Marshals Service have to do with it?

All good questions. Unfortunately he couldn't answer any of them. Secrecy was the crucial element that made the Federal Witness Protection Service so successful. Breach that, and everything that had been gained in the battle against organized crime would be lost.

His cell buzzed and he turned away to answer it. "McGraw."

"You wanted the address for the woman's next of kin?" asked one of his investigators.

"Right." Ruby had a twin sister, he knew. She'd have to be notified. Since she lived back east, at least he wouldn't be the one to do that.

"Jade Summers. Librarian. Current address is 45 Rock Lane, White Rock, Montana."

For an instant Micah froze. "Are you sure of that?"

"'Course I'm sure."

After he hung up, Micah turned to stare once more at the empty shell that had been Ruby Summers. She'd made mistakes in her life, plenty of them, but she'd done the right thing in the end when she'd testified against the mob. She hadn't deserved to end up lifeless on a cold concrete floor.

As for her sister...

What exactly was an easterner like Jade Summers doing in a small town in Montana? If there was an innocent reason, he couldn't think of it.

Ruby must have tipped her off to her location. That was the only explanation, and the deed violated one of the major principles of witness protection.

Ruby had known the rules. Immediate family could be relocated with her. If they chose not to, no contact was permitted—ever.

Ruby's twin had moved to Montana. White Rock was probably forty miles or so east of Billings. Not exactly around the corner from her sister.

But the fact that she was in Montana had to mean that they'd been in contact. And that contact just might have led to Ruby's death.

He glanced at his watch. Once his team arrived, he'd get back on the road toward Billings and beyond, to White Rock. To find Jade Summers and get some answers.

\* \* \* \* \*

*Will Micah get to Jade in time to save*
*her from a similar fate?*
*Find out in TWIN TARGETS,*
*available January 2010*
*from Love Inspired Suspense.*

# Love Inspired.
# HISTORICAL
## INSPIRATIONAL HISTORICAL ROMANCE

Drake Amberly, duke of Hawk Haven, came to the colonies for revenge—to unmask the spy who killed his brother. Yet he finds himself distracted from his mission by the beautiful and spirited Elise Cooper. But as Drake's pursuit of the "Fox" brings him dangerously close to Elise's secrets, she must prove to him that love and forgiveness are all they need.

## Look for
# The Duke's Redemption
## by
# CARLA CAPSHAW

*Available January*
*wherever books are sold.*

www.SteepleHill.com

Steeple
Hill®

LIH82828

# REQUEST YOUR FREE BOOKS!

## 2 FREE INSPIRATIONAL NOVELS
## PLUS 2
## FREE
## MYSTERY GIFTS

*Love Inspired.*
# HISTORICAL
### INSPIRATIONAL HISTORICAL ROMANCE

**YES!** Please send me 2 FREE Love Inspired® Historical novels and my 2 FREE mystery gifts (gifts are worth about $10). After receiving them, if I don't wish to receive any more books, I can return the shipping statement marked "cancel". If I don't cancel, I will receive 4 brand-new novels every other month and be billed just $4.24 per book in the U.S. or $4.74 per book in Canada. That's a savings of over 20% off the cover price. It's quite a bargain! Shipping and handling is just 50¢ per book.* I understand that accepting the 2 free books and gifts places me under no obligation to buy anything. I can always return a shipment and cancel at any time. Even if I never buy another book, the two free books and gifts are mine to keep forever.  102 IDN EYPS  302 IDN EYP4

---

Name _____ (PLEASE PRINT) _____

Address _____ Apt. #

City _____ State/Prov. _____ Zip/Postal Code

---

Signature (if under 18, a parent or guardian must sign)

### Mail to Steeple Hill Reader Service:
**IN U.S.A.:** P.O. Box 1867, Buffalo, NY 14240-1867
**IN CANADA:** P.O. Box 609, Fort Erie, Ontario L2A 5X3

Not valid to current subscribers of Love Inspired Historical books.

### Want to try two free books from another series?
Call 1-800-873-8635 or visit www.morefreebooks.com

* Terms and prices subject to change without notice. Prices do not include applicable taxes. Sales tax applicable in N.Y. Canadian residents will be charged applicable provincial taxes and GST. Offer not valid in Quebec. This offer is limited to one order per household. All orders subject to approval. Credit or debit balances in a customer's account(s) may be offset by any other outstanding balance owed by or to the customer. Please allow 4 to 6 weeks for delivery. Offer available while quantities last.

**Your Privacy:** Steeple Hill Books is committed to protecting your privacy. Our Privacy Policy is available online at www.SteepleHill.com or upon request from the Reader Service. From time to time we make our lists of customers available to reputable third parties who may have a product or service of interest to you. If you would prefer we not share your name and address, please check here. ☐

LIH09

*Love Inspired.*

# HISTORICAL

## TITLES AVAILABLE NEXT MONTH

### Available January 12, 2010

**HIGH PLAINS BRIDE by Valerie Hansen**
*After the Storm: The Founding Years*

When a tornado tears their wagon train apart,
Emmeline Carter's father is killed, her mother and sister
are injured and the family's twin wards go missing.
There's nowhere to turn but the fledgling Kansas settlement
of High Plains. Will Logan, the town's handsome founder,
steps in to help the Carters find a new home...and bring
Emmeline a new love.

**THE DUKE'S REDEMPTION by Carla Capshaw**
His faith in God has been shattered, and now Drake Amberly
wants nothing but revenge on the colonial spy who killed his
brother. But when courageous Elise Cooper turns out to be
the enemy he seeks, will forgiveness and love be enough to
save them both?

LIHCNMBPA1209